BEST SCIENCE FICTION
TWO

Edited by Ellen Datlow

OMNI Books
Greensboro, North Carolina

CONTENTS

INTRODUCTION

Omni, first published in October 1978, is the first (and still only) glossy mass-market magazine to provide science fiction and fantasy with the forum and format it deserves. Since its premier issue, *Omni* has showcased some of the most entertaining and thought-provoking sf and fantasy of our times. Just as important, *Omni* has brought science fiction to readers who have never read it before. The circulation of *Omni* is larger than all the traditional science fiction markets combined. *Omni*'s enormous success encouraged writers such as Robert Silverberg to return to short fiction and novelists such as Terry Bisson, Paul Park, and K. W. Jeter to begin writing short fiction.

Omni came into being during a fertile period for the science fiction short story. A new generation of imaginative, energetic, and prolific writers was emerging. By the mid-eighties, this new generation, including such talents as Lucius Shepard, Connie Willis, Pat Cadigan, Michael Swanwick, Pat Murphy, William Gibson, Bruce Sterling, and Karen Joy Fowler, had become increasingly visible in the genre, consistently appearing on award ballots for the Hugo and Nebula Awards. Most of these writers, who either started out or became popular in the eighties, were more influenced by outside literary sources and popular culture than were many of their predecessors. And a few were consummate prose stylists, an aspect of writing all but ignored by most sf writers. And some, such as Lucius Shepard and William Gibson and Bruce Sterling, brought a whole different perspective to the literature of the field by setting their fiction in cultures other than the North American one to which readers were accustomed.

One of the most satisfying jobs of an editor is to call a writer with the news that you want to buy his or her story, particularly if it is a first sale. Two authors in this anthology, Tom Maddox and Gregg Keizer, made first sales to me at *Omni*. Two others, Dan Simmons and Maggie Flinn, made their second sales to me. You can read about their subsequent accomplishments in the individual introductions to their stories.

In this second anthology of original and reprint fiction from *Omni,* there is science fiction, science-fantasy, and a bit of horror. "The Pear-Shaped Man," by George R.R. Martin, is the most straight-out horror story included here, and it was the winner of the first Bram Stoker Award for Best Achievement in the novelette. A couple of the other stories are science fiction with definite horrific elements.

We hope you, the reader, will come along with *Omni* magazine into the nineties to discover and support the best new writers of this decade as we continue to showcase sharply etched original science fiction.

Ellen Datlow

All the Perfumes of Araby

by Lucius Shepard

Lucius Shepard burst onto the science fiction and fantasy scene in the early 1980s and became one of the most prolific and influential writers of that decade. He won the John W. Campbell Award in 1985 as Best New Writer and has consistently been on the final ballot for one major award after the other, often in more than one category. In 1987 he won the Nebula Award for his novella "R & R," and in 1988 he won the World Fantasy Award for his collection *The Jaguar Hunter.* His first novel, *Green Eyes,* was part of the revived Ace Special series, his second was the critically acclaimed *Life During Wartime.* His latest, *The Golden,* described by Shepard as a "vampire-detective-coming-of-age novel," will be published by Bantam during the summer of 1993. Shepard was born in Lynchburg, Virginia, and now lives in Seattle, Washington.

Shepard writes sharp-edged science fiction and lush fantasy and horror. *Omni* has published several stories by him including the World Fantasy Award–nominated "Life of Buddha" (May 1988) and "A Little Night Music" (March 1992) and his narrative poem "Pictures Made of Stones" (Sept. 1987). His most recent story for *Omni,* a commissioned science fiction short-short called "Victory" (May 1992), could be considered a prequel to "All the Perfumes of Araby," a novelette appearing in this volume for the first time. As with much of Shepard's fiction, at its center is a troubled relationship between a man and woman.

ALL THE PERFUMES OF ARABY

Lucius Shepard

For nearly two years after my arrival in Egypt, I put off visiting the Pyramids. I had seen them once, briefly at sunset, while en route by car from Alexandria to Cairo. Looming up from the lion-colored sands, their sunstruck sides ignited to a shimmering orange, as if the original limestone veneer had been magically restored, and the shadows in their lee showed a deep mysterious blue, almost purple, like the blood of Caesar's Rome. They diminished me, those ancient tombs. Too much beauty for my deracinated spirit, too much grandeur and immensity. They made me think of history, death, and folly. I had no wish to endure the bout of self-examination a longer visit might provoke. It would be best, I thought, to live a hard, modern life in that city of monuments, free of ponderous considerations and intellectual witness. But eventually curiosity got the best of me, and one afternoon I traveled out to Giza. This time, swarmed by tourists, displayed beneath an oppressive gray sky, it was the Pyramids that looked diminished: dull brown heaps like the spoor of a huge, strangely regular beast.

I wandered about for more than an hour. I regarded the faceless mystery of the Sphinx and managed to avoid having a video taken atop a camel by a ragged teenager with an old camcorder and the raw scar of an AIDS inoculation on his bicep.

3

At length I leaned up against my Land Rover and smoked a hand-rolled cigarette salted with hashish and opium flakes. I thought in pictures, my eyes closed, imagining ibis gods and golden sun boats. When a woman's voice with more than a touch of Southern accent spoke from nearby, saying, "You can smell that shit fifty feet away," I was so distanced I felt only mild resentment for this interference in the plotlessness of my life, and said, because it required little energy, "Thanks."

She was tall and slender and brown, with a slightly horsey face and generous features and a pronounced overbite, the sort of tomboyish look I'd always found attractive, though overall she was a bit sinewy for my tastes. Late twenties, I'd say. About my age. Her skin, roughened by the sun, was just starting to crack into crowsfeet, her cheekbones were sharply whittled, and her honey-brown hair, tied back with a bandana, was streaked blond and brittle at the ends. She had on chino shorts and a white T-shirt and was carrying a net bag that held a canteen, a passport wallet, and some oranges.

"Aren't you goin' to put it out?" She gestured at my cigarette.

"Guess I better," I said, and grinned at her as I ground out the butt, expecting her to leave now that her prim mission had been accomplished; but she remained standing there, squinting at me.

"You're that smuggler guy, right?" she said. "Shears."

"Shields. Danny Shields." I was not alarmed that she knew my business—many did—but I was annoyed at not being able to recall her. She had nice eyes, dark brown, almost oriental-shaped. Her legs were long, lean and cut, but very feminine. "Sorry," I said. "I don't remember your name."

"Kate Corsaro," she said after a moment's hesitation. "We've never met. Just somebody pointed you out to me in a night club. They told me you were a smuggler." She left a pause. "I thought you looked interestin'."

"First impressions," I said. "You can never trust 'em."

"Oh, I don't know 'bout that." She gazed off toward the Great Pyramid; then, after a second or two: "So what do you smuggle? Drugs?"

"Too dangerous. You run drugs, you're looking at the death penalty. I have something of a moral problem with it, too."

"Is that right?" She glanced down at the remains of my cigarette.

"Just because I use doesn't mean I approve of the business."

"Seems to me that's tacit approval."

"Maybe so, but I see a distinction. Whatever else pays, I'll deal with it. Diamonds, exotic software, hacksaw blades ... whatever. But no drugs."

"Hacksaw blades?" She laughed. "Can't be much profit in that."

"You might be suprised."

"Been a while since anything's surprised me," she said.

A silence stretched between us, vibrant as a plucked wire. I wanted to touch the soft packs of muscle that bunched at the corners of her mouth. "You've come to the right place," I said. "I'm surprised all the time here."

"Is that so?"

"Like now," I said. "Like this very minute, I'm surprised."

"This here?" she said. "This is just doin' what comes naturally."

Despite her flirtatious tone, I had an idea she was getting bored. To hold her interest I told stories about my Arab partner in the old bazaar, about moving robotic elements and tractor parts. It's odd, how when you come on to someone, even with the sort of half-assed move I was making, you invest the proceedings with unwarranted emotion, you imbue every action and thought with luminous possibility, until suddenly all the playful motives you had for making the move begin to grow legitimate and powerful. It is as if a little engine has been switched on in your heart due to some critical level of heat having been reached. It seems that random and impersonal, that careless. Not that I was falling in love with her. It was just that everything was becoming urgent, edgy. But soon I began to bore myself with my own glibness, and I asked Kate how she had ended up in Egypt.

"I was in the Middle East nine years ago. I had an itch to see it again."

"In Egypt?"

"Naw, I was in Saudi. But I didn't want to go back. I couldn't walk around free like here."

I was just putting those two facts together, 1990 and Saudi Arabia, when the sun came out full, and something glinted on the back of her right hand: three triangular diamond chips embedded in the flesh. I noticed a slight difference in coloration between the wrist and forearm, and realized it was a prosthesis. I had seen similar ones, the same pattern of diamond chips, all embedded in artificial limbs belonging to veterans of Desert Storm. Kate caught me staring at the hand, shifted it behind her hip; but a second later she moved it back into plain view.

"Somethin' botherin' you?" she asked flatly.

"Not at all," I said.

She held my eyes for a few beats. The tension in her face dissolved. "It bothers some," she said, flexing the fingers of the hand, watching them work. She glanced up at me again. "I flew a chopper, case you're wonderin'."

I made a noncommittal noise. "Must have been tough."

"Yeah, maybe, I don't know. Basically what happened was just plain stupid." She lapsed into another silence, and I grew concerned again that I might be losing her interest.

"Would you like to go somewhere?" I asked. "Maybe

have a drink?"

She worried her lower lip. "A drink's not all we're talkin' about here, is it?"

I was pleased by her frankness, her desire to move things along. Like her ungilded exterior, I took this to indicate inner strength. "I suppose not."

She let out a breath slowly. "Know why I came back to this part of the world? I want somethin' from this place. I don't even know what exactly. Sometimes I think it's just to feel somethin' strong again, 'cause I've been so insulated against feelin' the past nine years. But whatever, I don't wanna be hangin' around anybody who's goin' to hold me back." Another sigh. "It's probably weird, me sayin' all this, but I don't want any misunderstandin's."

"No, it's not weird. I can relate." I was careful not to let the words sound too facile, sad for her, because though I *did* understand her, I no longer believed in what she thought was out there. I felt I should make a stab at honesty. "Me, I'm not looking for anything," I told her. "I just try to accept what comes."

"That's more than most," she said glumly.

Overhead the contrail of a fighter became visible, arrowing east toward Syria and the latest headlines. Seeing it appeared to brighten Kate.

"Well," she said, shouldering her bag. "I reckon I'll take you up on that drink."

Around midnight I got up from my bed and went into the living room, to a telephone table by French doors that stood open onto a balcony, where I dialed the Belgian girl whom I had been fucking for the past year. When she answered I said, "Hey, Claire."

"Danny? Where are you?"

"Out and about." I tried to think of something else to say.

She was helping to install an advanced computer in one of the mosques, one of those projects cloaked in secrecy. I found the whole thing immensely boring, but now I thought talking about it might be distracting. "How's work?" I asked.

"The usual. The mullahs are upset, the technicians are incompetent."

I imagined I could hear her displeasure in the bursts of static on the line. It was a cool night, and I shivered in the breeze. Sweat was drying on my chest, my thighs. Faint wailing music and a chaos of traffic noises from the street below. A slant of moonlight fell over the tile floor, a thin tide that sliced across my ankles and bleached my feet bone white. Beyond the light, two chairs and a sofa made shadowy puzzles in a blue darkness.

"You're with somebody, aren't you?" Claire said.

"You know me," I said.

"Perhaps I should come over. Make it a threesome."

"Not this time." But I could not help picturing them together. Claire, soft and white, black hair and large, startling indigo eyes, the submissive voluptuary, the intellectual with a doctorate in artificial intelligence. Kate, all brown and lithe, passionate and violently alive.

"Who is she?"

"An American. She just got a divorce, she's doing some traveling."

A prickly silence. "Why did you call?"

"I wanted to hear your voice."

"That's bullshit," she said. "You're worried about something. I always get these calls when something's not going the way you planned."

I hung my head, listening to the little fizzing storms on the line.

"Is she getting to you, Danny? Is that it?"

Through the French doors I could see a corner of the building that housed police headquarters on Tewfik Square, and facing it, reddish brown under the arc lights, the colossal statue of Ramses II, marooned on a traffic island, ruler now of a tiny country of parched grass and chipped cement, a steady stream of traffic coursing around it.

"That's why you called," Claire said. "Maybe you're falling in love a little bit, and you wanted . . . what do you say? A reality check. Well, don't worry, Danny. The world's still just like it was this morning. The big ones still eat the little ones, and you and I, we have our arrangement. We still"—she let rancor creep into her voice—"we still are there for each other."

"It must be the drugs that make you so wise," I said, both irritated and comforted that she knew me so well.

"That's it! That's it, exactly. And you, lover. It's been an education with you."

I heard a noise behind me. Kate was standing in the bedroom door, a sheet wrapped around her body, her face in shadow.

"I've got to go," I said to Claire.

"Duty calls, eh? All right, Danny. I know you'll be busy for a while, but give me a call when you get tired of it. Okay?"

"Okay."

"Who was that?" Kate asked as I hung up.

"I was breaking a date," I said.

"For tomorrow?" She came toward me, holding the sheet closed at her breasts. The cloth was dazzlingly white in contrast to her tan. With her hair tumbled about her shoulders, she had acquired an animal energy that had not been noticeable earlier. There was a sullen wariness in her face.

"For tonight," I said.

"That wasn't very thoughtful." She put her right hand on my chest; I could feel my heart beating against it.

"I'm not a very nice guy," I said.

She frowned at that. "I'm s'posed to believe 'cause you say you're not a nice guy, you really are? I'm s'posed to overlook the fact that after rollin' around with me, you hop outta the sack and call another woman?"

"I think," I said, "you should probably take it to heart."

Saying this affected me like a confession, the blurting out of a truth that until then I had only dimly perceived, and I felt heavy with the baggage of my trivial past, my deceits and delusions, the confidence game I had made of ordinary days and nights.

Kate studied me for a second or two. Her eyes looked all dark. Then she moved her hand lower, her fingers trailing across my stomach. "Hell, I'm fed up with nice guys," she said, and curled her fingers around my cock.

This made me a little nervous. That right hand of hers was a marvel. Earlier that evening she had crushed an ice cube into powder between her forefinger and thumb to win a bet, and had flicked off the top of a beer bottle as easily as I would have flicked a piece of lint from my jacket. She might, I thought, want to punish me because of the phone call. But she only caressed me, bringing my erection to life. The sheet slid to the floor, and I touched her breasts. They were small, with puffy coral-colored aureolae. I let their soft weights cozy in my hands. "Ah, baby," she said, a catch in her voice. "Baby." I could feel her trembling. She drew me to the sofa, perched on the back of it, and hooked her legs about my waist. My cock scored the crease of her, nuzzled the seep of juices. She guided me inside, worked me partway in. Her head came forward to rest on my shoulder, and her mouth pressed against my throat, breathing a moist, warm circle on my skin. She held me motionless, hands clamped to my buttocks. I pushed against her, trying to seat myself more deeply.

"No!" She pricked me with her nails. "Stay like this a minute."

"I want to be all the way in you," I said. She laughed happily, said, "Oh, I thought I had it all," and angled herself to accommodate me. I went in deeper with that silky glide that makes you think you are going to flow along with it forever, like the entry of a diver or the dismount of a gymnast, so perfect and gravityless, it should mark the first stage of a journey and not merely an abrupt transition into a clumsier state. I needed to feel it again, and I fucked her heavily, supporting her with both hands. She quit trying to hold me and thrust with her hips, losing her balance and putting a strain on my arms. We wobbled, nearly tumbled off the sofa. It was clear we were not going to make a success of things in this position.

"Let's go back in the bedroom," I said.

"Stay inside me," she said, and threw her arms around my neck. "I need you there. Carry me."

I lifted her and went weaving toward the bedroom, into the thick darkness, lurching sideways but managing to keep the tip of my cock lodged inside her; then I lowered her carefully, awkwardly, onto the cool, rumpled sheet. We wriggled about until we were centered on the bed, and I sank into her again. She bridged up on her elbows. I thought she would kiss me, but she only put her lips to my ear and whispered, "Do everything to me."

Those words seemed so innocent, as if she were new to all this sweet struggle, they made me feel splendid and blessed and full of love. But as I moved in her again, caution ruled me, and though I told her I loved her, I spoke in the softest of voices, a windy phrase almost indistinguishable from a sigh, and not so she could hear.

Two days later as we explored the old bazaar, the Khan al Khalili, idling along the packed, dusty streets among beggars, acrobats, men selling holograms of the Sphinx and plastic cartouches, ox-carts laden with bricks, hooting taxis, more beggars, traveling through zones of garbage stink, spicy cooking odors, perfumes, incense, hashish, walking through a thousand radio musics in the elaborate shade of mosques and roof warrens, past bamboo stalls and old slave markets with tawny arched facades and painted doors in whitewashed walls that might lead into a courtyard populated by doves and orange trees and houris or the virtual reality of a wealthy businessman with violet skies and flames bursting from black rock and djinn in iron armor, it occurred to me that while I had come to know a great deal about Kate during the past forty-eight hours, incidents from her armed service, sundry drab episodes from her marriage, her family in Virginia, she knew next to nothing about me. Having identified me as "that smuggler guy" appeared to have satisfied her curiosity. Not that there was anything more salient to know—my life had gone unchanged for almost a decade, and the colors of my youth had no real bearing on the man I had become, aimless and pleasure-seeking and competent in unimportant ways. I recognized that Kate was hoping to recapture the intensity she had experienced during her war, the talent for intensity that had been shrouded by marriage, and I realized now it was my occupation, not my winning personality, that had attracted her. I was to be the centerpiece of her furious nostalgia, a sinister element of the design. This comprised an irony I did not believe she would appreciate, for I was far from the adventurous soul she assumed me to be. My success in business was due to an attention to detail and the exercise of caution. The urge to play Indiana Jones was not in my canon. On the other hand, a large portion of what had attracted me to her was more or less the same quality she thought to perceive in me: her drive toward the edge, her consuming desire to put herself in harm's way on both emotional and physical levels. Because of the imbalance of our involvements, I knew that by allowing myself to become obsessed—and I had already developed a pounding fascination with her—I was opening myself up to a world of hurt; but that, too, the possibility of emotional risk, was part of her appeal. In ways I did not understand, I was committed to whatever course she cared to choose. It was as if when I first looked at her and saw the glitter of that impersonal desire in her eyes, that lust for whatever would excite her, I'd heard the future roaring in my ears and said to myself, Now, old son, now you can throw your life away for no reason at all.

The interior of the shop belonging to Abdel Affifi, my partner in crime, was a nondescript clutter: glass display counters ranked with bottles of various essences, shelves laden with toy camels and cotton shirts, cheap luggage, gilt bathrobes, fly whisks, bearded plastic heads with tiny fiberoptic memories that recited verses from the Koran, trays heaped with fraudulent antiquities. A beggar peered in through the window, his wizened face visible between two camel saddles, an artifact of the culture more authentic than any the shop had for sale. Abdel himself was a hook-nosed old man clad in a fez and a shabby suit coat worn over a gallibeya. He made a fuss over Kate, who had on a summery print dress and looked very pretty; he served her mint tea and insisted she try his most expensive essence. He failed to notice her prosthesis and seized her right hand; before she could object, he applied a drop of the oily stuff to the inside of her wrist. The perfume, designed to react with the skin to form a unique fragrance, gave off scarcely any odor at all. She pretended to be delighted, but moments later I caught her staring grimly at the wrist, and when I tried to console her, she shook me off.

Not long afterward a plump, animated, middle-aged Arab entered the shop, a man whom I knew as Rollo. Sleek black hair; flourishing mustache; western-style suit. He and Abdel struck up a conversation by the door. This did not please me. Rollo had been trying to involve us in drug trafficking in the Sinai. I wanted nothing to do with him, but Abdel, who was under some heavy financial pressure, had showed signs of weakening. I must admit I was also tempted by the money, but I had refused to give in to temptation. My policy of not dealing drugs was one of the few fixed points remaining on my moral compass; I needed to maintain it, I thought, in order to maintain my separateness from the chaotic amorality of my environment . . . though it may be that a form of superstitious fear, perhaps an apprehension that I would expose myself to karmic peril if I breached the policy, had supplanted any true moral feeling.

"Who's that?" Kate asked, and when I told her, she said, "Rollo? That's hilarious!"

"His father was a guide for the Brits in World War II. He taught Rollo the King's English, or at least some fishwife's version of it. The name'll make sense when you hear him talk."

After a minute or so Rollo came toward us, beaming like an uncle who had just spied his favorite nephew—this despite the fact he knew I detested him. "Danny!" he said joyfully, giving me a hug, enveloping me in an aura of flowery cologne. Then, turning his white smile on Kate, he said in the ripest of Cockney accents, " 'Oo's the bird?"

Kate managed to keep a straight face during the introductions and the exchange of pleasantries that followed, but after Rollo had drawn me aside I saw her over his shoulder, laughing silently.

"Look 'ere, mate," Rollo was saying. "My friend Abdel and Oi 'ave made us an agreement, but we can't do nuffin' 'less you're part of it. Oi need you to settle things with the Israelis. They've 'eard of you, and they'll be 'appier finkin' a Yank's in charge."

"Fuck off," I said.

"Listen to his offer, my friend," Abdel said, making a plaintive face.

With an air of vast self-importance, Rollo took a notepad from the pocket of his suit coat, scribbled on it and then showed me the percentages he had written. I tried to look blasé and told him I wasn't interested.

"Nao, you're not interested!" said Rollo. "Your eyes 'alf bugged out, they did!"

"He's only asking for you to make some arrangements," said Abdel in a wheedling tone. "You won't be carrying drugs."

"Damn right I won't." Abdel started to say something more, but I cut him off. "There's worse than Israeli troops out in the Sinai. With or without drugs, what he's asking is risky as hell. I don't know shit about these people. They might take a dislike to me and blow my fucking head off."

Abdel continued trying to persuade me, and this put me in a thorny position. I could have made my own way in Cairo without much difficulty, but Abdel had taken me under his wing, treated me more like a son than a partner, and as a result I was doing very well indeed. He was no saint, God knows; but compared to Rollo he was an innocent. I did not want him to get in over his head. Yet it was hard to deny him, knowing he was in trouble. I'd had dealings in the Sinai before, and I believed I could deal with Rollo's people. Crossing the border was no problem—though detection systems should have made such crossing impossible, there were many Israelis these days willing to look the other way for a price. It was the Palestinians who concerned me. Since the Intifada had failed, all manner of eccentric fundamentalism, some of it arcane in nature, had come to flourish in the camps and villages of the Sinai, and I had heard stories that gave me pause.

"I'll think it over," I said at last, figuring that if I could put him off, some wiser business opportunity might arise.

He spread his hands in a gesture of acquiescence, but Rollo, tactful as ever, brayed at me, saying, "Yeah, g'wan, fink it over! We'll just await your pleasure, shall we?"

After we had left Abdel's I explained to Kate what had happened. We were walking along a narrow street of open-front shops, ignoring the pleas of the beggars. The sun had lowered behind a mosque on our left, and the golden light had the mineral richness of the light you often get in the tropics when the sun is shining through rain clouds. As we neared the edge of the bazaar Kate leaned into me, pressed her breast against my arm, and said coyly, "Can't we go? I'd like to watch you in action."

"You want to go with me?" I chuckled. "Not a chance!"

She pulled back from me, angry. "What's so funny? I've been in the desert before. And I know how to handle myself. Maybe better than you!"

"Maybe," I said, trying to mollify her. "But you've never dealt with people like this. I wouldn't want to be responsible for what could happen."

That stirred her up even more. "Let's get this straight," she said. "I'm nobody's responsibility but my own, okay? Just 'cause we're screwin', that doesn't mean. . . ."

"Kate," I said, uncomfortable with the crowd that was gathering, the taxi honking at us to clear the way. We were standing beside a store that sold baskets, and the owner and customers had come out to watch. A trolley so clotted with humanity, people stuffed inside, hanging all over the outside, that you could scarcely see the green enamel finish of the car, passed on the street adjoining the entrance to the bazaar, and it seemed all those brown arms were waving at me.

"That doesn't mean," she went on, "you got any papers on me. Do you understand? I don't want you to be confused!"

I was startled by the intensity of her anger. She was enraged, her face flushed, standing with hands on hips, continuing her harangue. Some of the onlookers had begun to make jokes about me; the taxi driver was leaning out his window and laughing. Even the beggars were grinning.

I caught her by the arm. She tried to wrench away, but I hauled her along, pushed her into an alley, pinned her against the wall. "You can get all over me back at the place if you want," I said. "But not here. I work down here. People see me humiliated in public by a woman, word gets around, and I lose respect. That may sound sexist, but that's how it is in this culture. Respect's the main currency in my business. I can't afford to lose it."

She grew instantly contrite, telling me she understood, apologizing, not backing away from her statement of independence, but saying that she should have known better than to cause a scene, she was just a real bitch on that particular subject.

I had expected her anger to abate, yet not so quickly, and it was not until later I realized that her sudden shift in mood was due less to my logic than to the fact that I had acted like the character she fancied me instead of like the man I was. And perhaps I *had* been putting on an act. If Claire had done to me what Kate had, I would have simply walked away from her. But of course Claire would never have acted that way.

At the time I understood little of this. I believe now that I did not want to understand, that I knew I would have to play a role in order to keep the affair on course, to satisfy Kate's demands, and I am certain that this talent for self-deception was partly responsible for all that came to happen.

All that next week I tried to distract Kate from what had become a preoccupation with illegal adventure by showing her Cairo, a city that, with its minarets and roof warrens, its modern bridges and timeless river, ubiquitous flies, computerized calls to prayer, crushing poverty and secret pleasures, seemed to embody all the toxins and exaltations of life. But Kate, though exhilarated, was not distracted. One evening as we sat surrounded by old men smoking waterpipes in a back alley club— Claire's favorite, as it happened—a place constructed of ornate carpets draped over a bamboo frame, with folding chairs and little metal tables, all centered about a makeshift stage upon which a drugged young girl wearing street clothes, her cheeks pierced by silver needles, sang a song that prophesied glory for

Islam, Kate grew surly and silent, and as she often did when depressed, bent coins between the thumb and forefinger of her right hand. There was a great deal I loved about her, but this fixation on her prosthesis disturbed me no end. Once she had slit open a seam that ran across the palm, peeled back folds of plastic skin, laying bare a packed complexity of microcircuits, and demonstrated how, by stripping a wire that ran to the power pack, she could short out an electrical system. I was not happy to think that the woman with whom I was sleeping could electrocute me on a whim.

I understood her fixation—at least I sympathized with it—but there was much I did not understand about her reaction to war. I had known men of my father's generation, veterans of Vietnam, who had exhibited a similar yearning for the terrible pleasures of the battlefield; yet they had been brutally used and discarded by their country, whereas the veterans of Kate's war had been celebrated as American saints. Even if I accepted the idea that all combat veterans longed for such intensity, that did not explain the feverish quality of Kate's longing, and I thought my inability to understand her might stem from my failure to understand Desert Storm, a fabulous victory that had achieved next to nothing in terms of *realpolitik,* unless you considered the deaths of a hundred thousand Iraqis, the restoration of a cruel oligarchy in Kuwait, and the drastic upgrading of Syria's missile capacity to be achievements. Could the inconclusiveness of the action be responsible for the sickness that preyed upon Kate? Or could it be in that delirious sky over Bagdad, with white streaks and flares whirling in the electric blue of the nightscope like a kind of strange cellular activity, the darting of sperm in an inky womb, the mysterious associations of organelles, that some magic had been at work, infecting those who fought beneath it with unending dissatisfaction? I had asked Kate questions that addressed these and other notions, but she would only talk about the war in terms of anecdote, mostly humorous, mostly undermining the popular conception that Desert Storm had been an exercise of phenomenal precision, telling of crates of missiles left untended in the middle of nowhere, tank commands roaming aimlessly, misdirected platoons. Watching her that night, unable to comprehend her motives—or my own, for that matter—I acknowledged that my relationship with her was intrinsically concerned with the exploration of those motives, and so I told her that I was going into the Sinai, that she could go with me.

She glanced up from her pile of bent piastres; for an instant something glowed and shifted in her face, as if she were in the grip of an emotion that had the fierce mutability of a fire burning out of control.

"All right!" she said, and took my hand.

I had expected more of a reaction, but perhaps she too had known it was inevitable.

The young girl's song was ending. She swayed under the necklace of light bulbs that illuminated the stage, her hands describing delicate passages in the air, not a drop of blood spilling from her pierced cheeks, singing of how Muhammed returned to reign in Mecca and the blessing of Islam spread throughout the infidel world and flowers bloomed in the desert. All around me, wreathed in hashish smoke, old men were nodding, weeping, speaking the name of God. That was what I most loved about the Arabs of the bazaar, their capacity to cast aside the duplicitous context of their lives and find within themselves some holy fiber that allowed them to reduce the pain of the world to an article of faith. I shed no tears, yet I felt as one of them, wholly embracing a glorious futility, given over to the thunderous joy of belief, though I realized that the truth to which I had surrendered myself was meager and blighted and could not long sustain me.

*   *   *

Two nights later as we approached our rendezvous point, which lay less than a kilometer from the abandoned Palestinian village of El Malik, I began to smell perfume. I pulled Abdel's jeep onto the shoulder, in among some thorn bushes. Kate asked what was wrong, and I told her, Nothing. But perfume was often used by smugglers to disguise the scent of opium, and I was afraid that we had been set up. The cushion of the back seat was drenched with attar of roses. I sliced the upholstery with my pocket knife, groped inside the cushion, and along with wet stuffing and perfume vials and broken glass—apparently the last pothole had done the damage—I felt thin hard cakes wrapped in paper. Opium. And not a little of it.

Somewhere out in the darkness, among the barren hills that bulked up against the stars, an engine kicked over; I had to assume that the Israelis had spotted us, were puzzled by our having stopped, and were coming for their goods. A chill bloomed between my shoulder blades, and my legs grew feeble. I could feel the great emptiness of the Sinai solidifying around us, as malefic as a black tower in whose keep we stood. That no one had told me about the drugs made it clear that my survival was not a *fait accompli*. Rollo had viewed me as an impediment to his association with Abdel; alone, he would be able to manipulate Abdel, and he might have arranged to have me eliminated by the Israelis. An overly imaginative scenario, perhaps. But I had no desire to test its inaccuracy.

I listened to the approaching engine. Judging by its sound, the Israelis were driving something far more powerful than the Jeep. We would not be able to outrun them.

"Get the guns," I said to Kate; I dug out some of the opium and stashed it in my pack, along with several dozen of the vials, thinking I could use them for currency. Once again she asked me what was wrong. I shoved her aside and fished the guns— Belgian SMGs—out from beneath the front seat. I tossed one to her, said, "Let's go," and set off at a jog into the hills.

She caught up to me, grabbed my arm. "You goin' to tell me what the hell's goin' on?"

Until that moment I had controlled my fear, but her touch broke my control, and I was galvanized with terror, furious at her for having led me into this mess, at myself for having followed, for letting her so distract me that I had neglected to take basic precautions. "You stupid fucking bitch!" I shouted. "You're so hot to die, stay here. Otherwise get your ass moving." Her face was pale and stunned in the starlight. I felt a flicker of remorse, but only a flicker. "You wanted this," I said. "Now deal with it."

We had climbed about a third of a mile, I'd guess, when small arms fire sounded from the road. But no bullets struck close to us. After a few more bursts, there was a loud explosion and a fireball at the base of the hill. The Jeep. Shortly thereafter I heard the Israelis' engine roar away. As I had hoped, they were satisfied with the opium and not sufficiently zealous to fulfill their part of what I assumed to have been a contract. Nevertheless I continued climbing toward El Malik, which offered decent cover and where I planned to spend the night. The next morning I intended to hook up with my own Israeli contacts and negotiate our passage back to Cairo.

The moon was rising as we came into the village, descending a slope strewn with boulders, and in that milky light, the whitewashed houses with their vacant black windows and walls gapped by Israeli artillery, looked like the shards of enormous skulls. From the eastern edge of the place we gazed out across a valley figured by the lights of Israeli settlements, the formless constellations of a lesser sky. There was a heady air of desolation, a sense of lives violently interrupted yet still, in some frail, exhausted way, trying to complete their ordinary tasks, souls perceptible as a faint disturbance that underscored the silence, a vibration unaffected by the gusting of a cold wind.

We sheltered in a house with a packed dirt floor that offered a view of a public square and a ruined fountain. Kate, who had spoken little during the climb, sat against a wall and stared at me despondently.

"I'm sorry," she said after a while. "This is all my fault."

"Not all of it," I said, dropping beside her. "Anyway, the worst is over. Tomorrow, if we're careful, we should be able to get in touch with friends of mine. They'll help us."

She said nothing for almost a minute, then: "I've got to be crazy. To want this, I mean."

I chose not to absolve her of insanity, but I put an arm about her. I believe I felt then what she wanted to feel. To be in that gutted doom of a place, lent a memorial beauty by the moonlight, all its ruin seeming to burn white and bulge with living shadow; to have survived folly and betrayal—and I was not concerned that what had happened would hurt my business, I was simply interested in paying the betrayers back in kind; to be in the company of a woman who, though I did not love her, had put a lover's charge in me, a woman with whom I could practice a perfect counterfeit of passion; it was as if the events of that night had exposed a romantic core in me, and I was now entirely in the world, alive as I had not been for years.

She glanced up at me and said, "You look happy."

I laughed and kissed her. The kiss deepened. I touched her breasts, startled to find that anything could feel so soft and luxurious in this harsh, empty place.

Kate pulled back and gave me a searching stare. The vitality had returned to her face. After a second she jumped to her feet, backed away until she was standing in the chute of light spilling through the door.

I came to one knee, intending to go after her, but she held up a hand to ward me off and began unbuttoning her shirt. She smiled as she shrugged out of the shirt, and watching her work her jeans down past her hips, eyes focused on the dark tangle between her thighs, visible through the opaque material of her panties, I felt heavy in my head, thick and slow, full of a red urge, like a dog restrained from feeding by its mistress's command.

I saw the man behind her a moment before he reached the doorway, but I was so stupefied, I was unable to react, only registering him as a slight figure holding an automatic rifle, wearing jeans and a windbreaker. And a mask. He shoved Kate toward me, sending her toppling, and we fell together onto the floor. By the time I managed to disengage from her, he had been joined by four others, all masked. They were evil-looking things, the masks: curved sheets of white plastic with mouth slits and eyeholes, adorned with painted symbols and religious slogans.

"Tell the whore to clothe herself," one said in Arabic.

They watched without comment as Kate dressed; she stared back at them, not defiant, but cold, measuring. An admirable pose, but I had no urge to hand her a medal. We had, I believed, come to the end of it. The men who held us captive had lost everything, and their sole remaining ambition was to go down in flames while exacting a terrible vengeance. Oddly enough, at that moment I thought of Claire.

They collected our packs and guns and escorted us to the ruin of a small mosque, where another seven or eight masked men were assembled. Moonlight streamed through rents in the domed roof, applying a design of sharp shadows and blazing light to the floor tiles; the same fierce slogans decorating the masks had here been painted on the walls. A cooking fire burned in a shell crater. The men stationed themselves along the wall; then another man, unmasked, a sharply featured individual dressed in a striped robe, stepped out from a door at the rear of the building. He had a bronzed complexion and a neat beard salted with gray and one blind eye, white as marble. He was carrying a long, gracefully curved sword. He took a position at the center of the room, directly beneath a gap in the roof, so that a beam of moonlight, separate and distinct, shone like a benediction upon him, and stared at us with disdain. I could feel the fanatical weight of his judgment as surely as if it were a form of radiation.

One of the others handed him my pack, whispered in his ear. He inspected the contents, removed a vial of perfume. He moved close to me, smiling, his blind eye glowing like a tiny moon. "Thief," he said in a voice like iron, "my name is Mahmoud Ibrahim, and I am he who prepares the way. Thou hast stolen from me and given nothing in return. Yet because thou hast been touched by the city of Saladin, I will spare thee everything but pain." He opened the vial and poured the contents over my head. He took out a second vial, a third, and repeated the process. I shut my eyes. The oily stuff ran into my mouth, thick and bitter, trickling cold down my cheeks, drowning the stink of my fear in a reek of flowers and humiliation.

Mahmoud took one of the cakes of opium, pinched off a substantial fragment. "Eat," he said, holding it out. I let him place it on my tongue like a communion wafer.

When he was satisfied that I had swallowed, he smiled, nodded. Then he gestured at Kate and handed his sword to the man who had brought him my pack. "The woman first," he said.

Kate shrieked as three men threw her onto the floor and positioned her right wrist atop a block. Another stood by with a torch, while the man wielding the sword laid the edge of it on her wrist, then lifted it high. The traditional Arab punishment for stealing, the lopping off the right hand—I imagined it sheared away, blood spurting, and perhaps in her fright, Kate had also forgotten the prosthesis, for she twisted her head about, trying to find me, screaming, "Danny! Help me!" But I was targeted by seven rifles, and I could only stand and watch, the scene burning into my brain—the stark shadows of the ruin, the men in their strange white masks, the calm prophet with his glowing eye, and Kate writhing, her face distorted by panic.

Then, with a windy noise, the sword flashed down.

As the blade bit into Kate's prosthesis, slicing through plastic and microcircuitry, there was a sizzling noise, and a rippling blue-white charge flowed up the steel, outlining blade and hilt in miniature lightnings. Sparks showered around the man holding it, and there was so much confusion and shouting I am not sure whether or not he screamed. He stood for a second or two, shivering with the voltage passing through him; smoke trickled between his fingers. Then he fell. The sword flew from his grasp and went spinning across the floor to my feet.

It was reflex that moved me to pick up the sword, and it was dumb luck that Mahmoud had recoiled from the electrocution and wound up beside me. But I did not waste the opportunity. I slid the blade under his neck, making a yoke of it, and dragged him toward the rear door. Kate was sitting up, dazed, her prosthesis dangling horribly from a spaghetti of charred wires; but when I called to her, she got to her feet and came weaving toward me. More than half the men had fled, terrified by the witchery of her hand, but the remainder were closing on me. I pulled the blade tight against Mahmoud's Adam's apple, making him stiffen and gasp.

"*Emshi!*" I shouted, and his men backed away.

With Kate at my side, I guided Mahmoud through the rear door into a small room whose back wall had been obliterated. Three cars were parked outside. Kate leaned against the wall beside me; her face was empty, slack.

"Keys," I said to Mahmoud.

He groped in the pocket of his robe, fingered them out. "The Peugeot," he said, gritting out the words.

"Can you drive?" I asked Kate.

She did not answer.

I kicked her hard in the calf. She blinked; her head

25

wobbled.

"Drive!" I told her. "Take the keys and drive."

Though the men harassed us, aiming their rifles, threatening us, we made it to the car, Mahmoud and I taking the back seat. I sat turned toward him, barring his throat with the blade. Then we were bumping along the cratered streets, jouncing over potholes, past the last houses and out onto a rocky, precipitous road that wound down into the moonstruck valley. No headlights showed behind us. Once the land began to flatten out, I removed the blade from Mahmoud's throat. His men would not risk confronting the Israeli patrols. I was shaking, rattled with adrenaline, yet at the same time I felt woozy, drifty, as if a cloud were building in the center of my brain. I remembered the opium.

"Shit!" I said.

Mahmoud seemed as calm and content as a hawk with a dead mouse. Kate was staring straight ahead, her good hand clenching the wheel; her skin was pasty, and when she glanced back I had the impression that she looked shocky.

"You okay?" I asked.

She muttered something; the car swerved wildly onto the shoulder.

It was definitely the opium coming on. I was having trouble feeling the tips of my fingers, and my head was turning into a balloon. Everything I thought left a vague color in the air. Smoking opium was a fairly smooth sail, albeit a long ocean voyage; eating it, however, was a rocket to the moon. I was still lifting slowly from the launch pad, but in a minute or two I was going to have all the physical capacity of a cantaloupe. Or maybe a honeydew. I couldn't decide. Something round and gleaming and very, very still. I had intended to turn Mahmoud over to the Israelis; I was sure they wanted him, and I hoped that his capture would help them overlook our illegal entry. But now, with the opium taking control and Kate on the wobbly side, I could not chance having him along.

"Stop the car," I said.

I had to repeat myself twice before she complied, and by the time she did, I had almost forgotten why I wanted her to stop.

"Get out," I said to Mahmoud. That blind eye of his had acquired the nacreous depth of pearl, and I was beginning to see things in it. Beautiful things, amazing things. I told him again to get out. Or maybe I didn't. It was difficult to distinguish between speech and thought. Everything was so absorbing. The dark, the distant lights of a kibbutz. The attar of roses smell that clung to me. I could lose myself in any of it. Then something touched me on the brow, leaving a cool spot that went deep inside my head.

"From thy poison I have made thee a vision of the time to come," Mahmoud said. "What thou will have of it, I know not. But it is a gift of the Prophet, may His name be praised, and he planteth no seed that doth not bear fruit."

In the interval between these words and when next he spoke, I heard a symphony compounded of breath and night sounds and metallic creaks that implied an entire secret history hitherto unknown to man. Then there was a whisper, as sinister as a violin tremolo in a minor key: "Thou will not evade my punishment this night."

I thought I heard the car door slam shut.

"Kate," I said. "Can you get us somewhere? A town. Some place. . . ."

I never heard her reply, for I was walking along the crest of a green hill shaped like a dune. A verdant plain spread in every direction, picked out here and there by white stone houses formed into elaborate shapes, and by deep blue lakes along whose edges flamingos stalked and lions with men's voices took their ease, and by white cities where no one cried for meat and in whose highest tower lofty questions were put to a wonderful machine that had summoned and now embodied the soul of the Prophet. White clouds the size of small kingdoms floated overhead, and flying among them were golden shining things that whirled and darted like swallows, yet were made of metal not flesh. At long last I came to a pool shaped like a deep blue eye, almost purple, that lay in the midst of a bamboo thicket, with the ancient statue of an enthroned pharaoh at one end, worn faceless by the wind and the sand. I made to drink from the pool, but when I dipped my hand into the water, it began to stir and to ripple, and strange lights glowed beneath the surface illuminating an intricate thing of silver fibers and rods and other structures whose natures were not clearly revealed, and I heard a voice in the air, the voice of this silver thing, saying, "I am the Oracle of the Past. Ask and I will tell thee where thou hast been."

And I said to her, for it was the voice of a woman, "Of what use is this? I wish to know the Future."

"Truly," she said, "the Future is already known. This is the time of Paradise long prophesied, the time without end when all men live as brothers. Only the Past remains a mystery, and indeed, it has always been thus, for no man can know himself by knowing his future. It is from the Past that the greatest wisdom derives."

"Then tell me who I am," I said.

There was a silence, and finally the voice said, "Thou art Daniel, the infidel who is known as The Arm of Ibrahim, and thou hast struck down many enemies of Allah and also many enemies of the sons of Abraham. Thou hast faced peril and known terrible strife, yet thou hast survived to wield great power in the service of peace and righteousness, though thy life is as secret to the world as a stone at the bottom of the Nile." The voice paused, then said, "I do not understand thee, for it seems thy past and thy future are the same."

(At this point I heard a scream, a tremendous noise, and felt a tearing pain in my right arm; but I was overwhelmed by the opium and it was as if these things had happened to someone else to whom I was somehow remotely physically connected.)

I, of course, understood the Oracle's confusion. Was not her past my future, and vice versa? "What must I now do?" I asked.

"Thou must return to the city of Saladin, and there thou will build a city within the city, and all I have told you will come to pass."

"And who will sustain me against the peril and strife that you have prophesied?"

"I will," said the voice. "I will sustain thee."

"Tell me who you are," I said.

"I am the Oracle, the soul of the machine," the voice said. "Yet I am also, and this I do not understand, the love of thy life come across the centuries to find thee."

And from the pool there emerged a woman all of white metal save only her right hand which was bone and blood and milky flesh, and her eyes had the shape of the pond and were of a like color, indigo, and it seemed I had known her for many years, though I could not call her to mind. I took her hand, and as I did, the flesh of her hand began to spread, devouring the metal, until she stood before me, a woman in all ways, complete and mortal.

(I heard anxious voices, "Where's the driver?" "She was thrown out," "Have you got him?" "Oh, God! I can't stop the bleeding!", and felt even more intense pain. The vision had begun to fade, and I saw flashes of red light, of concerned faces, the interior of a van.)

And I lay down with the woman among the bamboo stalks, and we touched and whispered, and when I entered her she gave a soft cry that went out and out into the world, winding over the green plain and into the dark valley like the wail of a siren or a call to prayer, and in our lovemaking it seemed we were moving at great speed past strange bodies of light and towers, heading for a destination beyond that of pleasure and release, a place where all my wounds would be healed and all my deepest questions answered.

The doctors in Haifa tried to save my right arm, but in the end they were forced to amputate. It took me six months to adapt to a prosthesis, six months in which I considered what had happened and what I should do next. Kate had also been in the hospital, but she had returned to America by the time I was well enough to ask for her. She left a note in which she apologized for the accident and for involving me in her "misguided attempt to recapture what I never really lost." I felt no bitterness toward her. She had failed herself far more than she had failed me. My fascination with her, the psychological structure that supported strong emotion, had died that night in the ruined mosque, its charge expended.

Neither did I feel bitter toward Mahmoud Ibrahim. In retrospect, it seemed he had been no ordinary fanatic, that his poise had been the emblem of a profound internal gravity, of peacefulness and wisdom. Perhaps I manufactured this characterization in order to justify my folly in terms of predestination or some other quasi-religious precept. Yet I could not wholly disbelieve that something of the sort may have been involved. How else could Mahmoud have known that I came from Cairo, the city of Saladin? Then there was his prophecy of my "punishment," the vision with its curiously formal frame and futuristic detail, so distinct from the random lucidity of the usual opium dream.

A gift from the Prophet?

I wondered. I doubted, yet still I wondered.

Claire came to Haifa, distraught, horrified at my injuries. She slept in the hospital room with me, she washed me, she tended me in every human way. The similarity between her and the woman of my vision was not lost upon me, nor was the fact that her studies in artificial intelligence and her secret project with the mosque gave rise to some interesting possibilities and paradoxes concerning the Oracle; yet I was reluctant to buy into something so preposterous. As the months passed, however, I could not ignore the way that things were changing between us, the tendrils of feeling that we had tried to kill with drugs and cynicism now beginning to creep forth and bud. If this much of the vision had a correspondence with reality, how then could I ignore the rest of it? The life of power and strife, the building of a city within a city: my business? It occurred to me that I had only played at business all these years, that now I was being tempted to get serious. There was much one could effect on an international level through the agency of the black market. But if I were to get serious, it would call for an increased ruthlessness on my part, a ruthlessness informed by a sense of morality and history, something I was not sure I had in me.

I did not know what I would do on my return to Cairo, but on my second night back I went for a walk alone through a secluded quarter of the Khan al Khalili, heading—I thought—in no particular direction, idling along; yet I was not altogether surprised when I came to a certain door in a certain whitewashed wall, the retreat of a wealthy businessman. I hesitated. All the particulars of Mahmoud's vision came before my eyes, and I began to understand that, true or not, it offered me a design for life far superior to any I had contrived. At length I opened the door, which was locked, with no great difficulty, and stepped into a courtyard with a tiled fountain and lemon trees. I moved quietly into the house beyond, into a long study lined with books, furnished with a mahogany desk and leather chairs. I waited in the shadows for the man, idly playing with the coins in my pocket, a habit I had picked up during my rehabilitation. I left one of the coins on the desk for him to find. I knew he was a poor sleeper, that soon he would wake and come into the study. When at last he did appear, yawning and stretching, a plump fellow with a furious mustache and sleek black hair, I did not hate him as much as I had presumed; I saw him mainly as an impediment to my new goals.

He sat at the desk, switched on a lamp that cast a pool of light onto the writing surface, shuffled some papers, then spotted the ten piastre coin that I had left for him. He picked it up and held it to the light. The coin was bent double, the image on its face erased by the pressure of my right thumb and forefinger. It seemed an article of wonder to him, and I felt a little sad for what I must do. He was, after all, much the same as I, a ruthless man with goals, except my ruthlessness was a matter of future record and my goals the stuff of prophecy.

There was no point, I realized, in delaying things. I moved forward, and he peered into the darkness, trying to make me out, his face beginning to register the first of his final misgivings. I felt ordered and serene, not in the least anxious, and I understood that this must be the feeling one attains when one takes a difficult step one has balked at for years and finds that it is not so difficult at all, but a sweet inevitability, a confident emergence rather than an escalation of fear.

"Hello, Rollo," I said. "I just need a few seconds of your time."

The Robot and the One You Love

by Tom Maddox

Tom Maddox's first story, "The Mind Like a Strange Balloon," was published in *Omni* (June 1985) and introduced some of the ideas and themes that have preoccupied Maddox in his fiction ever since: artificial intelligence, the maelstrom of male-female relationships, and the individual vs. the large corporate entity. Maddox's first novel, *Halo,* was published in 1991 by Tor. Maddox is a native Virginian now living in Olympia, Washington. "The Robot and the One You Love," originally published in *Omni* (March 1988), is a fast-paced and hard-edged story about loyalty, jealousy, and betrayal.

THE ROBOT AND

THE ONE YOU LOVE

Tom Maddox

Black polycarbon tentacles hissing across concrete, the diener robot continued along M Street, warmed by the July sun. Its shell was made of porcelain the color of a blue sky, the color of dreams. Sitting in the controller egg at home, Jerome squirmed, feeling as if someone were scraping his skin from the inside. The clear path along the sidewalk turned into cratered moonscape, street sounds to electric charivari. The fragile interlink between him and the diener robot was breaking up in a burst of neurological static.

"You pulling anything interesting?" Jerome asked, fighting to stay oriented. His perceptions shifted from room to street and back again, like a TV monitor flashing aimlessly from camera to camera.

"No," the diener robot said, its voice coming from Jerome's back teeth through conduction speakers vibrating behind his ears. The diener carried unobtrusive optical and acoustical recorders for the passing scene, electronics to capture data from surveillance cameras and filch transmissions from police, private security firms, corporate spies, Peeping Toms.

"I need to quit," Jerome said. "I'm getting crazy."

"I am sorry you are troubled," the diener said. "I will return."

That night Jerome sat next to the controller, viewing CROME disk records of the day's take. Around him free-form shapes in pale rose flowed from ceiling to wall and floor. They changed, and dark mauve outlines shifted with them, as the decorating program displayed its abstractions. Between the viewing console and the controller—a dark padded chair with a chrome sphere forming its upper half—the diener robot stood motionless.

"This was not a good day," the diener said in a voice that over the past two years had acquired some of Jerome's characteristic inflections.

"A horseshit day," Jerome said. "But I've gotta look."

Jerome was a freelance information broker. He moved lightly across the web of information that the city generated, stopping from time to time to pull at a few among the millions of threads. He had sold to congressional aides, lobbyists, policemen, and pimps. Sifting through the city's chaos, he looked for a treasure trove . . . whispered word of a deal going down, evidence of felonies old and new, rumors of sicknesses, love affairs, changes of allegiance. Even the smallest of indiscretions could be worth something in a city where information was practically an autonomous currency. On a whim he would trail people selected at random for a week, a month, or more— would create dossiers more complete than the National Data Bank's or the FBI's. Jerome was obsessed by characteristic details . . . a man's liking for eating hot dogs from Sabra street vendors while sitting in the sun next to the Dupont Circle fountain, then drinking small cups of Turkish coffee at a sidewalk cafe before entering a hotel room where he would lie nude—prone and helpless, weeping and fulfilled—beneath black-clad legs and spike heels.

Compared with Jerome, voyeurs were casual, uninterested. Compared with his needs, theirs were direct and uncomplicated. What he was trying to learn even he did not know, but he kept at it, capturing what most people never looked for and so didn't see. . . . In a shadowed alley near P Street, an old man in a long green coat blackened with dirt pissed steadily against sooty brick and then collapsed into the puddle. A cat with grease-smeared yellow fur stopped to sniff the puddle, then the man, looked around as though aware it was being watched, moved on.

At the corner of Wisconsin and M stood a man and woman in their early twenties. They were almost identical—hair dyed black, flowing yellow silk scarves, soft blue leather boots. Locked together in a moment of pain—carefully groomed faces, red and tear streaked—they were oblivious to dense crowds surging around them. At this point the diener lost interest.

Jerome froze the frame, ran a sound-isolation program on the couple, wanting to understand the passion that isolated and transformed them, but they stood there speechless and so beyond his ability to probe. At the edge of the picture a woman was caught in mid-stride, holding a cold bag of crumpled white foam. Near the cream plastic U of the handle, black numerals against a silver ground read thirty degrees F.

He closed in on her face.

In profile she had a strong nose, an overbite, a hint of a coming double chin. Her eyes were brown, liquid. Her clothes— black blouse, tan straight skirt with dark blotchy stains—seemed thrown on her, not worn. She looked like nothing special, but . . . . He scanned her image from pale streaked hair to black spike shoes. If you spend most of your life watching and listening, perhaps it's inevitable—this helpless, feckless thing—that you'll find the key to the code written so deep that it might be in your genes; in the tattered phrase, you'll find *the one you love*.

He painted her face into Search Chip Memory. It began its routines, matching her face against local hotels' register tapes, district police updates to the National Data Bank, composite travel records compiled from trains, buses, airplanes. And there, on the passenger list of a United flight that had come in three days earlier from Miami, she turned up. But Jerome was asleep when that happened. Only the diener was awake to hear the bell ring, and it moved with a ripple of black tentacles across rose and watched her face begin to expand across the paintscreen, color and shape flowing as if someone were dropping pigment into invisible set forms. The diener extruded a black cable and plugged into the Search Chip interface, which gave all it had on Connie Stone.

From atop the Riggs Bank at the corner of M and Wisconsin, a flat, black camera sat on the golden dome and watched for any of eight "Sons of Bright Water"—descendants of Hiroshima survivors rumored heading for the base of the Washington Monument with two-kiloton suitcase bombs. This was a CIA search program, and Jerome had piggybacked it to look for Connie Stone. It was not, however, the CIA's camera but a Safeway's "sidewalk sentry"—a blue aluminum box surrounded by fine wire mesh—that spotted her getting into a Yellow Cab on Wisconsin Avenue near the National Cathedral. She still carried the cold bag, and in closeup her eyes were red shot, tired, and wary.

Jerome's search programs had a fix. They sounded the alarm to tell Jerome she had been found.

Jerome sat at his console and watched the cab's coordinates trace a path along Connecticut Avenue toward downtown. Now he had her. What should he do?

When the cab dropped her on K Street in front of the New Millennium Hotel, eighteen stories of silvered glass, he was watching through the hotel's entrance monitor, and he thought,

First, Connie Stone, I've got to find out who you are.

Until three years ago, she had been just another medial lab assistant. Then, according to the National Data Bank, her employment history went off record and stayed that way. She did not marry or otherwise change her name and did not appear on unemployment compensation, welfare, or disability rolls. More peculiar yet, she had disappeared from credit records as well. *The state of California might forget her,* Jerome thought, *but Masterchip, VisaBanque, Amex? No way.*

He had to dig in forbidden ground to find her. A quick raid, very quick—their reprisals were vicious—on the IRS records indicated a complex arrangement with a company named American Bioforms, which somehow was not her real employer. The IRS knew this but didn't mind; it was getting its cut of her salary.

The Dow Jones computer coughed up a string of parent companies and blinds terminating in a Caribbean bank. Home free: The bank's computer told him she was working for I.G. Biochemie in the Dominican Republic. Finally the CEO Intel Digest told him that the I.G. Biochemie compound was located on the Dominican Republic's northern coast near a little town called Sosua, a place with a strange history. In 1940 Rafael Trujillo, an almost forgotten twentieth-century dictator, had invited German Jews to come to the Dominican Republic and promised them sanctuary and their own town, Sosua. A few Jews had come, but over the years their numbers dwindled, so that by the end of the twentieth century there were none left.

A few decades later, in came I.G. Biochemie and a horde of Germans, very few of them Jews. And a few years later, in came Connie Stone.

Looking at life as a secret sharer had put some very strong torque on Jerome's already strange worldview. He walked a path signposted with paranoid conceits and occult symbols—

some real, some at least arguably real, others purely delusional. Connie Stone's blind employment history; associations with genocide, old dictators, German cartels—it all reeked of geoconspiracy, multicorporate plot. Jerome lit up like yellow phosphorus in sunlight.

"Locate I.G. Biochemie Sosua data processing station," he said, beginning the instructions to his computer. "Call and institute mole programs. Compile user data, establish operating-system codes. Load virus and execute. Terminate on unforeseen interrupt, and restart only on verbal authorization." It might take days to penetrate the corporation's security shells, but he was betting the I.G. Biochemie computer would fall.

Connie Stone sat beneath a green, white, and red umbrella. Blown in summer breeze, her hair was tangled around a red plastic barrette above her left ear. She wore a tropical print dress—red and blue and green flowers on a white background—that rode to her thighs as she sat with her foot touching the white bag of crumpled foam beneath her table. Her skin was pale white, lightly freckled; her look was vague.

Speaking out of bright sunshine, Jerome said, "Hello." The diener robot stood beside him. "My name is David Jerome. You have a problem."

Perhaps she thought of running—her knees clattered against metal struts beneath the table. "Go away," she said, hostile but still sitting, presumably concluding that he was no threat nor was his robot.

"I don't know what's in the bag," Jerome said, "but it must be perishable, so you can't carry it around much longer."

"What are you talking about?"

"I.G. Biochemie." He had leaned over the table to whisper the name to her. "Whatever that is, I guess you stole it from them. If you play around, they'll find you—"

The diener watched. She was half up from the table now,

the muscles of her face taut with something that could be either fear or outrage. Jerome still leaned over her, and in that moment the diener's tentacles moved beneath it in agitation: Something it didn't understand was going on here.

They sat in Jerome's living room. White light from the walls was shaded to purple in translucent polycarbonate couch, chair, and settees. Red speaker film framed in chrome stood next to a clear rack of AV equipment in matching red and a silver two-meter screen. Purple holographic letters dangled in space over sliding glass doors, asking ARE WE NOT MEN?

"You want in on the money," Connie said.

"Sure, but look what I'm worth to you," Jerome said. "You've been hung up, stuck with whatever you've got there ... maybe some help you were expecting, somebody you were expecting, didn't show." He waved away her attempt to answer. "That doesn't matter. I can arrange things so that I.G. Biochemie won't find you, and I can put the money anywhere in the world you want it. You won't be sorry."

"There's one thing you have to tell me," Connie said. "It's too creepy otherwise. How did you find me?"

"I saw you on the street ... I saw you, and I wondered why you were carrying that thing, who you were . . . it's hard to explain. Come here and let me show you." In the hallway the decorating program was restrained—it merely placed a rose tint over white walls, a dark purple border along the wallboards. Jerome said, "Let me in," and the door opened. "In here," he said. "Here's where I found you."

Jerome set Connie's two black, hard-shell suitcases on his living room floor and said, "I'll take them in the spare bedroom later." The cold bag lay across the living room couch. Connie ran her finger along the bag's seam, and it split, the sheets of crumpled white foam opening like petals of a giant flower.

Inside lay a black plastic cube the size of a fist, the compressor that forced cold air into the bag's foam cells. Next to it was a small sheet of white foam folded around something smaller and tied off in gray tape. On it in faint red marker was written a single numeral: 6. The package frosted as she held it out to him. "Do you want to look?" she asked.

"Is there anything to see?" he said.

"Not really. And you might contaminate it. So here—" She pulled a small silver disk from a fold in the crumpled white. "Here's all you'll need. Transmit this, and they'll know what you're selling. It's encoded, of course, but that's all right. Maybe the less you know, the better."

Silver whipspring coils snapped out of section joints in blue porcelain, and shining steel blades on the coils' tips flashed under fluorescent kitchen light, slicing away yellow skin and fat, cutting to the bone.

"That's a real floor show," Connie said. She walked out of the kitchen to find Jerome looking out the window onto R Street ten floors below. "Probably pretty good for self-defense, too." She sat on the purple-tinged couch.

"Sure," Jerome said, "if I want to stand trial for assault or involuntary manslaughter. If the diener hurts anyone, I'm responsible, just like I was driving a car."

The knife blades kept moving, but the diener was having trouble—inexplicable vertigo of robot visions. Half an ounce of flesh was sheared away with breastbone.

A new kind of awareness had been growing these past few months, out of the controller bond between the diener and Jerome, and it thought: *You are responsible, you say, but are you?*

Steel clanged against ceramic, blade against countertop.

Jerome called, "You got a problem, diener?"

"No," it said. "There is no problem. I was going too fast."

"Work within your limits, pal," Jerome said, then turned to Connie and said, "What did you say?"

"How long?" she asked again. "How long before you can finish this?"

"Hard to say. Could go a week if their security shells are really good, and they might be, especially now. But more likely we'll get in within the next thirty hours. No special reason for them to look for a computer burn on top of—"

"A theft," Connie said. "I'm a biolab technician specializing in cold-spot asepsis, and I'm a goddamn thief." Her voice was speeding up like a disk player with a faulty power supply, and Jerome knew it was all going to come out of her now. She said, "I took their *six*."

Jerome lay on the padded floor in the workroom. The diener was plugged in again for recharging and from time to time twitched like a dreaming dog. Opposite them both, a two-meter wallscreen ran mixed windows. From the news window came the voice and face of Latoh Bernie, one of the more popular computer-constructs. Below red wolf eyes, pale lips moved, and Latoh Bernie's voice said, "The Hunterian Museum of the Royal College of Surgeons in London reported today the theft of the brain of Charles Babbage, nineteenth-century pioneer in computer science. He was the man who first envisioned an all-purpose computer, which he called the Analytical Engine."

Babbage, Jerome thought, the man with the gears and cams and pulleys, inventor of, call it the "zeroth" computer generation, the one that never happened. Start counting generations, and you get to five by the beginning of the twenty-first century—systems like the diener robot. It walked, it talked, it performed a fair number of tasks with enormous skill. . . . But fifth-generation machines came up short in important ways—within limits they were hell, but they still weren't worth a damn at a Turing test.

Here an impish voice whispered inside him, *Oh, yeah, then what about the diener?* Because Jerome had stopped thinking of the diener as a machine long ago, never mind its limitations.

The way most people saw it, however, you were unlikely to mistake a fifth-generation machine for an intelligent being under any but the most restricted conditions. So for anyone with a professional stake in the matter, the magic number had become six. Information-dense transfer states, many-mind theory—researchers were working at the edge of things, where reality's fuzziest states connected to nature's complex systems, and there was a feeling that soon something would have to tumble.

If Connie was right, something had: I.G. Biochemie had hit the jackpot, an organic artificial intelligence. Then it *died,* this little bit of flesh, poisoned by a series of metabolic irregularities that IGB desperately wanted to examine. And they would have if Connie hadn't stolen the remains.

"Signing off, babies," Latoh Bernie said. "Let's hear it for Charley, eh? So bring back the brain, whoever you are." Latoh Bernie giggled.

"Christ," Jerome said. "All off." Wallscreen windows faded to rose.

"David," Connie said. "What are you doing?" She stood backlit in the doorway, wearing baggy pants and a blouse of crushed white cotton.

"Come on in," he said. She sat next to him on the padded floor and leaned back against the wall.

"I've been thinking," she said. "Now that you understand what's going on, maybe you want out."

And to himself Jerome said, *What I* want *no longer matters; you're what I* need.

"We'll see," he said. "If things get too strange, I'll tell you. But for the moment, no problem, I said I'd do it; I'll do it."

"That's very nice of you."

She gave a kind of sigh as he put his hands on her shoulders.

The events of the next few hours were as inevitable as the path of a freely falling object. As they took place, the diener remained motionless and apparently oblivious to what went on. But perhaps it was aware.... *There,* as Jerome was bent between her thighs and she cried out, was the diener moving; did it make a sound?

Jerome walked along Q Street near Dupont Circle. An old woman selling flowers out of white crockery vases arranged in a line along the sidewalk called to him, her tongue a blotch of dark red behind toothless gums. She said, "Come on, roses for your lady, mister." As if she knew.

In the middle of the next block, a tall, thin man in a green plastic jacket was bouncing plasma balls against cement steps. Flashes of electric gold exploded under sick amber streetlights. Jerome stopped and yelled, "Hey, 2-Ace!" The man gestured for him to come on. 2-Ace was shirtless under the jacket. Bones of chest and rib cage stood in clear outline, and chrome stars set into the meager flesh of his left pectoral gleamed in the streetlight. His eyes were bright, and even standing still, he seemed in motion—his left hand jerked back and forth in quick, unconscious arcs. 2-Ace did a fair amount of speed.

"Man," he said. "Jerome." A small maroon velveteen bag dangled from his waist, and he shook it gently. "Good shit," he said.

"I hope so," Jerome said. 2-Ace was selling credit chip blanks and recent codes—the necessary ingredients to cook up instant credit in whatever name he might choose and so have untraceable means. Jerome, Connie, and the diener might have to move in a hurry, and in an almost pure credit economy, cash in any significant amount would attract unwanted attention.

Jerome wanted to buy a rose from the old woman, but she had gone.

Nighttime is usually when the deal goes down, so Jerome wasn't surprised when he heard the message relay chirping around three A.M. Coming in through electronic dead drops in Europe, switched through the West Coast, it was I.G. Biochemie's reply. Then came an unexpected series of nonsense syllables. Jerome was wondering what they would have encrypted and why, when the system alarm went off—beeps and screams laced with urgent subsonics, the kind of message your central nervous system knows it never wants to hear.

Then there was FATAL ERROR on every screen, words that died even as he looked, as the machines were burned down to the ROM level, "eaten by the weasel" it was called, and Jerome had never seen it done—had not believed really that it *could* be done. But there it was: a whole system trashed, chips fried, CROME disks and WORM memories wiped.

The diener's bulbous front poked through the door with Connie just behind. "What's up?" she said. "What's wrong?"

"Grab what you've got," Jerome said. "But make it quick."

The door slid sideways as the elevator sighed to a stop at the first floor, and the stocky, sallow-faced man in a dark suit who waited just outside pulled his coat back and took a Colt Magnamatic from an upside-down shoulder holster.

There was an electric crackle, and the man collapsed: A small silver dart high on his left cheek led along a nearly invisible wire to a port in the diener's nose. "Nice work," Connie said.

Jerome said, "A man's got a right to defend his property." Flip, cool, false: more shock than anything. Jerome was already much deeper into bad shit than he'd ever dreamed of being.

Connie was on her knees by the prone man, taking the gun from his hand. She put the dark Kevlar barrel to the man's mouth and whispered, "I ought to just kill you." Paralyzed, he looked at her through hatred and pain. "What's going on?" Jerome asked. Connie looked at him, something crazy in her eyes. "No!" the diener said, its small-voiced cry punctuated by one subsonic pop as she fired. Back spatter put red lacework on her white sleeve. Blood and fluid leaked across black-and-white tile.

"Come on," she said. "Don't just stand there, come on!"

Carrying emerald-green methamphetamines and a handful of bogus credit chips in more names than either of them could remember, they were ready to run. The rented Pontiac sat in bright morning sunshine, silver clamshell doors sprung open, ceramic engine clattering as it came up to operating temperature. Dust motes danced in the light, and Jerome stood looking at the white plastic bag emitting its soft hum. He pressed down on the trunk lid, and it hissed shut.

Somewhere in Pennsylvania, where the sky was a dull gray that filtered the light and leached the color out of rolling farmland, Jerome said, "You've got to explain that...what you did."

Connie lay with her seat back, reclining almost on top of the diener, which filled most of the rear. Her face was toward the car's ceiling, her eyes closed. "David," she said, "I had to kill him. Christ, he knew what we look like, what we were wearing ...he even saw the robot, which by the way is going to be a big liability."

"Never mind that. Him or us, right?"

"That's what I'm trying to tell you."

The diener burned with a new set of perceptions. Over and over, it saw itself freezing the man with a taser dart, dropping him to the ground, and Connie Stone killing him *over and over.*

Who is responsible, and what could I have done? it wanted to know.

They bypassed Chicago, where the black Sears Tower sat in a foul petrochemical haze, looking like home base for the Evil Empire. Interstate 80 (Aut) had become a hot magnetic tube that sucked them along. The pilot was off, and red numbers on the dash flickered in the nineties—hopes for invisibility not forgotten exactly, just mislaid in the moment's burn.

By the next day the Midwest had been chewed up, and so had they, as the miles rolled under the Pontiac, and the chemicals they were eating fired a million tiny darts up and down their spines and dumped huge glass vats of acid into their stomachs. Jerome figured they had to stop sometime. So in Wyoming, in a shitty little town that was half neon fast-food strip and half lunar landscape, they pulled in under a clear sky that was rapidly fading into twilight and stopped at the 80 Autotel.

The diener followed Jerome and Connie into the motel room, where they took a Demerol each and slept ten straight hours, falling out of the amphetamine haze and into a dark sleep like death. The diener stood in its own darkness, possessed by the memory of that one event, working through what in a human would have to be called the trauma of it, the pain.

The next afternoon, clouds hanging on the surrounding mountains laid down a chill drizzle as they dropped into Salt Lake City. Half an hour later Jerome had gone to manual and was driving the Pontiac along the edge of the overflowing Salt Lake, where dikes of rock and dirt had cut the road to two slow-moving lanes wet with seepage from the overflow. Robot cranes—giant mantises ringed with camera eyes—worked the tops of the dikes while flagmen in yellow plastic suits urged the bottlenecked traffic onward. Farther west the road drew a straight line across the flooded salt flats, where gray sky and clouds and brown mountains were reflected in a giant watery mirror, two orders of being intersecting seamlessly, nature's excess flowing free into an unexpected beauty.

Jerome chewed a green capsule, gagged as it went down, then choked and spit into his hand. "I think I know what we're going to do," he said, then licked fragments of bitter amphetamine from his palm. "The diener here can send these assholes a phone message: *Fuck with us one more time, and we leave the rotting carcass of your "six" on the roadside for the coyotes to eat. So pay now. Do it fast and safe—encrypt, squeeze, and squirt.* I made a bad mistake the last time; I went after them like they were into some kind of ordinary security routine; but I forgot how much they might have to protect."

"And I forgot how quick they are," Connie said. "And how mean."

"Yeah. Anyway, I think we've run about far enough."

Jerome had always had apocalyptic associations with Nevada. Words like *test range, underground explosion,* and *dead sheep* came to mind. But that's where they ended up, in a small town just over the border, burning under the day's fading sun, where signs promised investors cheap entry into the "Next Las Vegas." All were faded to near illegibility.

Their room had steel furnishings, eggshell blue walls. The lobby of the Flowing Sands had been late-twentieth-century pseudo-luxe: white ceramic and red Naugahyde, chrome, multicolored lasers running mindlessly through their programs.

Jerome lay on the bed, feeling strange.

Old blues, half remembered . . . songs about guns and knives and women—*She's got a thirty-eight special,* and *Hey momma, please stop breakin' down*—he thought one of them might be somehow appropriate.

She stepped out of the bathroom wearing a light pink towel, crystal beads of water from the shower on her skin—

The one I love—

And she opened a black drawer and lifted a dark blue silky gown from it and put the towel aside—
put a pistol in a man's mouth—
She slid the gown over her head—
and pulled the trigger—
When her hot, damp skin pushed against him it erased an infinity of doubts—
(some special kind of blues).

The diener reached inside itself and pulled out a blue plastic lead with a silver plug on its end. Spring-loaded, the lead pulled taut as the diener stretched it and snapped it into the base of the phone. "You wish me to transmit now?" it asked.

"Sure," Jerome said.

And in the moment of the relay's closing, as circuits began to come together from Nevada to the Dominican Republic, it knew what it must say, now, and to whom.

A few seconds later, Jerome said, "That's it. It's all over. Let's get a drink." And to the diener he said, "You should recharge."

"I will do so," it said. It had further material to ponder: In light of its recent experience of irreversible change—irreversible choice—it considered what likely would happen next.

Quick and mean, she had said.

Connie and Jerome were sitting over room-service breakfast the next morning when the door opened and two men in hotel uniforms—maroon jumpsuits with gold trim—stepped inside. The tall one held a small black automatic pistol like the Colt in Connie's handbag. The short one went to the closet and pushed the button, and the mirrored door slid aside. He reached into the white-lit interior and pulled the cold bag from behind stacked black suitcases. He laid the cold bag on the double bed, split the opening seam, and took out the package. He unwrapped the package and with a small scalpel carved away a sliver of the lump of pink flesh inside and placed the sliver in a small black tube.

Connie looked at the diener, which was plugged into a wall socket. "I'm sorry," Jerome said, but she ignored him; she was looking wildly about as if for something that was not there.

The short one nodded his head and began to repack the cold bag. The tall one fired a shot that hit Connie in the middle of the forehead. The impact slammed her against the wall, and the shooter walked over to where she sprawled with her legs and arms flung wide, and put another shot into the inside curve of her left breast, into the heart.

"Go home," he said to Jerome in the flat voice of a poker player taking the dealer for two cards. "Someone will be along to take care of things—the woman, the car. Don't say anything to anybody, and don't ever bother us again. Understand?"

With her blood on him and the smell of her death in his nostrils, Jerome understood. The two men didn't wait for him to say so. They were gone.

The shuttle to Reno lifted straight up from a pad of cracked cement on the edge of the almost-town. Inside the old swing-wing jet, the stink of sweat came off tattered green upholstery. Over the mountains the plane swayed and bucked in rough air that penetrated Jerome's stunned grief and guilt and made him white with nausea.

In Reno the airport was bright blue cement, red steel, and a forest of mirrors, and Jerome and the diener were insignificant among thousands returning east, most having blown sensible amounts, a few telling stories of big casino wins, a few more nursing the gut ache that comes with big-time loss, the one you can't afford.

"You're sure the compartment is pressurized," Jerome said to the woman behind the United counter. The diener had already been checked through, but Jerome was anxious.

"Hey, Jackie," the woman said. "This guy's shipping a robot. You wanna talk to him? I'm busy." She was in her early twenties with bright, sexy eyes, and obviously did not give a shit.

"Fuck you," Jerome said, and walked away.

"Next," the woman said.

On the flight to Washington, the cabin was dark, and Jerome sat sleepless in the gloom, confronting the blank recognition that he had known little about Connie Stone, and he wondered who she was, and more . . . wondered about them . . . what were the odds that their passion would have endured past the moment's hot radioactive burn? At Dulles there was rain and fog and crowds dispersing quickly off two incoming flights.

The diener rolled up a ramp into the rear compartment of an airport limo; Jerome sat among the half-dozen glum people inside. As the limo moved along the Dulles Parkway, no one said a word, which was fine with Jerome. He could barely imagine trying to talk to anyone about anything.

Late afternoon the following day, Jerome sat on the minute terrace outside his bedroom. Through open glass doors he could hear the quiet swish of the diener as it moved through the room.

Jerome's voyeurism was gone, its energies extinct. He thought that maybe his curiosity had gone with it, though he did wonder about one thing.

"Diener," he called, and the robot came onto the terrace. "How do you think I.G. Biochemie found us?" Jerome asked. He breathed in the burned hydrocarbons from the street ten stories below. The diener stayed silent. "I used to think I was pretty good at this game," Jerome went on, "but they burned me down, they caught us."

"No," the diener said. "Not your fault."

"Of course it is."

"No. I told them."

Coming out of the chair, Jerome put his hands under the edge of the diener's porcelain shell. He thought, *Of course you did,* in a moment more of recognition than of discovery. He grunted as he levered the diener's body sideways so that it rested against the white-painted terrace railing. The diener's tentacles quivered like agitated black worms.

"To save your life," the diener said. "I made a deal with them. They would never have forgotten you, they would have killed you. Why do you worry about that woman? She was a thief, a murderer."

"You little shit."

Under the diener's weight and Jerome's push, the rail came free, and the diener tumbled in bright sunlight. Smashing through a sculpture of black wrought iron, it plunged through rippling water, and its body shattered on the fountain's concrete and sandstone bottom.

Over the chatter of people gathering around the fountain, Jerome's wail could be heard coming from high above.

Chimera Dreams

by Gregg Keizer

Gregg Keizer's first story, "I Am the Burning Bush," was also published in *Omni* (May 1982). Keizer's fiction continued to demonstrate a quirkiness I greatly admired, and I subsequently published three other short stories by him, including this one, "Chimera Dreams" (June 1983). Unfortunately for his fiction fans, Keizer became an editor at *COMPUTE!* magazine and began writing nonfiction in the late '80s. He has produced virtually no short fiction since then but rumor has it he might be getting back into it. Keizer lives in Eugene, Oregon.

"Chimera Dreams" is what I would consider science fantasy because although one of the characters in this love triangle is a werewolf, this condition is explained by scientific (albeit fuzzy) means.

CHIMERA DREAMS

Gregg Keizer

On the other side of the door the werewolf howled. He wanted in. Enough to scrape at the wood and even throw himself against it, sending shudders through the frame. I sat in the deep chair on the far side of the room, my legs and dress tucked under me. I swallowed the last of the wine and threw the shimmering crystal against the door. For a second the sound of the spinning fragments drowned out his yells.

"God damn it, Kirt, you were told not to come here again," I yelled as loudly as I could, hoping that the werewolf would hear me over his own howling.

I got up from my chair, reached for the thick wooden cane that leaned against it, and walked a bit unsteadily across the room. I'd drunk too much, and my feet kept catching in the wrinkles of the rug. The werewolf—no, Kirt actually—kept up his yowl. *How can he stand to listen to himself?* I thought as I began unlatching the door. Another shudder went through the wood frame. Then I flung the door open and lifted the cane.

"Shut up, shut up, do you hear me?" I screamed, swinging the cane as hard as I could across his shoulder. The silver handle, in the shape of a bison, slammed into the thick hair. I didn't have the strength to really hurt him. But Kirt still shrieked in pain. Fake pain; he'd seen the cane's silver head and

54

screamed because the drug he'd taken forced him to. By legend, silver was agony to werewolves, and so Kirt, who thought himself a werewolf while he was on fantacin, screamed.

As he recoiled from the blows, he retreated across the corridor until his back was against the papered wall, his paws before his face. I put my hands on my knees and bent over, trying to draw sweeter air into my lungs. A snarl from the werewolf forced me to look up over the rim of my glasses, and I tightened my grip on the cane. But he didn't lunge, only stood warily five feet away.

He was tall and rangy, at least six feet tall if one counted the tufts of fur at the top of his ears. His face was only vaguely wolflike; it had as many human characteristics as lupine. An overlarge nose jutted from the matted hair around the circles of his eyes, and his chin was decidedly cleft. Wolves' chins were not like that; I had seen photos of the last wolves found in northern Canada. His ears were pointed and a bit bent at the tips. Huge canines dropped over the lower lip, but they appeared more awkward than dangerous. And Kirt's paws had opposing thumbs, something evolution hadn't given the wolf.

It was all part of the chimera cloak Kirt wore. Just an illusion fabricated by the living crystals woven into the cloak's fabric. Cloak was a poor word, for it was more a tight-fitting shirt that ended above the waist. Depending on the pattern and type of crystals, the holographic projection the cloak manufactured forced the viewer to believe different things. Kirt had chosen a chimera cloak made to show a werewolf, and so that image was what I saw. I *knew* that it was really Kirt who stood in front of me behind the fur and crooked limbs, but my eyes could see only the twisted vision.

And Kirt. Even *he* saw himself this way. Not only that, but fantacin, the drug he was on, convinced him that he *was* a werewolf. When he ran on two legs, fantacin made him feel he loped on four. When he let loose an all-too-human cry, he imagined a wolf's bay. It was what made him fear my silver-headed cane. To those of us who changed to were-animals each night, fantacin was our release. We remembered our humanity only when we tried something impossible. The first chimera werewolf who thought his canines were real had been shocked when five teeth broke as he tried to crack the femur of an antelope in the zoo compound.

Kirt was coming off the fantacin. Fear always makes one come down faster. He did not metamorphose slowly into his human shape, as in some poorly done dissolve in an old movie. He stayed a werewolf, for his chimera cloak was still on, but his movements and gestures became subtly human. His paw groped at his chest as if he were searching for cigarettes.

Then he was Kirt, the cloak a piece of glittering black cloth he held in his hands. He brushed blond hair from his eyebrows and slumped to the floor, rubbing his shoulder and neck where I'd caned him. Sweat slid down his face, and he wiped it with the chimera cloak. The hallway smelled thick, a strange sweetness that hung in the air. He grinned idiotically at me.

"Have fun, Courtney?" he asked, pointing a finger at the cane I still held.

"You're a bastard, Kirt. You really are," I said, smiling back at him, and watched his grin disappear.

"I just wanted to get in to see her."

"She's not home, Kirt," I said. "She told you never to come here again. Especially this way." I shuddered at the thought of what he might have done if he'd gotten inside the apartment while fantacin burned in him.

"I wasn't going to do anything," he said, eyeing the cane. He still seemed wary of it. "I knew I'd come down off the drug before I got inside."

"It's not that accurate, Kirt. Don't you think I know?" I asked. I swallowed the dark red capsules, too, but I played a different part. I glanced down at the bison head on the cane's tip.

"You don't have any more control over fantacin than anyone else. Don't lie to me, Kirt. I'm not stupid."

"Where is she, Courtney?" He stood up slowly, using the wall as a brace.

"You don't seem to understand. Hellea doesn't want to see you again. Not when you're real, not when you're that," I said, pointing at the chimera cloak he held. "If you come around again, Kirt, I'll use the revolver." His face drained of color. He was free of the drug, and his fear was now of metal bullets, not the self-made fright of silver that fantacin manufactured.

"Why do you play these games, Courtney?" he asked finally. "Hellea still loves me. You took her away from me, and I want her back. You'd see she still loves me if you just let me talk to her." I drew a breath and forced my voice beyond a whisper.

"You want her back, Kirt? For what? So you can beat her again? Hellea's told me everything, Kirt. You're violent. Insane and violent. She'll never go back to you." I paused and drew another breath. "Don't come here again. Stay away."

"Everything?" he asked. "She told you all of it?" I nodded. He was quiet for several seconds. "We're not so very different, I think. We both want Hellea. But I want her enough to kill you to get her." I backed up a step toward the apartment door, the cane now held before my breasts. He stayed on the other side of the corridor and kept his gaze on the silver bison tip as he spoke. "It doesn't matter where she goes. I'll find her even if she hides behind you."

"How?" was all I could manage.

He touched his nose, once on each side of his nostrils. "I'm a werewolf, Courtney. A *real* werewolf. Scent will lead me."

I couldn't help staring, and I heard my voice catch in the rear of my throat. "God, you *are* insane." Then Kirt pointed with the hand that held the chimera cloak, and I followed its direction until I saw the thing on the floor. It was a small animal of some kind. All I could see was its twisted throat and the slight dark line on the floor. That was what I'd smelled, I realized. Its death smell.

"For Hellea," he said, moving his hand to indicate the small, dead form. "Tell her I was here." I held my hands at my mouth to keep the sourness inside me. I knew I was shaking my head, and the moan that I heard must have been mine. "And for you, Courtney. Take it as a warning."

A shrill, faraway howl came through the thick walls from outside, and Kirt laughed softly as he looked at me. Then he was running down the hall, heading for the darkness at the head of the stairs. In the dim light just above the first step, I thought I saw him hesitate and slip his chimera cloak on once more. Then only his footsteps remained, their sounds broken finally by the howling from outside.

I heard the key turn in the lock and hefted the cane in my hand, moving slightly in the chair as I braced my feet on the floor. If it wasn't Hellea I would be ready.

"What's that?" Hellea asked as she closed the door behind her. I still held the silver-tipped cane, but now it felt only foolish. "Do you want me to move out already?" And she smiled, that Hellea smile that made my anxieties and the memories of Kirt's face wither and fall from my mind.

"He was here again," I said, my eyes on her lips. They were nothing like the thin streaks of Kirt's mouth. "I had to use this to drive him away."

"I'd hoped he wouldn't come back," she said. She stood in the center of the room and seemed awkward and stiff as she spoke. "I told him he shouldn't come here again. I told him I didn't love him." She paused. "I wonder how he found us?"

Although we'd been lovers for almost two months now,

Hellea had moved into my apartment only four days before. Last night Kirt pounded on the door, shouting for her. Their screaming argument in the hallway hadn't been hard to hear through the door.

Then I told her what had happened between Kirt and me. When I mentioned the small, dead thing still in the hallway, of how its throat was torn open, she looked away from me.

"He said it was a gift for you and a warning for me." Hellea was silent and stared at the closed door. "I'm calling the p.o.'s."

Finally she moved toward my chair and knelt beside it. I put the cane down on the other side of the chair. Her hand was on my shoulder, warm and comfortable. She brushed her finger along my eyebrows, circled the edges of my ears. I felt the blood warm my face.

"They won't want to talk to us about it." Her voice was soft.

"Perhaps. But he's killed something. That may make a difference." I pulled her hands from my face, stood, and walked to the phone. She followed me.

"Once they find out chimera is involved, they'll make excuses. You know that; everyone does. They'll apologize and say they'll send someone out to investigate, but no one will show. They never do."

"But Kirt's insane. He killed. . . ."

"Murder they'll listen to, even if you tell them chimera is part of it," she said, her hands on my shoulders again. "They have to come then. But for a lover's quarrel? A dead animal caught in the park? Hardly."

It was true. Crimes were almost impossible to solve when chimera cloaks were involved because they made perfect disguises. That was why the p.o.'s concentrated on murders or rapes. Minor violations of the law were ignored, for the most part. They weren't worth the time.

"Just let me call and tell them what he's done. Once they hear what he said to me, they'll at least listen." I picked up the phone.

"What did he say?" Hellea asked. Her hand tightened almost imperceptibly on my shoulder.

"That he'd track us by our scent," I said, punching numbers on the phone.

"What else?"

"That he was a real werewolf."

Her hand twitched again. When Hellea said nothing, I turned to her. She was still, her eyes closed.

"He *is* insane," she whispered, and I heard her breath hiss from between her teeth. Her hand closed over mine and pushed the phone receiver back into its cradle. "Don't bother with the p.o.'s. They won't bother with us." She paused. "We'll deal with Kirt ourselves. I promise."

"If that's what you want," I said. She nodded. I couldn't understand her hesitancy in calling the p.o's, but she was upset. I shrugged and let the matter drop.

"I want something else, Courtney." She was not very subtle in leading me from the talk of Kirt and madness and the p.o.'s, but again I said nothing, for she was suddenly pressed against me, her curious perfume enveloping me, her hands busy at my neck, then at my waist. Her touch was so delicate and sure that it drove the fear from me, and for those moments I was only in love.

In the coolness of our sheets we lay next to each other, shoulders touching. Hellea's smell was everywhere, even on my fingers when I lifted them to my nostrils. Pungent, yet intoxicating.

"Like it?" she asked, and her voice was deeper, more in the back of her throat.

"Yes."

"I'm glad," Hellea whispered, her voice almost unintelligible because of its deepness. She licked her lips quickly several times, her tongue slapping against her teeth. For a moment, in the dim moonlight from the windows, I thought I saw canines. Memories of Kirt and his chimera cloak—that was all. "We'll get rid of him," Hellea said softly.

"Yes," I said, thinking only of Hellea, wondering why she was so against involving the p.o.'s. Hellea, for all our intimacy, was still a stranger. I'd met her at work and fallen in love straightaway. But she already had a lover, she'd said. Kirt. And then, gradually, she'd told me of how he beat her when he was on fantacin, how he was insane and violent. I talked to her for long hours and finally persuaded her to leave him and live with me. That had been only four days before, and already Kirt had found her. Scent would lead him, he had said in the corridor.

"I'm glad I came here," Hellea whispered. She moved her fingers, brushed my eyelids and lips with them. The odor of her was smothering. "Do you love me, Courtney?" she asked, her voice still deep. I barely caught her words and could only nod. *Scent,* Kirt had said, and I breathed deeply of Hellea's extraordinarily perfumed skin.

I suddenly felt far colder than the pleasant warmth of my bed could allow.

The tram to work was crowded, and Hellea and I had to push our way between two obese women to get through the doors before they closed. One woman nodded to me, but I was not in the mood for chatter, even though I recognized her. She lived in our building, a floor or two down. I remembered her as a wildebeest at night.

I had managed to sleep, finally, the night before, but only after deciding Kirt was genuinely insane. That he knew of Hellea's unusual perfume was not unlikely; if he believed himself enough of a werewolf to lose his sanity, he could believe himself able to track scents. Insanity made anything possible. Yet I had dreamed of Kirt and imagined his claws on my breasts. They had ripped me open in my nightmare; they'd been real, not just chimera illusion. Hellea's warmth beside me when I woke had been the only thing that had kept me from screaming.

"Did you see the program on video last night?" one obese woman asked another. "That old one, with the birds. You know, the birds that died way back."

I wanted to tell her that all of them were dead. The large ones had been the first to vanish, eighty-odd years ago. Somehow, the birds were the first. Or perhaps we only noticed them before the rest. We had looked up and realized that almost all the large animals were gone. They'd been on endangered lists for decades, centuries for some of them, but we hadn't paid enough attention. There were plenty of small mammals, the things that multiplied quickly, but that was all. No lionesses creeping through grasses, no lumbering elephants, no white-furred bears in the Arctic. I'd seen photographs of them.

We were lonely, in a way. It was difficult to feel kinship with the small, scurrying things. The chimera cloak came first, and people wore the animal they most admired. Then fantacin, and one could become another creature, at least for a while, and at least in one's own imagination. Everyone did it now. Everyone who could afford it. The others watched video and dreamed of being something else when night came.

Perhaps we felt guilty about our carelessness. So now there were animals again, though they weren't real. And some people were like Kirt, who used the chimera and fantacin to hide their insanity. People looked the other way when someone wore a chimera and played at being a rutting, aggressive beast in the night. The p.o's, with their stunners and laws to enforce, rarely bothered with people in chimera. As long as you were not too violent, the p.o.'s left you alone. They had enough trouble simply solving the chimera murders that crowded the dockets.

"I'm going to look for a new cloak tomorrow," a voice beside me said. I turned, but it was only the second fat woman, talking to the other. "The one I've got is so old and shabby. Arron told me he could see my real face through it last night," she said, her voice almost a giggle. I watched her stroke the thick skin beneath her eye, rubbing the layers of fat there. Perhaps she was a starving antelope in the night. It would be a way to forget her obesity for a few hours.

The tram stopped in front of our office building, and we worked our way to the open doors. As I stepped to the ground the man in front of me stumbled, and I reached out a hand to steady him. I saw his face go white and turned to see what he looked at.

She was spread awkwardly on the pavement, her head canted oddly to one side. Her face was hidden from me, but I could not help staring at the back of her neck, for a line of blood started there and flowed to the gutter. A circle of people was drawn around her, but no one touched the dead woman, not even the p.o. who stood off to one side, his hand resting on the butt of his stunner. He seemed to be waiting for his superiors before he disturbed her.

"Oh, my god," I heard Hellea whisper. Her eyes were wide as she stared at the body. "How could he do this?"

I felt a sudden chill on my arms and realized the dead woman looked familiar, even from the back. Her hair was auburn, her limbs long, and her hands large for her wrists. I walked around the edges of the circle until I could see her face. Through her contorted grimace and the already-drying blood on her throat, I recognized her face. I recognized her because she looked so much like me.

"Somebody's idea of a joke, I suppose," the p.o. investigator said as he drew back the chimera cloak from the woman on the ground. The outline of the shape on the pavement shimmered for a moment and then solidified. It wasn't human. It was the body of a sheep. A sheep in human guise. The zoo-compound markings on the animal's chest were plain to see, even through the darkening from the torn throat.

"I don't understand," I said.

"Someone killed this poor creature, wrapped this cloak around it," the investigator said, holding the chimera in his hand at arm's length, as if it were contagious, "and then dumped the carcass here. Have any idea why?" He looked at me, and when I said nothing he went on. "The cloak is of you. Or close enough not to matter. Custom-made, by the looks of it. Shouldn't be too hard to trace back to whoever commissioned it. Someone you know enjoy killing zoo-compound animals? Against the law, you know. You wear these?" And he held up the chimera again. I felt Hellea's hand on my arm.

"Yes, yes I do."

"I suppose all your friends do, too," he said, looking at Hellea, his disgust not quite concealed. He was like most p.o.'s; he hated all chimera for its ability to hide the guilty. "You have no idea who might have done this?" He pointed to the dead sheep that still lay on the pavement. Perhaps it was only imagination, but I thought I smelled the same odor as in the hallway the night before. Death smell.

"Can't you see the shock she's had?" Hellea asked. "Of course she doesn't know who did this. Leave her alone." She glared at the p.o. investigator, who was silent and blinked his eyes often.

"I apologize," he said finally. "But we have to investigate. A zoo-compound animal's not killed and just forgotten . . . ."

"Is it more important than she is?" Hellea asked. She stepped forward and tried to push me behind her.

"Stop it," I said. "Stop it." I pulled Hellea's hand from my arm and looked at the p.o. investigator. "Yes, I think I know who did this. He's threatened me before. Last night, in fact." I could sense Hellea's eyes on me, so I turned to her. "Let me talk. This is the only way we can get rid of him." Back to the investigator again. "He's insane. He's jealous because Hellea left him. He brought some dead thing to our apartment last night and said it was a warning for me. To let Hellea go back to him, I suppose. His name is Kirt. What's his last name, Hellea?"

She glanced at me for a moment, and it wasn't hard to see the fury in her face. But she answered. "Gallins. Kirt Gallins."

"He thinks he's a werewolf. A *real* one," I said. I heard Hellea inhale quickly.

"Obviously," the investigator said, and when I shook my head in confusion, he bent down beside the sheep's carcass. "Unusual wound," he said, pushing his fingers into the ripped throat of the sheep. "See the ragged edges? Here and here? Didn't use a blade, that's plain. Something blunter, rounder perhaps. Like a tooth."

Had he actually placed his mouth on the thing's throat when he killed it? Could he be that mad?

"May I go home now?" I finally asked. He looked at the place where the sheep lay, turned back to me, and nodded.

"I'd stay in tonight if I were you," he said, pointing to the bison's-head ring on my left index finger. Though his advice was sound, I knew I wouldn't take it. "We'll see what Kirt Gallins has to say about this. Shouldn't be hard to find him. Call if you think of anything we might want to know?" His eyebrows edged up and stayed there.

"Certainly, if we think of anything." I turned then and walked to the tram stop, glad to be among a crowd, even in the daylight. I didn't wait for Hellea to move with me. The group made me comfortable, for it felt as if someone were standing just outside my view, waiting for me to step outside the crush of others. But every time I looked around, the only familiar face I saw was Hellea's.

"Why did you tell him?" Hellea asked. "We could have

dealt with Kirt ourselves. Now the p.o.'s know everything."

I stared at her. A madman had killed an animal and dressed it in a cloak to make it look like me. The meaning was less than subtle. Yet she still thought we could do something about him ourselves.

"That's the point," I said slowly. "What can *we* do? Kill him? I don't have the stomach for that, Hellea. The p.o.'s will find him and lock him away."

She grabbed my arm and pulled me to her until her lips were only inches from mine. "No," she said, and I could feel her breath hot on my face. "I'll deal with him myself. He's mine, and I'll do what we've always done with those like him."

"*We've* done?" I asked, feeling her hand still tight around my arm. But she wouldn't look at me, even when she spoke.

"He's insane, Courtney. But don't let the p.o.'s force him to see that. Let me."

She might as well have continued with her unspoken words. *Let me, because I still love him.* That was why she did not want the p.o's involved. She was afraid for Kirt. I wanted her to speak those unspoken words, but I was afraid she would answer and put an end to everything.

She seemed to read my mind. "Please, Courtney. No more questions. Just let me take care of Kirt."

"Let's go home," I said, suddenly afraid of losing her.

Damn Kirt, damn him, I thought, and for a second I even believed I could do him harm to keep Hellea with me.

I gazed stupidly across the park meadow and imagined I chewed on the grass. It was not the prairie that I dreamed of, but it was the best in the city, the widest expanse of open ground. Someday I would make it to the plains, but not tonight. I was only a bison in the city tonight.

There were at least three dozen others around me, people I knew vaguely in their human forms, better in their chimera cloaks. The great shaggy bull toward the treeline was Mestern; the young cow beside me was Hellea. It was my herd, my group, and the sense of security was thick in the air as we moved slowly through the grasses.

I'd taken a low dose of fantacin and so kept sliding in and out of myself. Most of the time I realized I was human dressed in chimera; occasionally I lost track and only knew when I came out of the blankness that I'd truly thought of myself as bison. We are a stupid animal, really, but one with group instinct. I was an animal I liked to be.

In that brief moment of human consciousness I caught the scent of Hellea on my skin. We'd gone to the apartment from the scene of the p.o.'s and the chimera-cloaked sheep to make love. Hellea had said nothing, only made love to me with furious energy. When we were done and exhausted on the sheets, she massaged my back, rubbing our mixed perspiration into my skin. She'd seemed nervous then, but still said little to me. Now that her strange perfume was rubbed deep into me, I felt secure in her love. Perhaps all my misgivings were only lover's paranoia.

The comforting warmth of the herd as we closed up made me slip from my humanity then, but I recovered quickly. Even knowing what I was, the sense of protection overwhelmed me until I felt every worry, every anxiety fall from my busy mind, until it was emptied and confident. Nothing could harm me here in the herd.

A nervous flicker seemed to run through all of us. I looked down, and though the chimera I wore made me see the thick shoulders of a bison, I knew I was human and was really only glancing at my waist. Still, I saw my matted hair move again as the flesh beneath it twitched. We'd smelled something wrong in the air.

A short howl from the trees told me what it was. Wolves: either ones that ran on four feet or werewolves. Both kinds would be chimera-driven. The members of the herd moved closer together, three of the bulls on the outside of the ragged circle, calves in the middle. I slipped into the dream-world of fantacin and lost my thoughts.

I awoke to see Kirt's werewolf face filling my sight. He peered at me through yellow eyes, his nose wrinkled up as he inhaled deeply. His massive head shook as if he were confused. I caught a trace of a strange odor when he breathed in my face. Again the fantacin pulled me from consciousness. My eyes finally opened, and even though I knew they were only human teeth wrapped around the throat of Hellea's imaginary bulk, I couldn't help but scream inside myself as she struggled against the werewolf who sawed at her neck.

Fantacin again touched me, and I could only stare dumbly as the werewolf tore my lover's throat with immense canines that glinted in the dim moonlight. He dropped her body, her carcass, then seemed to stare into my eyes. I tried to blink but could not, for fear was in my mouth and squeezed my face tight until I felt my temples throb. He leaned on his heels, arched his head back hard, and howled at the half-moon. I stepped back, turning to my left, bringing my immense head directly in line with him. I would not die easily. But Kirt did nothing but howl once again, wave a hand to indicate Hellea beside him on the ground, whirl, and run for the trees.

Driven away by the fear-crested adrenaline, fantacin burned from my body, and I peeled off my chimera cloak and held it in my hand. Several of the others in my herd were doing the same. The ones still playing bison snuffed around the spoor of the vanished werewolves. Hellea had been the only casualty.

And then the enormity of what Kirt had done stuck me. He'd murdered her; the p.o.'s would hunt hard for him now. A howl echoed from the tree line, and the sheer sound of it made me sick. I was on the grass, my hands splayed in front of me, mouth gasping for air as I vomited. For a moment, I even forgot what he'd done to Hellea. I was next. I was sure of it. But I still did not know why he'd left me for last.

The p.o.'s that came and knelt on the grass to look at Hellea's still-cloaked body told me they would search for Kirt but not to expect too much. It was going to be hard finding him when chimera cloaks could be donned at will. I knew they were right.

A p.o. went home with me on the tram and even walked me up the stairs to my door, but after I opened it and he thrust his head inside, he simply withdrew and shrugged his shoulders. No Kirt. Nothing.

I waited until he'd left, then closed the door, leaving it unlocked. The ancient revolver lay heavy in my hands as I crouched in the darkness at the far end of the corridor, my eyes on the stairway where Kirt would have to show himself. I checked the revolver. All I had to do was pull back the hammer and yank on the trigger. It was better than doing what the p.o. recommended: spend the night with him and wait until Kirt was found. They might never find him. I wanted an end to it, but the images of the false woman on the pavement, blood under its throat, and of Hellea's bulk, silent on the meadow grass, kept interfering and urging me to flee. I sat, nevertheless. Perhaps it was the bison in me.

He crept up the stairs. I could hear his hind paws on the landings. Pulling back on the hammer, I felt better after I'd heard it click into place. But it was not Kirt who slunk along the walls, one side of his face in the shadows. It couldn't be Kirt, for the face was all wrong. There was no cleft in the chin, the nose did not jut from the flatness of the face, and the canines no longer looked merely awkward. They looked like they could tear flesh.

I held the image of the sheep-woman in my mind, then tasted the same sourness in my mouth as when I'd been in the park where Hellea had died. This man was mad. He thought himself a real werewolf, an animal that had never existed except in the imagination of chimera-wearers. And now he'd bought another chimera. Still werewolf but slightly different. I'd never seen one like it, but it had to be a cloak. There was no other explanation.

I thought of Hellea, felt her touch, delicate even in my imagination, on my throat and face. This man, this thing, had murdered her. I pulled hard on the revolver's trigger, listening to the roar of it as it fired. The darkness I hid in was illuminated by the flash, and in the brief glare I saw Kirt stagger and heave against the wall. He was down on the floor now, slumped in the junction of floor and wall.

"Kirt?" I asked. He nodded after what seemed too long a pause.

"Does this mean you don't love me, Hellea?" he asked, his breathing labored as he moved one furred hand to hold the wound at his side. The corridor was filled with his odor. It was the same clinging scent I'd smelled before. But there was no small dead thing in the corner now. There was only Kirt. "I came to you, Hellea. We belong together, you and I. We've no choice now. I know the others want me dead. They want you dead, too, for consorting with a human. She's dead now, and there's only me. You can't go back to the others; they'll kill you." His speech was understandable but only barely so, for his voice was surprisingly deep and filled with noises from the back of his throat.

"Hellea is dead, Kirt. You killed her. Don't you remember? In the park tonight."

He was silent for the longest time.

"Kirt?"

"No. I killed the other one. The human who wore the bison. I smelled her, Hellea. At first I thought she was one of us. Her smell fooled me. But she was human."

Memories came to me of Hellea and me lying together, her

fingers pressing her odors into my back, our scents mixed in our lovemaking. I breathed the corridor's smell and knew it was near Hellea's perfume. Not identical, just as a woman smells vaguely different from a man, but near. Hellea's perfumed scent, Kirt's too-sweet odor. Female and male.

"Hellea is dead. I'm Courtney," I hissed, knowing now what he was here for.

"No, you *are* Hellea," he whispered. "I wear the chimera," he said, pulling two of the cloaks from the clenched fingers of his other hand. "One is for this," he said. Slowly and in obvious pain, he pulled one over his head until it was straightened. For a moment his outline shimmered gently, as everyone's does when a chimera is first put on. Then the image solidified, and he was Kirt, the blond hair hanging over the eyes, his chest thin, his hands delicate and long fingered. There was still a blotted stain at his side. "The other one makes me this," he whispered hoarsely, removing the human chimera and pulling on the other cloak. As soon as his outline cleared, I could see the werewolf face he'd always shown me. It had the cleft chin, the jutting nose, the vaguely human features. He pulled it off quickly, then threw them both in front of me. He was the werewolf again, the different one, the one with few human characteristics. No cleft chin, no thrusting nose. He grimaced, and canines showed.

I looked at the heavy revolver in my hand. The bullet had not been silver, yet he was wounded. That meant he had staged the fear and pain from my cane's silver head to make me believe he was a *human* werewolf, a fantacin-driven imitation.

"You are one of us," Kirt said. "I love you, Hellea. You never should have left me."

"You're mad," I whispered.

"I won't touch you again, I promise," he said softly. "I know why you left me. It was because I told them what I was. There's no harm in that anymore. The humans don't believe in us, Hellea. They think we're only wearing these." He waved to the dark cloaks in front of me. "There's no danger in telling them what we are. We're finally safe. Don't you see that?" He stopped, drawing breaths in short gasps.

"You're mistaken, Kirt," I said softly. "I'm not one of you, whatever you are."

"I smelled you. I'm not wrong. There was werewolf scent from your apartment. You were clever to room with a human, Hellea. Very clever," he said, his breath sounding loud in the close corridor.

This thing, this madman, had smelled Hellea? "You got confused by the chimera, Kirt," I said slowly. "You smelled my scent on Hellea, hers on me. You made a mistake, Kirt. You killed her instead of me."

"No, you're wrong. I killed the right one. You are Hellea. Take off the chimera," he said, sliding his body toward me. "Let me see you for what you are."

Even though I knew now what Hellea had been, even though I now realized why she had not wanted to involve the p.o.'s, I knew I had loved her. She had tried to conceal herself by living with me, by mixing my human scent with hers. She had even tried to hide me from Kirt by rubbing her scent on me, but it had only resulted in her own death. I pulled the hammer of the revolver back once again. There were no silver bullets, but there were still five more with lead tips. They would do. "NO!" I screamed. "There is nothing more!" And I yanked hard on the trigger, hearing the explosion three times before I could pull my finger from the weapon. I tugged and tugged on the bloodied fur of Kirt's arm and chest, but there was no chimera cloak to pull off. He had been telling me the truth. He was a werewolf. Had they always existed, or had they slid into the world when chimera and fantacin made the boundaries of man and beast blurry and vague?

I thought of my fear of Kirt when he'd pounded on my

door. I had worried about what he would do if he got inside, not knowing there was already one like him in my bed.

Kirt and Hellea's kind were outnumbered by the humans who dressed as them. Hellea had left him because he was insane, daring to let humans know the truth. Who else besides me had he told? But he'd been right; it was a safe time for them. Hide amongst those who look like you, and no one will hunt you down. They prospered in this time of illusion. What was another werewolf in a crowd of chimera?

I left Kirt there on the floor of the corridor, pooled darkness around him. Someone would have called the p.o.'s when the revolver fired, and I had to be far from here when they arrived. Who could I trust? Who was real when any could hide behind the chimera? What if a werewolf, a friend of Kirt's, wore a chimera that disguised him as a p.o. investigator?

I wanted to go to the morgue, where Hellea's body was waiting for cremation. They were sure to find that she was not human when they pulled off her bison chimera for the autopsy. What would they think? Would they hunt down the real werewolves? How? The p.o.'s could never ban chimera cloaks, and those like Kirt would always hide behind them. I was the only one who could identify them when they wore chimera. Hellea's and Kirt's peculiar scents could not be forgotten. And even if I did want to help the p.o.'s, which I did not, they wouldn't be able to protect me forever. Sooner or later one like Kirt would reach me. But there was no time to see Hellea as she really was, so I slipped out of my building and walked into the cool streets. Shadows moved on the far side of the pavement, shadows that slithered away too easily to be chimera-driven men playing at being wolves. The others that Kirt had talked about, no doubt. The other werewolves who wanted him and Hellea dead. Who did they wait for now? Kirt or his murderer?

I walked quickly to the tram stop, hearing my heels click on the pavement, wondering when I would hear the first howl.

But it was silent, and they never came any closer than when I'd first seen them. *Perhaps they still smell werewolf on me,* I thought, as I looked down at my hands, black in the dim light from Kirt's blood. *There's no time to be sick. No time for anything,* I thought, *but running.*

I snort and feel the air rush into my throat. Breathing out, the noise sounds loud in my ears. My hands are thick hooves, my wrists heavy forelegs that scuff at the dirt, send it billowing into the still air. The dust motes glint slightly in the three-quarter moon's light. I've swallowed a low dose of fantacin again and so slide in and out of myself. It is always like this lately. Not because I want to feel human but because I have no choice; I have little of the drug left, and I cannot go back to the village ten miles away. The last time I was there I'd overheard someone ask for me. It was not a p.o., for they have a certain look about them. This man was thin, blond-haired, and reminded me of Kirt.

My head swings slowly, and I feel grass in my mouth. Is it really there, or is it only fantacin that makes me feel it? I'm not sure.

I always think of Hellea, except when I have fantacin to make me forget. Involuntarily I shudder, feeling my bulk move in the night. I had loved her.

The prairies. I am finally here, though not for the reasons I'd once wanted. Wolves, real wolves, had tracked their meat for days, weeks sometimes. Werewolves are not so different. They are intelligent and can feel the rush of revenge as they think of one who can expose them, who knows how to identify them. They want to remain unknown, as they'd always been. They know I am the only one who can help the p.o.'s track them down. That is why they follow me across the grasslands.

Or is it only to thank me? The werewolves had wanted Kirt dead as much as I had. Perhaps they follow to simply thank me for doing what they were ready to do themselves. I hope that, but I do not believe it. I am too dangerous to them while alive. The sudden howl from the gully to the south is piercing and makes the entire herd shuffle in the dust, nervous at the sound. There are no real wolves alive. And that is not a coyote's call.

They will not make a mistake again. I have no werewolf smell on me this time, for it has been months since I'd last loved one of them. Unknowingly loved, I remember.

The howl comes again, shorter this time, closer to the edges of the herd. I vaguely hear a bull bellow—once, twice. They are creeping toward me from the gully. A scent drifts to me. Both male and female track me, I can tell. They have not even bothered to come from downwind.

I wish that it were chimera, not reality, which stalks me. But bison do not wish, do not think. Stupid animals.

If only I can make it clear that I had loved one of them. *I've killed the madman among you. I will not help the p.o.'s hunt you. Only leave me alone and alive.* She'd loved me too, I want to tell them. Hellea had tried to protect me. If one of you could love me, what harm can I do to you? But I don't think they'll listen to me. I delude myself with false hope. They settle matters with violence; what rumors we have of them have told me that.

And as I feel myself slip into the grasp of fantacin, I wonder if I will feel it when they come to worry my throat. I wish not.

The Pear-Shaped Man

by George R. R. Martin

Born in Bayonne, New Jersey, George R. R. Martin now divides his time between New Mexico and Los Angeles. He made his first fiction sale in 1971 and soon established himself as one of the most popular writers of the seventies, winning his first Hugo Award in 1975 for his novella "A Song for Lya." In 1980 he went on to take three more major awards: his novelette "Sandkings" won both the Nebula and the Hugo, and his short story "The Way of Cross and Dragon" won a Hugo as well, making Martin the first author ever to receive two Hugo Awards for fiction in the same year. Both stories were published in *Omni*. His novella "The Skin Trade" won the World Fantasy Award in 1989. Martin's books include the novels *Fevre Dream, The Dying of the Light, The Armageddon Rag,* and five short story collections. He is also editor of the Wild Card's mosaic novel series and was co-supervising producer for the popular TV series *Beauty and the Beast.*

"The Pear-Shaped Man" (*Omni,* Oct. 1987) won the first Bram Stoker Award given for achievement in the horror novelette. It is a dark urban fantasy in which a particular junk food is prominently featured. Once you read this story, you'll never again think of this item in the same way.

THE PEAR-SHAPED MAN

George R. R. Martin

The Pear-shaped Man lives beneath the stairs. His shoulders are narrow and stooped, but his buttocks are impressively large. Or perhaps it is only the clothing he wears; no one has ever admitted to seeing him nude, and no one has ever admitted to wanting to. His trousers are brown polyester double knits, with wide cuffs and a shiny seat; they are always baggy, and they have big, deep, droopy pockets so stuffed with oddments and bric-a-brac that they bulge against his sides. He wears his pants very high, hiked up above the swell of his stomach, and cinches them in place around his chest with a narrow brown leather belt. He wears them so high that his drooping socks show clearly, and often an inch or two of pasty white skin as well.

His shirts are always short-sleeved, most often white or pale blue, and his breast pocket is always full of Bic pens, the cheap throwaway kind that write with blue ink. He has lost the caps or tossed them out, because his shirts are all stained and splotched around the breast pockets. His head is a second pear set atop the first; he has a double chin and wide, full fleshy cheeks, and the top of his head seems to come almost to a point. His nose is broad and flat, with large, greasy pores; his eyes are small and pale, set close together. His hair is thin, dark, limp, flaky with dandruff; it never looks washed, and there are those who say that he cuts it himself with a bowl and a dull knife. He has a smell, too, the Pear-shaped Man; it is a sweet smell, a sour smell, a rich smell, compounded of old butter and rancid meat and vegetables rotting in the garbage bin. His voice, when he speaks, is high and thin and squeaky; it would be a funny little voice, coming from such a large, ugly man, but there is something unnerving about it, and something even more chilling about his tight, small smile. He never shows any teeth when he smiles, but his lips are broad and wet.

Of course you know him. Everyone knows a Pear-shaped Man.

Jessie met hers on her first day in the neighborhood, while she and Angela were moving into the vacant apartment on the first floor. Angela and her boyfriend, Donald the student shrink, had lugged the couch inside and accidentally knocked away the brick that had been holding open the door to the building. Meanwhile Jessie had gotten the recliner out of the U-Haul all by herself and thumped it up the steps, only to find the door locked when she backed into it, the recliner in her arms. She was hot and sore and irritable and ready to scream with frustration.

And then the Pear-shaped Man emerged from his basement apartment under the steps, climbed onto the sidewalk at the foot of the stoop, and looked up at her with those small, pale, watery eyes of his. He made no move to help her with her chair. He did not say hello or offer to let her into the building. He only blinked and smiled a tight, wet smile that showed none of his teeth and said in a voice as squeaky and grating as nails on a blackboard, "Ahhhh. *There* she is." Then he turned and walked away. When he walked he swayed slightly from side to side. Jessie let go of the recliner; it bumped down two steps and turned over. She suddenly felt cold, despite the sweltering July heat. She watched the Pear-shaped Man depart. That was her first sight of him. She went inside and told Donald and Angela about him, but they were not much impressed. "Into every girl's life a Pear-shaped Man must fall," Angela said, with the cynicism of the veteran city girl. "I bet I met him on a blind date once."

Donald, who didn't live with them but spent so many nights with Angela that sometimes it seemed as though he did, had a more immediate concern. "Where do you want this recliner?" he wanted to know.

Later they had a few beers, and Rick and Molly and the Heathersons came over to help them warm the apartment, and Rick offered to pose for her (wink wink, nudge nudge) when Molly wasn't there to hear, and Donald drank too much and went to sleep on the sofa, and the Heathersons had a fight that ended with Geoff storming out and Lureen crying; it was a night like any other night, in other words, and Jessie forgot all about the Pear-shaped Man.

But not for long.

The next morning Angela roused Donald, and the two of them went off, Angie to the big downtown firm where she was a legal secretary, Don to study shrinking. Jessie was a freelance commercial illustrator. She did her work at home, which as far as Angela and Donald and her mother and the rest of Western civilization were concerned meant that she didn't work at all. "Would you mind doing the shopping?" Angie asked her just before the move, so as not to have a lot of food to lug across town. "Seeing as how you'll be home all day? I mean, we really need some food."

So Jessie was pushing a full cart of groceries down a crowded aisle in Santino's Market, on the corner, when she saw the Pear-shaped Man the second time. He was at the register, counting out change into Santino's hand. Jessie felt like making a U-turn and busying herself until he'd gone. But that would be silly. She'd gotten everything she needed, and she was a grown woman, after all, and he was standing at the only open register.

Resolute, she got in line behind him. Santino dumped the Pear-shaped Man's coins into the old register and bagged up his purchase: a big plastic bottle of Coke and a one-pound bag of Cheez Doodles. As he took the bag, the Pear-shaped Man put the brown paper sack inside a shapeless leather bag of the sort that schoolboys use to carry their books, gathered it up, and waddled out of the store. Santino, a big grizzled man with thinning salt-and-pepper hair, began to ring up Jessie's groceries. "He's something, ain't he?" he asked her.

"Who is he?" she asked.

Santino shrugged. "Hell, I dunno. Everybody just calls him the Pear-shaped Man. He's been around here forever. Comes in every morning, buys a bottle of Coke and a big bag of Cheez Doodles. Once we run out of Cheez Doodles, so I tell him he oughta try them Cheetos or maybe even potato chips, y'know, for a change? He wasn't having none of it, though."

Jessie was bemused. "He must buy something besides Coke and Cheez Doodles."

"Wanna bet, lady?"

"Then he must shop somewhere else."

"Besides me, the nearest supermarket is nine blocks away. Charlie down at the candy store tells me the Pear-shaped Man comes in every afternoon at four-thirty and has himself a chocolate ice-cream soda, but far as we can tell, that's all he eats." He rang for a total. "That's seventy-nine eighty-two, lady. You new around here?"

"I live just above the Pear-shaped Man," Jessie confessed.

"Congratulations," Santino said.

Later that morning, after she lined the shelves and put away the groceries, set up her studio in the spare bedroom, made a few desultory dabs on the cover she was supposed to be painting for Pirouette Publishing, ate lunch and washed the dishes, hooked up the stereo and listened to some Carly Simon, and rearranged half of the living room furniture, Jessie finally admitted a certain restlessness and decided this would be a good time to go around the building and introduce herself to her new neighbors. Not many people bothered with that in the city, she knew, but she was still a small-town kid at heart, and it made her feel safer to know the people around her. She decided to start with the Pear-shaped Man down in the basement and got as far as descending the stairs to his door. Then a funny feeling came over her. There was no name on the doorbell, she noticed. Suddenly she regretted her impulse. She retreated back upstairs to meet the rest of the building.

The other tenants all knew him; most of them had spoken to him at least once or twice, trying to be friendly. Old Sadie Winbright, who had lived across the hall in the other first-floor apartment for twelve years, said he was very quiet. Billy Peabody, who shared the big second-floor apartment with his crippled mother, thought the Pear-shaped Man was creepy, especially that little smile of his. Pete Pumetti worked the late shift and told her how those basement lights were always on, no matter what hour of the night Pete came swaggering home, even though it was hard to tell on account of the way the Pear-shaped Man had boarded up his windows. Jess and Ginny Harris didn't like their twins playing around the stairs that led down to his apartment and had forbidden them to talk to him. Jeffries the barber, whose small two-chair shop was down the block from Santino's, knew him and had no great desire for his patronage. All of them, every one, called him the Pear-shaped Man. That was who he was. "But who is he?" Jessie asked. None of them knew. "What does he do for a living?" she asked.

"I think he's on welfare," Old Sadie Winbright said. "The poor dear, he must be feebleminded."

"Damned if I know." said Pete Pumetti. "He sure as hell don't work. I bet he's a queer."

"I think he might be a drug pusher," said Jeffries the

barber, whose familiarity with drugs was limited to witch hazel.

"I betcha he writes them pornographic books," Billy Peabody surmised.

"He doesn't do anything for a living," said Ginny Harris. "Jess and I have talked about it. He's a shopping-bag man; he has to be."

That night, over dinner, Jessie told Angela about the Pear-shaped Man and the other tenants and their comments. "He's probably an attorney," Angie said. "Why do you care so much, anyway?"

Jessie couldn't answer that. "I don't know. He gives me goose bumps. I don't like the idea of some maniac living right underneath us."

Angela shrugged. "That's the way it goes in the big, glamorous city. Did the guy from the phone company come?"

"Maybe next week," said Jessie. "That's the way it goes in the big, glamorous city."

Jessie soon learned that there was no avoiding the Pear-shaped Man. When she visited the laundromat around the block, there he was, washing a big load of striped boxer shorts and ink-stained short-sleeved shirts, snacking on Coke and Cheez Doodles from the vending machines. She tried to ignore him, but whenever she turned around, there he was, smiling wetly, his eyes fixed on her or perhaps on the underthings she was loading into the dryer.

When she went down to the corner candy store one afternoon to buy a paper, there he was, slurping his ice-cream soda, his buttocks overflowing the stool on which he was perched. "It's homemade," he squeaked at her. She frowned, paid for her newspaper, and left.

One evening when Angela was seeing Donald, Jessie picked up an old paperback and went out on the stoop to read and maybe socialize and enjoy the cool breeze that was blowing up the street. She got lost in the story, until she caught a whiff of something unpleasant, and when she looked up from the page, there he was, standing not three feet away, staring at her. "What do you want?" she snapped, closing the book.

"Would you like to come down and see my house?" the Pear-shaped Man asked in that high, whiny voice.

"No," she said, retreating to her own apartment. But when she looked out a half hour later, he was still standing in the same exact spot, clutching his brown bag and staring at her windows while dusk fell around him. He made her feel very uneasy. She wished that Angela would come home, but she knew that wouldn't happen for hours. In fact, Angie might very well decide to spend the night at Don's place.

Jessie shut the windows despite the heat, checked the locks on her door, and then went back to her studio to work. Painting would take her mind off the Pear-shaped Man. Besides, the cover was due at Pirouette by the end of the week.

She spent the rest of the evening finishing off the background and doing some of the fine detail on the heroine's gown. The hero didn't look quite right to her when she was done, so she worked on him, too. He was the usual dark-haired, virile, strong-jawed type, but Jessie decided to individualize him a bit, an effort that kept her pleasantly occupied until she heard Angie's key in the lock.

She put away her paints and washed up and decided to have some tea before calling it a night. Angela was standing in the living room, with her hands behind her back, looking more than a little tipsy, giggling. "What's so funny?" Jessie asked.

Angela giggled again. "You've been holding out on me," she said. "You got yourself a new beau and you didn't tell."

"What are you talking about?"

"He was standing on the stoop when I got home," Angie said, grinning. She came across the room. "He said to give you these." Her hand emerged from behind her back. It was full of fat, orange worms, little flaking twists of corn and cheese that curled between her fingers and left powdery stains on the palm of her hand. "For you," Angie repeated, laughing. "For you."

That night Jessie had a long, terrible dream, but when the daylight came she could remember only a small part of it. She was standing at the door to the Pear-shaped Man's apartment under the stairs; she was standing there in darkness, waiting, waiting for something to happen, something awful, the worst thing she could imagine. Slowly, oh so slowly, the door began to open. Light fell upon her face, and Jessie woke, trembling.

He might be dangerous, Jessie decided the next morning over Rice Krispies and tea. Maybe he had a criminal record. Maybe he was some kind of mental patient. She ought to check up on him. But she needed to know his name first. She couldn't just call up the police and say, "Do you have anything on the Pear-shaped Man?" After Angela had gone to work, Jessie pulled a chair over by the front window and sat down to wait and watch. The mail usually arrived about eleven. She saw the postman ascend the stairs, heard him putting the mail in the big hall mailbox. But the Pear-shaped Man got his mail separately, she knew. He had his own box, right under his doorbell, and if she remembered right it wasn't the kind that locked, either. As soon as the postman had departed, she was on her feet, moving quickly down the stairs. There was no sign of the Pear-shaped Man. The door to his apartment was under the stoop, and farther back she could see overflowing garbage cans, smell their rich, sickly sweet odor. The upper half of the door was a window, boarded up. It was dark under the stoop. Jessie barked her knuckles on the brick as she fumbled for his mailbox. Her hand brushed the loose metal lid. She got it open, pulled out two thin envelopes. She had to squint and move toward the sunlight to read the name. They were both addressed to Occupant.

She was stuffing them back into the box when the door opened. The Pear-shaped Man was framed by bright light from within his apartment. He smiled at her, so close she could count the pores on his nose, see the sheen of the saliva on his lower lip. He said nothing.

"I," she said, startled, "I, I . . . I got some of your mail by mistake. Must be a new man on the route. I, I was just bringing it back."

The Pear-shaped Man reached up and into his mailbox. For a second his hand brushed Jessie's. His skin was soft and damp and seemed much colder than it ought to be, and the touch gave her goose bumps all up and down her arm. He took the two letters from her and looked at them briefly and then stuffed them into his pants pocket. "It's just garbage," squeaked the Pear-shaped Man. "They shouldn't be allowed to send you garbage. They ought to be stopped. Would you like to see my things? I have things inside to look at."

"I," said Jessie, "uh, no. No, I can't. Excuse me." She turned quickly, moved out from under the stairs, back into the sunlight, and hurried back inside the building. All the way, she could feel his eyes on her.

She spent the rest of that day working, and the next as well, never glancing outside, for fear that he would be standing there. By Thursday the painting was finished. She decided to take it in to Pirouette herself and have dinner downtown, maybe do a little shopping. A day away from the apartment and the Pear-shaped Man would do her good, soothe her nerves. She was being overimaginative. He hadn't actually done anything, after all. It was just that he was so damned *creepy.*

Adrian, the art director at Pirouette, was glad to see her, as always. "That's my Jessie," he said after he'd given her a hug. "I wish all my artists were like you. Never miss a deadline, never turn in anything but the best work, a real pro. Come on back to my office, we'll look at this one and talk about some new assignments and gossip a bit." He told his secretary to hold his calls and escorted her back through the maze of tiny little cubicles where the editors lived. Adrian himself had a huge corner office with two big windows, a sign of his status in Pirouette Publishing.

He gestured Jessie to a chair, poured her a cup of herb tea, then took her portfolio and removed the cover painting and held it up at arm's length.

The silence went on far too long. Adrian dragged out a chair, propped up the painting, and retreated several feet to consider it from a distance. He stroked his beard and cocked his head this way and that. Watching him, Jessie felt a thin prickle of alarm. Normally, Adrian was given to exuberant outbursts of approval. She didn't like this quiet. "What's wrong?" she said, setting down her teacup. "Don't you like it?"

"Oh," Adrian said. He put out a hand, palm open and level, waggled it this way and that. "It's well executed, no doubt. Your technique is very professional. Fine detail."

"I researched all the clothing. It's all authentic for the period; you know it is."

"Yes, no doubt. And the heroine is gorgeous, as always. I wouldn't mind ripping her bodice myself. You do amazing things with mammaries, Jessie."

She stood up. "Then what is it? I've been doing covers for you for three years, Adrian. There's never been any problem."

"Well," he said. He shook his head, smiled. "Nothing, really. Maybe you've been doing too many of these. I know how it can go. They're so much alike, it gets boring, painting all those hot embraces one after another; so pretty soon you feel an urge to experiment, to try something a little bit different." He shook a finger at her. "It won't do, though. Our readers just want the same old shit with the same old covers. I understand, but it won't do."

"There's nothing experimental about this painting," Jessie said, exasperated. "It's the same thing I've done for you a hundred times before. *What* won't do?"

Adrian looked honestly surprised. "Why, the man, of course," he said. "I thought you'd done it deliberately." He gestured. "I mean, look at him. He's almost *unattractive*."

"What?" Jessie moved over to the painting. "He's the same virile jerk I've painted over and over again."

Adrian frowned. "Really now," he said. "Look." He started pointing things out. "There, around his collar, is that or is that not just the faintest hint of a double chin? And look at that lower lip! Beautifully executed, yes, but it looks, well, gross. Like it was wet or something. Pirouette heroes rape, they plunder, they seduce, they threaten, but they do not drool, darling. And perhaps it's just a trick of perspective, but I could swear"—he paused, leaned close, shook his head—"no, it's not perspective, the top of his head is definitely narrower than the bottom. A pinhead! We can't have pinheads on Pirouette books, Jessie. Too much fullness in the cheeks, too. He looks as though he might be storing nuts for the winter." Adrian shook his head. "It won't do, love. Look, no big problem. The rest of the painting is fine. Just take it home and fix him up. How about it?"

Jessie was staring at her painting in horror, as if she were seeing it for the first time. Everything Adrian had said, everything he had pointed out, was true. It was all very subtle, to be sure; at first glance the man looked almost like your normal Pirouette hero, but there was something just the tiniest bit off about him, and when you looked closer, it was blatant and unmistakable. Somehow the Pear-shaped Man had crept into her painting. "I," she began, "I, yes, you're right, I'll do it over. I don't know what happened. There's this man who lives in my building, a creepy-looking guy, everybody calls him the Pear-shaped Man. He's been getting on my nerves. I swear, it wasn't intentional. I guess I've been thinking about him so much it just crept into my work subconsciously."

"I understand," Adrian said. "Well, no problem, just set it right. We do have deadline problems, though."

"I'll fix it this weekend, have it back to you by Monday," Jessie promised.

"Wonderful," said Adrian. "Let's talk about those other assignments, then." He poured her more Red Zinger, and they sat down to talk. By the time Jessie left his office, she was feeling much better.

Afterward she enjoyed a drink in her favorite bar, met a few friends, and had a nice dinner at an excellent new Japanese restaurant. It was dark by the time she got home. There was no sign of the Pear-shaped Man. She kept her portfolio under her arm as she fished for her keys and unlocked the door to the building.

When she stepped inside, Jessie heard a faint noise and felt something crunch underfoot. A nest of orange worms clustered against the faded blue of the hallway carpet, crushed and broken by her foot.

She dreamed of him again. It was the same shapeless, terrible dream. She was down in the dark beneath the stoop, near the trash bins crawling with all kinds of things, waiting at his door. She was frightened, too frightened to knock or open the door, yet helpless to leave. Finally the door crept open of its own accord. There he stood, smiling, smiling. "Would you like to stay?" he said, and the last words echoed, *to stay to stay to stay to stay,* and he reached out for her, and his fingers were as soft and pulpy as earthworms when he touched her on the cheek.

The next morning Jessie arrived at the offices of Citywide Realty just as they opened their doors. The receptionist told her that Edward Selby was out showing some condos; she couldn't say when he'd be in. "That's all right," Jessie said. "I'll wait."

She settled down to leaf through some magazines, studying pictures of houses she couldn't afford.

Selby arrived just before eleven. He looked momentarily surprised to see her, before his professional smile switched on automatically. "Jessie," he said, "how nice. Something I can do for you?"

"Let's talk," she said, tossing down the magazines.

They went to Selby's desk. He was still only an associate with the rental firm, so he shared the office with another agent, but she was out, and they had the room to themselves. Selby settled himself into his chair and leaned back. He was a pleasant-looking man, with curly brown hair and white teeth, his eyes careful behind silver aviator frames. "Is there a problem?"

Jessie leaned forward. "The Pear-shaped Man," she said.

Selby arched one eyebrow. "I see. A harmless eccentric."

"Are you sure of that?"

He shrugged. "He hasn't murdered anybody yet, at least that I know of."

"How much do you know about him? For starters, what's his name?"

"Good question," Selby said, smiling. "Here at Citywide Realty we just think of him as the Pear-shaped Man. I don't think I've ever gotten a name out of him."

"What the hell do you mean?" Jessie demanded. "Are you telling me his checks have THE PEAR-SHAPED MAN printed on them?"

Selby cleared his throat. "Well, no. Actually, he doesn't use checks. I come by on the first of every month to collect and knock on his door, and he pays me in cash. One-dollar bills, in fact. I stand there, and he counts out the money into my hand, dollar by dollar. I'll confess, Jessie, that I've never been inside the apartment, and I don't especially care to. Kind of a funny smell, you know? But he's a good tenant, as far as we're concerned. Always has his rent paid on time. Never bitches about rent hikes. And he certainly doesn't bounce checks on us." He showed a lot of teeth, a broad smile to let her know he was joking.

Jessie was not amused. "He must have given a name when he first rented the apartment."

"I wouldn't know about that," Selby said. "I've only handled that building for six years. He's been down in the basement a lot longer than that."

"Why don't you check his lease?"

Selby frowned. "Well, I could dig it up, I suppose. But really, is his name any of your business? What's the problem here, anyway? Exactly what has the Pear-shaped Man *done?*"

Jessie sat back and crossed her arms. "He looks at me."

"Well," Selby said, carefully, "I, uh, well, you're an attractive woman, Jessie. I seem to recall asking you out myself."

"That's different," she said. "You're normal. It's the *way* he looks at me."

"Undressing you with his eyes?" Selby suggested.

Jessie was nonplused. "No," she said. "That isn't it. It's not sexual, not in the normal way, anyhow. I don't know how to explain it. He keeps asking me down to his apartment. He's always hanging around."

"Well, that's where he lives."

"He bothers me. He's crept into my paintings."

This time both of Selby's eyebrows went up. "Into your paintings?" he said. There was a funny hitch in his voice.

Jessie was getting more and more discomfited; this wasn't coming out right at all. "Okay, it doesn't sound like much, but he's *creepy*. His lips are always wet. The way he smiles. His eyes. His squeaky little voice. And that smell. Jesus Christ, you collect his rent, you ought to know."

The realtor spread his hands helplessly. "Its not against the law to have body odor. It's not even a violation of his lease."

"Last night he snuck into the building and left a pile of Cheez Doodles right where I'd step in them."

"Cheez Doodles?" Selby said. His voice took on a sarcastic edge. "God, not *Cheez Doodles!* How fucking heinous! Have you informed the police?"

"It's not funny. What was he doing inside the building anyway?"

"He lives there."

"He lives in the basement. He has his own door, he doesn't need to come into our hallway. Nobody but the six regular tenants ought to have keys to that door."

"Nobody does, as far as I know," Selby said. He pulled out a notepad. "Well, that's something, anyway. I'll tell you what, I'll have the lock changed on the outer door. The Pear-shaped Man won't get a key. Will that make you happy?"

"A little," said Jessie, slightly mollified.

"I can't promise that he won't get in," Selby cautioned. "You know how it is. If I had a nickel for every time some tenant has taped over a lock or propped open a door with a doorstop because it was more convenient, well . . . ."

"Don't worry, I'll see that nothing like that happens. What about his name? Will you check the lease for me?"

Selby sighed. "This is really an invasion of privacy. But I'll do it. A personal favor. You owe me one." He got up and went across the room to a black metal filing cabinet, pulled open a drawer, rummaged around, and came out with a legal-sized folder. He was flipping through it as he returned to his desk.

"Well?" Jessie asked, impatiently.

"Hmmmm," Selby said. "Here's your lease. And here's the others." He went back to the beginning and checked the papers one by one. "Winbright, Peabody, Pumetti, Harris, Jeffries." He closed the file, looked up at her, and shrugged. "No lease. Well, it's a crummy little apartment, and he's been there forever. Either we've misfiled his lease or he never had one. It's not unknown. A month-to-month basis. . . ."

"Oh, great," Jessie said. "Are you going to do anything about it?"

"I'll change that lock," Selby said. "Beyond that, I don't know what you expect of me. I'm not going to evict the man for offering you Cheez Doodles."

The Pear-shaped Man was standing on the stoop when Jessie got home, his battered bag tucked up under one arm. He smiled when he saw her approach. *Let him touch me,* she thought; *just let him touch me when I walk by, and I'll have him booked for assault so fast it'll make his little pointy head swim.* But the Pear-shaped Man made no effort to grab her. "I have things to show you downstairs," he said as Jessie ascended the stairs. She had to pass within a foot of him; the smell was overwhelming today, a rich odor like yeast and decaying vegetables. "Would you like to look at my things?" he called after her. Jessie unlocked the door and slammed it behind her.

I'm not going to think about him, she told herself inside, over a cup of tea. She had work to do. She'd promised Adrian the cover by Monday, after all. She went into her studio, drew back the curtains, and set to work, determined to eradicate every hint of the Pear-shaped Man from the cover. She painted away the double chin, firmed up the jaw, redid those tight wet lips, darkened the hair, made it blacker and bushier and more wind tossed so the head didn't seem to come to such a point. She gave him sharp, high, pronounced cheekbones—cheekbones like the blade of a knife—made the face almost gaunt. She even changed the color of his eyes. Why had she given him those weak, pale eyes? She made the eyes green, a crisp, clean, commanding green, full of vitality.

It was almost midnight by the time she was done, and Jessie was exhausted, but when she stepped back to survey her handiwork, she was delighted. The man was a real Pirouette hero now: a rakehell, a rogue, a hell-raiser whose robust exterior concealed a brooding, melancholy, poetic soul. There was nothing the least bit pear-shaped about him. Adrian would have puppies. It was a good kind of tiredness. Jessie went to sleep feeling altogether satisfied. Maybe Selby was right; she was too imaginative, she'd really let the Pear-shaped Man get to her. But work, good hard old-fashioned work, was the perfect antidote for these shapeless fears of hers. Tonight, she was sure, her sleep would be deep and dreamless.

She was wrong. There was no safety in her sleep. She stood trembling on his doorstep once again. It was so dark down there, so filthy. The rich, ripe smell of the garbage cans was overwhelming, and she thought she could hear things moving in the shadows. The door began to open. The Pear-shaped Man smiled and touched her with cold, soft fingers like a nest of grubs. He took hold of her by the arm and drew her inside, inside, inside . . . .

Angela knocked on her door the next morning at ten. "Sunday brunch," she called out. "Don is making waffles. With chocolate chips and fresh strawberries. And bacon. And coffee. And O.J. Want some?"

Jessie sat up in bed. "Don? Is he here?"

"He stayed over," Angela said.

Jessie climbed out of bed and pulled on a paint-splattered pair of jeans. "You know I'd never turn down one of Don's brunches. I didn't even hear you guys come in."

"I snuck my head into your studio, but you were painting away, and you didn't even notice. You had that intent look you get sometimes, you know, with the tip of your tongue peeking out of one corner of your mouth. I figured it was better not to disturb the artist at work." She giggled. "How you avoided hearing the bedsprings, though, I'll never know."

Breakfast was a triumph. There were times when Jessie couldn't understand just what Angela saw in Donald the student shrink, but mealtimes were not among them. He was a splendid cook. Angela and Donald were still lingering over coffee, and Jessie over tea, at eleven, when they heard noises from the hall. Angela went to check. "Some guy's out there changing the lock," she said when she returned. "I wonder what that's all about."

"I'll be damned," Jessie said. "And on the weekend, too. That's time and a half. I never expected Selby to move so fast."

Angela looked at her curiously. "What do you know about this?"

So Jessie told them all about her meeting with the realtor and her encounters with the Pear-shaped Man. Angela giggled once or twice, and Donald slipped into his wise shrink face. "Tell me, Jessie," he said when she had finished, "don't you think you're overreacting a bit here?"

"No," Jessie said curtly.

"You're stonewalling," Donald said. "Really now, try and look at your actions objectively. What has this man done to you?"

"Nothing, and I intend to keep it that way," Jessie snapped. "I didn't ask you for your opinion."

"You don't have to ask," Donald said. "We're friends, aren't we? I hate to see you getting upset over nothing. It sounds to me as though you're developing some kind of phobia about a harmless neighborhood character."

Angela giggled. "He's just got a crush on you, that's all. You're such a heartbreaker."

Jessie was getting annoyed. "You wouldn't think it was funny if he was leaving Cheez Doodles for you," she said angrily. "There's something . . . well, something *wrong* there. I can feel it."

Donald spread his hands. "Something wrong? Most defi-

95

nitely. The man is obviously very poorly socialized. He's unattractive, sloppy, he doesn't conform to normal standards of dress or personal hygiene, he has unusual eating habits and a great deal of difficulty relating to others. He's probably a very lonely person and no doubt deeply neurotic as well. But none of this makes him a killer or a rapist, does it? Why are you becoming so obsessed with him?"

"I am not becoming obsessed with him."

"Obviously you are," Donald said.

"She's in love," Angela teased.

Jessie stood up. "I am *not* becoming obsessed with him," she shouted, "and this discussion has just ended!"

That night, in her dream, Jessie saw inside for the first time. He drew her in, and she found she was too weak to resist. The lights were very bright inside, and it was warm and oh so humid, and the air seemed to move as if she had entered the mouth of some great beast, and the walls were orange and flaky and had a strange, sweet smell, and there were empty plastic Coke bottles everywhere and bowls of half-eaten Cheez Doodles, too, and the Pear-shaped Man said, "You can see my things, you can have my things," and he began to undress, unbuttoning his short-sleeved shirt, pulling it off, revealing dead, white, hairless flesh and two floppy breasts, and the right breast was stained with blue ink from his leaking pens, and he was smiling, smiling, and he undid his thin belt, and then pulled down the fly on his brown polyester pants, and Jessie woke screaming.

On Monday morning, Jessie packed up her cover painting, phoned a messenger service, and had them take it down to Pirouette for her. She wasn't up to another trip downtown. Adrian would want to chat, and Jessie wasn't in a very sociable mood. Angela kept needling her about the Pear-shaped Man, and it had left her in a foul temper. Nobody seemed to understand. There was something wrong with the Pear-shaped Man, something serious, something horrible. He was no joke. He was frightening. Somehow she had to prove it. She had to learn his name, had to find out what he was hiding.

She could hire a detective, except detectives were expensive. There had to be something she could do on her own. She could try his mailbox again. She'd be better off if she waited until the day the gas and electric bills came, though. He had lights in his apartment, so the electric company would know his name. The only problem was that the electric bill wasn't due for another couple of weeks.

The living room windows were wide open, Jessie noticed suddenly. Even the drapes had been drawn all the way back. Angela must have done it that morning before taking off for work. Jessie hesitated and then went to the window. She closed it, locked it, moved to the next, closed it, locked it. It made her feel safer. She told herself she wouldn't look out. It would be better if she didn't look out.

How could she not look out? She looked out. He was there, standing on the sidewalk below her, looking up. "You could see my things," he said in his high, thin voice. "I knew when I saw you that you'd want my things. You'd like them. We could have food." He reached into a bulgy pocket, brought out a single Cheez Doodle, held it up to her. His mouth moved silently.

"Get away from here, or I'll call the police!" Jessie shouted.

"I have something for you. Come to my house and you can have it. It's in my pocket. I'll give it to you."

"No you won't. Get away, I warn you. Leave me alone." She stepped back, closed the drapes. It was gloomy in here with the drapes pulled, but that was better than knowing that the Pear-shaped Man was looking in. Jessie turned on a light, picked up a paperback, and tried to read. She found herself turning pages rapidly and realized she didn't have the vaguest idea of what the words meant. She slammed down the book, marched into the kitchen, made a tuna salad sandwich on whole wheat toast. She wanted something with it, but she wasn't sure what. She took out a dill pickle and sliced it into quarters, arranged it neatly on her plate, searched through her cupboard for some potato chips. Then she poured a big fresh glass of milk and sat down to lunch.

She took one bite of the sandwich, made a face, and shoved it away. It tasted funny. Like the mayonnaise had gone bad or something. The pickle was too sour, and the chips seemed soggy and limp and much too salty. She didn't want chips anyway. She wanted something else. Some of those little orange cheese curls. She could picture them in her head, almost taste them. Her mouth watered.

Then she realized what she was thinking and almost gagged. She got up and scraped her lunch into the garbage. She had to get out of here, she thought wildly. She'd go see a movie or something, forget all about the Pear-shaped Man for a few hours. Maybe she could go to a singles' bar somewhere, pick someone up, get laid. At his place. Away from here. Away from the Pear-shaped Man. That was the ticket. A night away from the apartment would do her good. She went to the window, pulled aside the drapes, peered out.

The Pear-shaped Man smiled, shifted from side to side. He had his misshapen briefcase under his arm. His pockets bulged. Jessie felt her skin crawl. He was *revolting,* she thought. But she wasn't going to let him keep her prisoner.

She gathered her things together, slipped a little steak knife into her purse just in case, and marched outside. "Would you like to see what I have in my case?" the Pear-shaped Man asked her when she emerged. Jessie had decided to ignore him. If she did not reply at all, just pretended he wasn't there, maybe he'd grow bored and leave her alone. She descended the steps briskly and set off down the street. The Pear-shaped Man followed close behind her. "They're all around us," he whispered. She could smell him hurrying a step or two behind her, puffing as he walked. "They are. They laugh at me. They don't understand, but they want my things. I can show you proof. I have it down in my house. I know you want to come see."

Jessie continued to ignore him. He followed her all the way to the bus stop.

The movie was a dud. Having skipped lunch, Jessie was hungry. She got a Coke and a tub of buttered popcorn from the candy counter. The Coke was three-quarters crushed ice, but it still tasted good. She couldn't eat the popcorn. The fake butter they used had a vaguely rancid smell that reminded her of the Pear-shaped Man. She tried two kernels and felt sick.

Afterward, though, she did a little better. His name was Jack, he said. He was a sound man on a local TV news show, and he had an interesting face: an easy smile, Clark Gable ears, nice gray eyes with friendly little crinkles in the corners. He bought her a drink and touched her hand; but the way he did it was a little clumsy, like he was a bit shy about this whole scene, and Jessie liked that. They had a few drinks together, and then he suggested dinner back at his place. Nothing fancy, he said. He had some cold cuts in the fridge; he could whip up some jumbo sandwiches and show her his stereo system, which was some kind of special super setup he'd rigged himself. That all sounded fine to her.

His apartment was on the twenty-third floor of a midtown high rise, and from his windows you could see sailboats tacking off on the horizon. Jack put the new Linda Ronstadt album on the stereo while he went to make the sandwiches. Jessie watched the sailboats. She was finally beginning to relax. "I have beer or iced tea," Jack called from the kitchen. "What'll it be?"

"Coke," she said absently.

"No Coke," he called back. "Beer or iced tea."

"Oh," she said, somehow annoyed. "Iced tea, then."

"You got it. Rye or wheat?"

"I don't care," she said. The boats were very graceful. She'd like to paint them someday. She could paint Jack, too. He looked like he had a nice body.

"Here we go," he said, emerging from the kitchen carrying a tray. "I hope you're hungry."

"Famished," Jessie said, turning away from the window. She went over to where he was setting the table and froze.

"What's wrong?" Jack said. He was holding out a white stoneware plate. On top of it was a truly gargantuan ham-and-Swiss sandwich on fresh deli rye, lavishly slathered with mustard, and next to it, filling up the rest of the plate, was a pile of puffy orange cheese curls. They seemed to writhe and move, to edge toward the sandwich, toward her. "Jessie?" Jack said.

She gave a choked, inarticulate cry and pushed the plate away wildly.

Jack lost his grip; ham, Swiss cheese, bread, and Cheez Doodles scattered in all directions. A Cheez Doodle brushed against Jessie's leg. She whirled and ran from the apartment.

Jessie spent the night alone at a hotel and slept poorly. Even here, miles from the apartment, she could not escape the dream. It was the same as before, the same, but each night it seemed to grow longer, each night it went a little further. She was on the stoop, waiting, afraid. The door opened, and he drew her inside, the orange warm, the air like fetid breath, the Pear-shaped Man smiling, "You can see my things," he said, "you can have my things," and then he was undressing, his shirt first, his skin so white, dead flesh, heavy breasts with a blue ink stain, his belt, his pants falling, polyester puddling around his ankles, all the trash in his pockets scattering on the floor, and he really was pear-shaped, it wasn't just the way he dressed, and then the boxer shorts last of all, and Jessie looked down despite herself and there was no hair and it was small and wormy and kind of yellow, like a cheese curl, and it moved slightly and the Pear-shaped Man was saying, "I want your things now, give them to me, let me see your things," and why couldn't she run, her feet wouldn't move, but her hands did, her hands, and she began to undress.

The hotel detective woke her, pounding on her door, demanding to know what the problem was and why she was screaming.

She timed her return home so that the Pear-shaped Man would be away on his morning run to Santino's Market when she arrived. The house was empty. Angela had already gone to work, leaving the living room windows open again. Jessie closed them, locked them, and pulled the drapes. With luck, the Pear-shaped Man would never know that she'd come home.

Already the day outside was swelteringly hot. It was going to be a real scorcher. Jessie felt sweaty and soiled. She stripped, dumped her clothing into the wicker hamper in her bedroom, and immersed herself in a long, cold shower. The icy water hurt, but it was a good clean kind of hurting, and it left her feeling invigorated. She dried her hair and wrapped herself in a huge, fluffy blue towel, then padded back to her bedroom, leaving wet footprints on the bare wood floors.

A halter top and a pair of cutoffs would be all she'd need in this heat, Jessie decided. She had a plan for the day firmly in mind. She'd get dressed, do a little work in her studio, and after that she could read or watch some soap or something. She wouldn't go outside; she wouldn't even look out the window. If the Pear-shaped Man was at his vigil, it would be a long, hot, boring afternoon for him.

Jessie laid out her cutoffs and a white halter top on the bed, draped the wet towel over a bedpost, and went to her dresser for a fresh pair of panties. She ought to do a laundry soon, she thought absently as she snatched up a pair of pink bikini briefs.

A Cheez Doodle fell out.

Jessie recoiled, shuddering. It had been *inside,* she thought wildly, it had been inside the briefs. The powdery cheese had left a yellow stain on the fabric. The Cheez Doodle lay where it had fallen, in the open drawer on top of her underwear. Something like terror took hold of her. She balled the bikini briefs up in her fist and tossed them away with revulsion. She grabbed another pair of panties, shook them, and another Cheez Doodle leapt out. And then another. Another. She began to make a thin, hysterical sound, but she kept on. Five pairs, six, nine, that was all, but that was enough. Someone had opened her drawer and taken out every pair of panties and carefully wrapped a Cheez Doodle in each and put them all back.

It was a ghastly joke, she thought. Angela, it had to be Angela who'd done it, maybe she and Donald together. They thought this whole thing about the Pear-shaped Man was a big laugh, so they decided to see if they could really freak her out. Except it hadn't been Angela. She knew it hadn't been Angela.

Jessie began to sob uncontrollably. She threw her balled-up panties to the floor and ran from the room, crushing Cheez Doodles into the carpet. Out in the living room, she didn't know where to turn. She couldn't go back to her bedroom, *couldn't,* not just now, not until Angela got back, and she didn't want to go to the windows, even with the drapes closed. He was out there; Jessie could feel it, could feel him staring up at the windows. She grew suddenly aware of her nakedness and covered herself with her hands. She backed away from the windows, step by uncertain step, and retreated to her studio.

Inside she found a big square package leaning up against the door, with a note from Angela taped to it. "Jess, this came for you last evening," signed with Angie's big winged A. Jessie stared at the package, uncomprehending. It was from Pirouette. It was her painting, the cover she'd rushed to redo for them.

Adrian had sent it back. Why?

She didn't want to know. She had to know.

Jessie ripped at the brown paper wrappings, tore them away in long, ragged strips, baring the cover she'd painted. Adrian had written on the mat; she recognized his hand. "Not funny, kid," he'd scrawled. "Forget it."

"No," Jessie whimpered, backing off.

There it was, her painting, the familiar background, the trite embrace, the period costumes researched so carefully, but no, she hadn't done that, someone had changed it, it wasn't her work, the woman was her, her, her, slender and strong with sandy blond hair and green eyes full of rapture, and he was crushing her to him, to *him*, the wet lips and white skin, and he had a blue ink stain on his ruffled lace shirtfront and dandruff on his velvet jacket and his head was pointed and his hair was greasy and the fingers wrapped in her locks were stained yellow, and he was smiling thinly and pulling her to him and her mouth was open and her eyes half closed and it was him and it was her, and there was her own signature, there down at the bottom.

"No," she said again. She backed away, tripped over an easel, and fell. She curled up into a little ball on the floor and lay there sobbing, and that was how Angela found her, hours later.

Angela laid her out on the couch and made a cold compress and pressed it to her forehead. Donald stood in the doorway between the living room and the studio, frowning, glancing first at Jessie and then in at the painting and then at Jessie again. Angela said soothing things and held Jessie's hand and got her a cup of tea; little by little her hysteria began to ebb. Donald crossed his arms and scowled. Finally, when Jessie had dried the last of her tears, he said, "This obsession of yours has gone too far."

"Don't," Angela said. "She's terrified."

"I can see that," Donald said. "That's why something has to be done. She's doing it to herself, honey."

Jessie had a hot cup of Morning Thunder halfway to her mouth. She stopped dead still. "I'm doing it to myself?" she repeated incredulously.

"Certainly," Donald said.

The complacency in his tone made Jessie suddenly, blazingly angry. "You stupid ignorant callous son of a bitch," she roared. "I'm doing it to myself, *I'm* doing it, *I'm* doing it, how *dare* you say that *I'm* doing it." She flung the teacup across the room, aiming for his fat head. Donald ducked; the cup shattered and the tea sent three long brown fingers running down the off-white wall. "Go on, let out your anger," he said. "I know you're upset. When you calm down, we can discuss this rationally, maybe get to the root of your problem."

Angela took her arm, but Jessie shook off the grip and stood, her hands balled into fists. "Go into my bedroom, you jerk, go in there right now and look around and come back and tell me what you see."

"If you'd like," Donald said. He walked over to the bedroom door, vanished, reemerged several moments later. "All right," he said patiently.

"Well?" Jessie demanded.

Donald shrugged. "It's a mess," he said. "Underpants all over the floor, lots of crushed cheese curls. Tell me what you think it means."

"He broke in here!" Jessie said.

"The Pear-shaped Man?" Donald queried pleasantly.

"*Of course* it was the Pear-shaped Man," Jessie screamed. "He snuck in here while we were all gone and he went into my bedroom and pawed through all my things and put Cheez Doodles in my underwear. He was *here!* He was touching my stuff."

Donald wore an expression of patient, compassionate

wisdom.

"Jessie, dear, I want you to think about what you just told us."

"There's nothing to think about!"

"Of course there is," he said. "Let's think it through together. The Pear-shaped Man was here, you think?"

"Yes."

"Why?"

"To do . . . to do what he did. It's disgusting. He's disgusting."

"Hmmm," Don said. "How, then? The locks were changed, remember? He can't even get in the building. He's never had a key to this apartment. There was no sign of forced entry. How did he get in with his bag of cheese curls?"

Jessie had him there. "Angela left the living room windows open," she said.

Angela looked stricken. "I did," she admitted. "Oh, Jessie, honey, I'm so sorry. It was hot. I just wanted to get a breeze, I didn't mean . . . ."

"The windows are too high to reach from the sidewalk," Donald pointed out. "He would have needed a ladder or something to stand on. He would have needed to do it in broad daylight, from a busy street, with people coming and going all the time. He would have had to have left the same way. And then there's the problem of the screens. He doesn't look like a very athletic sort, either."

"He did it," Jessie insisted. "He was here, wasn't he?"

"I know you think so, and I'm not trying to deny your feelings, just explore them. Has this Pear-shaped Man ever been invited into the apartment?"

"Of course not!" Jessie said. "What are you suggesting?"

"Nothing, Jess. Just consider. He climbs in through the windows with these cheese curls he intends to secrete in your drawers. Fine. How does he know which room is yours?"

Jessie frowned. "He . . . I don't know . . . he searched around, I guess."

"And found what clue? You've got three bedrooms here, one a studio, two full of women's clothing. How'd he manage to pick the right one?"

"Maybe he did it in both."

"Angela, would you go check you bedroom, please?" Donald asked.

Angela rose hesitantly. "Well," she said, "okay." Jessie and Donald stared at each other until she returned a minute or so later. "All clean," she said.

"I don't know how he figured out which damned room was mine," Jessie said. "All I know is that he did. He had to. How else can you explain what happened, huh? Do you think I did it *myself?*"

Donald shrugged. "I don't know," he said calmly. He glanced over his shoulder into the studio. "Funny, though. That painting in there, him and you, he must have done that some other time, after you finished it but before you sent it to Pirouette. It's good work, too. Almost as good as yours."

Jessie had been trying very hard not to think about the painting. She opened her mouth to throw something back at him, but nothing flew out. She closed her mouth. Tears began to gather in the corners of her eyes. She suddenly felt weary, confused, and very alone. Angela had walked over to stand beside Donald. They were both looking at her.

Jessie looked down at her hands helplessly and said, "What am I going to do? God. What am I going to *do?*"

God did not answer. Donald did. "Only one thing *to* do," he said briskly. "Face up to your fears. Exorcise them. Go down there and talk to the man, get to know him. By the time you come back up, you may pity him or have contempt for him or dislike him, but you won't fear him any longer, you'll see that he's only a human being and a rather sad one."

"Are you sure, Don?" Angela asked him.

"Completely. Confront this obsession of yours, Jessie. That's the only way you'll ever be free of it. Go down to the basement and visit with the Pear-shaped Man."

"There's nothing to be afraid of," Angela told her again.

"That's easy for you to say."

"Look, Jess, the minute you're inside, Don and I will come out and sit on the stoop. We'll be just an earshot away. All you'll have to do is let out the teeniest little yell, and we'll come rushing right down. So you won't be alone, not really. And you've still got that knife in your purse, right?"

Jessie nodded.

"Come on, then, remember the time that purse snatcher tried to grab your shoulder bag? You decked him good. If this Pear-shaped Man tries anything, you're quick enough. Stab him. Run away. Yell for us. You'll be perfectly safe."

"I suppose you're right," Jessie said with a small sigh. They *were* right. She knew it. It didn't make any sense. He was a dirty, foul-smelling, unattractive man, maybe a little retarded, but nothing she couldn't handle, nothing she had to be afraid of; she didn't want to be crazy; she was letting this ridiculous obsession eat her alive, and it had to end now. Donald was perfectly correct; she'd been doing it to herself all along and now she was going to take hold of it and stop it; certainly, it all made perfect sense and there was nothing to worry about, nothing to be afraid of; what could the Pear-shaped Man possibly *do* to her that was so terrifying? Nothing. Nothing.

Angela patted her on the back. Jessie took a deep breath, took the doorknob firmly in hand, and stepped out of the building into the hot, damp evening air. Everything was under control.

So why was she so scared?

* * *

Night was falling, but down under the stairs it had fallen already. Down under the stairs it was always night. The stoop cut off the morning sun, and the building itself blocked the afternoon light. It was dark, so dark. She stumbled over a crack in the cement, and her foot rang off the side of a metal garbage can. Jessie shuddered, imagining flies and maggots and other, worse things moving and breeding back there where the sun never shone. *No, mustn't think about that; it was only garbage, rotting and festering in the warm, humid dark; mustn't dwell on it.* She was at the door.

She raised her hand to knock, and then the fear took hold of her again. She could not move. *Nothing to be frightened of,* she told herself, *nothing at all.* What could he possibly *do* to her? Yet still she could not bring herself to knock. She stood before his door with her hand raised, her breath raw in her throat. It was so hot, so suffocatingly hot. She had to breathe. She had to get out from under the stoop, get back to where she could breathe. A thin vertical crack of yellow light split the darkness. *No,* Jessie thought, *oh, please no.*

The door was opening.

Why did it have to open so slowly? Slowly, like in her dreams. Why did it have to open at all? The light was so bright in there. As the door opened, Jessie found herself squinting. The Pear-shaped Man stood smiling at her.

"I," Jessie began, "I, uh, I . . . ."

"*There* she is," the Pear-shaped Man said in his tinny little squeak.

"What do you want from me?" Jessie blurted.

"I knew she'd come," he said, as though she wasn't there. "I knew she'd come for my things."

"No," Jessie said. She wanted to run away, but her feet would not move.

"You can come in," he said. He raised his hand, moved it toward her face. He touched her. Five fat white maggots crawled across her cheek and wriggled through her hair. His fingers smelled like cheese curls. His pinkie touched her ear and tried to burrow inside. She hadn't seen his other hand move until she felt it grip her upper arm, pulling, pulling. His flesh felt damp and cold. Jessie whimpered.

"Come in and see my things," he said. "You have to. You know you have to." And somehow she was inside then, and the door was closing behind her, and she was there, inside, alone with the Pear-shaped Man.

Jessie tried to get a grip on herself. *Nothing to be afraid of,* she repeated to herself, a litany, a charm, a chant, *nothing to be afraid of, what could he do to you, what could he do?*

The room was L-shaped, low ceilinged, filthy. The sickly sweet smell was overwhelming. Four naked light bulbs burned in the fixture above, and along one wall was a row of old lamps without shades, bare bulbs blazing away. A three-legged card table stood against the opposite wall, its fourth corner propped up by a broken TV set with wires dangling through the shattered glass of its picture tube. On top of the card table was a bowl of Cheez Doodles. Jessie looked away, feeling sick. She tried to step backward, and her foot hit an empty Coke bottle. She almost fell. But the Pear-shaped Man caught her in his soft, damp grip and held her upright.

Jessie yanked herself free of him and backed away. Her hand went into her purse and closed around the knife. It made her feel better, stronger. She moved close to the boarded-up window. Outside she could make out Donald and Angela talking. The sound of their voices, so close at hand—that helped, too. She tried to summon up all of her strength. "How do you live like this?" she asked him. "Do you need help cleaning up the place? Are you sick?" It was so hard to force out the words.

"Sick," the Pear-shaped Man repeated. "Did they tell you I was sick? They lie about me. They lie about me all the time. Somebody should make them stop." If only he would stop smiling. His lips were so wet. But he never stopped smiling. "I knew you would come. Here. This is for you." He pulled it from a pocket, held it out.

"No," said Jessie. "I'm not hungry. Really." But she was hungry, she realized. She was famished. She found herself staring at the thick orange twist between his fingers, and suddenly she wanted it desperately. "No," she said again, but her voice was weaker now, barely more than a whisper, and the cheese curl was very close.

Her mouth sagged open. She felt it on her tongue, the roughness of the powdery cheese, the sweetness of it. It crunched softly between her teeth. She swallowed and licked the last orange flakes from her lower lip. She wanted more.

"I knew it was you," said the Pear-shaped Man. "Now your things are mine." Jessie stared at him. It was like in her nightmare. The Pear-shaped Man reached up and began to undo the little white plastic buttons on his shirt. She struggled to find her voice. He shrugged out of the shirt. His undershirt was yellow, with huge damp circles under his arms. He peeled it off, dropped it. He moved closer, and heavy white breasts flopped against his chest. The right one was covered by a wide blue smear. A dark little tongue slid between his lips. Fat white fingers worked at his belt like a team of dancing slugs. "These are for you," he said.

Jessie's knuckles were white around the hilt of the knife. "Stop," she whispered.

His pants settled to the floor.

She couldn't take it. No more, no more. She pulled the knife free of her bag, raised it over her head. "*Stop!*"

"Ahh," said the Pear-shaped Man, "there it is."

She stabbed him.

The blade went in right to the hilt, plunged deep into his soft, white skin. She wrenched it down and out. The skin parted, a huge, meaty gash. The Pear-shaped Man was smiling his little smile. There was no blood, no blood at all. His flesh was soft and thick, all pale dead meat.

He moved closer, and Jessie stabbed him again. This time he reached up and knocked her hand away. The knife was embedded in his neck. The hilt wobbled back and forth as he padded toward her. His dead, white arms reached out and she pushed against him and her hand sank into his body like he was made of wet, rotten bread. "Oh," he said, "oh, oh, oh." Jessie opened her mouth to scream, and the Pear-shaped Man pressed those heavy wet lips to her own and swallowed all her sound. His pale eyes sucked at her. She felt his tongue darting forward, and it was round and black and oily, and then it was snaking down inside her, touching, tasting, feeling all her things. She was drowning in a sea of soft, damp flesh.

She woke to the sound of the door closing. It was only a small click, a latch sliding into place, but it was enough. Her eyes opened, and she pulled herself up. It was so hard to move. She felt heavy, tired. Outside they were laughing. They were laughing at her. It was dim and far-off, that laughter, but she knew that it was meant for her.

Her hand was resting on her thigh. She stared at it and blinked. She wiggled her fingers, and they moved like five fat maggots. She had something soft and yellow under her nails and deep dirty yellow stains up near her fingertips.

She closed her eyes, ran her hand over her body, the soft heavy curves, the thicknesses, the strange hills and valleys. She pushed, and the flesh gave and gave and gave. She stood up weakly. There were her clothes, scattered on the floor. Piece by piece she pulled them on, and then she moved across the room. Her briefcase was down beside the door; she gathered it up, tucked it under her arm; she might need something; yes, it was good to have the briefcase. She pushed open the door and emerged into the warm night. She heard the voices above her: ". . . were right all along," a woman was saying, "I couldn't believe I'd been so silly. There's nothing sinister about him, really, he's just pathetic. Donald, I don't know how to thank you."

She came out from under the stoop and stood there. Her feet hurt so. She shifted her weight from one to the other and back again. They had stopped talking, and they were staring at her, Angela and David and a slender, pretty woman in blue jeans and work shirt. "Come back," she said, and her voice was thin and high. "Give them back. You took them; you took my things. You have to give them back."

The woman's laugh was like ice cubes tinkling in a glass of Coke.

"I think you've bothered Jessie quite enough," Donald said.

"She has my things," she said. "Please."

"I saw her come out, and she didn't have anything of yours," Donald said.

"She took all my things," she said.

Donald frowned. The woman with the sandy hair and the green eyes laughed again and put a hand on his arm. "Don't look so serious, Don. He's not all there."

They were all against her, she knew, looking at their faces. She clutched her briefcase to his chest. They'd taken her things, he couldn't remember exactly what, but they wouldn't get her case; he had stuff in there, and they wouldn't get it. She turned away. He was hungry, she realized. She wanted something to eat. He had half a bag of Cheez Doodles left, she remembered. Downstairs. Down under the stoop.

As she descended, the Pear-shaped Man heard them talking about her. He opened the door and went inside to stay. The room smelled like home. He sat down, laid his case across his knees, and began to eat. He stuffed the cheese curls into his mouth in big handfuls and washed them down with sips from a glass of warm Coke straight from the bottle he'd opened that morning, or maybe yesterday. It was good. Nobody knew how good it was. They laughed at him, but they didn't know; they didn't know about all the nice things he had. No one knew. No one. Only someday he'd see somebody different, somebody to give his things to, somebody who would give him all their things. Yes. He'd like that. He'd know her when he saw her.

He'd know just what to say.

Kingdom Come

by Bruce McAllister

Bruce McAllister lives in Redlands, California, and is director of the writing program at the University of Redlands. He published his first story in 1963, when he was seventeen. His short fiction has been published in *Omni, Isaac Asimov's Science Fiction Magazine, The Magazine of Fantasy and Science Fiction,* and the anthologies *In the Field of Fire* and *Alien Sex.* His first novel, *Humanity Prime,* was in the original Ace Special series. His second novel, *Dream Baby* (Tor), is based on the Nebula Award–nominated novella of the same title.

"Kingdom Come" is a mysterious, surrealist story. The focus is on a relationship, one that shows the strains of constant bombardment by inexplicable outside forces. It was published in *Omni* in February 1987.

KINGDOM COME

Bruce McAllister

His wife shouted from the kitchen while outside angels died. He was working in the corner of their apartment's small living room, and he paid no attention. She shouted again, saying "Jesus *Christ!*" and at the word *Christ* there was an explosion, a shattering of glass. He got up and padded his way across the flattened pile of the aging Daylong rug. The shag had once been a smooth Eldorado Gold. Now it was mottled with broad, dark smears from months of sugary drinks and other spills. Nothing ever changes, he told himself. Nothing ever changes in here, even with the world outside what it is. He tried not to think of it, but long white wings flashed behind his eyes, and he couldn't help himself. It was always there. He came up behind her and sighed, letting the sigh lead into his first word. "What's the matter?" The shards of one of their last water glasses lay glittering at the base of the kitchen wall.

She turned her head slowly, the muscles and tendons taut on her neck, one blazing eye coming into sight first, then the other, her mouth in a sneer. "I'd tell you—if I thought you could understand," she said. The same childish sarcasm. Too many years with kids.

He looked away and closed his eyes. It was beginning again. All the lines they'd used before—one version or another—

and went on using, even with the world outside being what it was. The pale wings. The great door. The greater shadow.

He could feel her glaring at him, and he waited for the whisper of shoe on linoleum as she turned her back on him. It came. He opened his eyes and watched her move to the sink, where she began to fumble with something, as if purposefully.

He felt his jaw tighten, as always. "What are you talking about?"

She said nothing. He stared at the back of her head, at the wisps of dark hair at her neck, which he still found beautiful. He wondered what an angel's neck was like.

He looked around the kitchen slowly, seeing the leaking faucet, the fire-blackened wall above the stove. Neither was new. Then he saw the big black fingerprints on the wall, five or so feet above the glass shards, as if an oversized child had put them there. He tried to remember how—why—he had put his hands up there like that.

"I'm sorry about the fingerprints on the wall," he said. "It's generator oil."

"It's not just the fingerprints, Jerry." She didn't pause. "By themselves—taken alone," she went on, loving the sound of it, "big black fingerprints on the wall are almost pretty. On a lovely white wall like that."

He had closed his eyes again, dizzy with the familiarity of it all.

Was this simply how they coped—in the face of it? Wings, shadow, jaws, the sounds just beyond their walls.

"The baby craps in her diapers," the voice was saying, "but you're watching a blank TV screen, so I clean it up. You smear the walls, so I clean it up. Do you want to know why?"

Still blind, he knew she was turning. He opened his eyes. She stood before him with the can opener raised like a little ax, mouth open, words ready.

"Because you've trained me well, Jerry. Sometimes I'm

even *happy* doing it."

He thought of the creatures dying outside. *"All right!* I said I was sorry about the damn fingerprints, and I'm sorry about everything else, too. Let's drop it. I've got two hours left on the generators."

She was staring at him, shaking her head in slow motion. She wasn't saying anything; she was just shaking her head. It drove him crazy, as always.

"You're pathetic," he whispered.

"I'm what?"

"You're pathetic," he heard himself say again. "Go ahead. Shake your head while you think of something wonderful to—"

The Swing-a-way can opener left her hand and moved in slow motion past his head—close enough for sincerity but without any pretense of aim. He turned and watched it fall short of the drapes in their small dining room. He stared at it.

Even this tiny gesture of violence was familiar. It had been a plate the last time, a coat hanger before that, a fork—all offered in the same way.

A cry came from the stairwell, but neither of them stopped. The old rage began to fill him.

"You bitch," he told her.

He was glaring at her, and as he glared, the kitchen brightened as if a ball of ragged light had suddenly come through the walls. His eyes were wide open. His mouth was twisted. It had him now, the script, and he remembered his decision.

"Jerry, I'm sorry."

As always, the voice had changed. The eyes had changed.

"Dear God," he spat. How could anyone who'd run a preschool for seven years be so goddamn weak?

"Jerry, please." She was pained; she didn't want him angry at her anymore.

"Why do I ever listen to your bitching?" he was saying. "It's over in five minutes, but I listen. I take you seriously. I worry."

He began to move—toward the living room, the hallway, toward his decision.

"Jerry." The voice was loud, plaintive.

"The window," she pleaded. As far away as she was, as frightened as she was, it sounded like a whisper: "Please."

He stopped in the middle of the living room. He didn't want to. This time he just didn't want to. But there were times when she didn't want to either, and she went ahead and did it, didn't she? If she could do it, he could, couldn't he?

He felt a stab of old affection and then nothing. He turned to her, did not look at her eyes, and took one end of their Danish-plaid sofa. She took the other end, and they began to move it.

They moved it from the wall where the feathery crack in the plaster had begun to creep down behind the sofa. They arranged it so it faced the floor-length drapes in the living room. He turned off the light. She opened the drapes.

When they sat down, they did not touch. But once again—for the moment—they were on the same couch, nearly touching, looking out and wondering whether the scratchings at the door, the moans and cries and wordless pleas that sometimes came to the hallways outside would interrupt them. It had happened before.

Together they looked out at the world, the dream and nightmare of it.

Central Park was gone. In the perpetual twilight that held everything, they could see, down toward Ninety-sixth, the dark swaths of the few remaining trees and paths. Beyond that— reservoir, museum, lake, and zoo—the park was gone. From Columbus Circle to Ninety-sixth, it was gone.

The few trees and pathways that remained might have been comforting, but they were too distant and dim. In place of the park was what he had come to call The Door. What his wife called it, in her private thoughts, he did not know. They did not refer to it out loud; they did not have to. It was always there, whether the drapes were open or not.

Through The Door, its great edges shimmering like a black mirage, they could see the other universe—the dark, towering cliffs and darker sea; the eternal twilight; the twin moons; the spit of dim, barren land that somehow bridged the two worlds.

From the twilight of that other universe, from the moons and towering cliffs, the winged creatures streamed into their world. Like flocks of great birds they caught updrafts, banked and plummeted, and soared again, moving effortlessly between the two skies. But more than that, they played, tumbling and teasing, their bodies—all but the wings—so human, their heads thrown back in what he felt sure was laughter, the kind that children made.

And then it would change. Out of nowhere would come things barely visible, not unlike the creatures' own winged shadows, and darker than the twilight. A pair of wings would be struck, then another, and another; and each pale pair would drop through the twilight with its shadow, feathers trailing as if torn by invisible jaws.

The pale wings would flicker in and out of darkness. The bodies would twist, disappearing and reappearing, writhing. A few would eventually regain flight, flapping injuredly back to their world or on into this one. A few would fall to the earth, streaming light, and he would see them later wandering the land bridge between the two worlds, wingless and stumbling. But most would simply disappear in the first tumble, winking out into a darkness deeper than the twilight—as if taken.

Seen through the window glass, it was like a movie. It reached them, but it did not. They saw the distant pairs of wings but did not feel the wind those wings made. They saw the creatures struck, but did not feel the jaws that tore them. There was nothing to hear, nothing to smell. They took it in with their eyes and were safe. As long as they remained in their rooms— his generators working for them, the food and water and first-aid supplies replenishing themselves somehow in the storeroom he had built for them—they were safe.

When the great shadow passed overhead, however, it was different. The glass could not protect them. It was not a movie, not at all. Sometimes the thing came from the universe beyond The Door, from the endless twilight and dark cliffs. Sometimes it came from his own world, as if returning from a long journey. Whatever the direction, both worlds shook—cliffs and buildings and skies and Door—and the twilight flickered, turned grainy, and for a moment was blacker than any night.

He thought of it simply as The Shadow.

When it came, the building rocked. It reached through the glass; it grabbed them both by their very souls; and they trembled, knew fear, and forgot the old script.

The window was their agreement. It had worked for weeks.

They waited. They jerked. A single cry from the baby's room reached them; they held their breaths, and the cry did not come again. Sometimes the baby could sleep through the rocking of the building, the flickering of the universes. Sometimes the slightest sound would wake it.

Joanna was the baby's name. When he thought about her, it was as if she were someone else's. As if the woman beside him were someone else's wife. Had they ever laughed? He could not remember.

They waited. He felt her stiffen and thought it was coming at last. But then he heard what she was hearing. The scratching at the door. They held their breaths again, together. There was a cry—not from the baby's room this time—and then it was gone. Silence came back.

Once, a little later, he thought he could feel the building

tremble. But it was only the woman beside him, shifting on the couch. It wasn't going to come.

Even if it did, it wouldn't work this time.

He couldn't remember the last time it had worked—for him.

He felt her against him, her shoulder warm. It made no difference.

A tear in space. An Einstein intersection. Black hole, wormhole, parallel universes colliding, or literal gate into literal hell: He could not have said what it was—this Door. He was a high-school psych teacher who sometimes taught English, sometimes coached basketball; and he could not have said. He had simply gotten two cycle-fitted generators; built a storeroom in the back bedroom; stocked it well because the world had turned ugly; and was lying in bed with his wife when the universe seemed to end, when The Door appeared, and the three of them were suddenly alone.

It was the same night, according to Channel Eleven, that the Aryan Knights were going to try for Harlem again, using the same pit mortars and antipersonnel weapons The Takers had used against them weeks before. Two nights before that, three buildings on One Hundred Tenth had blazed with the pretty white phosphorus all the gangs liked, and the city's SWAT fire units never quite got the fires out, "Willy Peter" being the tenacious thing it was. They'd watched the stubborn glow from their window, but the strike on Harlem never came off. There were reports of new, black market Israeli Tamirins—the new generation of laser-aimed, infrared assault rifles—being used in the subways by the bankrolled mercs, and a story about a viral epidemic in Newark too perfect not to be a gene splice, but nothing in Harlem. They'd watched from their window, holding their breaths, and then finally had gone to bed.

They'd have left the city, but it was no better anywhere else. Boston, Chicago, and Atlanta were as bad. D.C. was a fortress where you couldn't move without paper, and the curfew started at six. The West Coast was being hit by imports as well as its own native sons, and L.A.'s streets, people said, belonged to high-tech urban warriors. Rural New England was swamped with refugees; the Midwest was blockaded; and you didn't leave the U.S. if you didn't want worse. No one knew why. It had started somewhere, of course—farm demonstrations in '86, the San Onofre melt-down, the Cabinet Hoax, a revolution in Mexico, all of these things—but how it had come this far no one seemed able to say.

Sarah's brother had taken a hollow-point bullet on Fifth Avenue, tearing the back of his skull off; and the next day Jerry had bought the generators and a manual on their use, had tripled their supplies, and had started on the storeroom with what lumber he could get from Max Cheney in the school's woodshop.

Was it only two months? Six? He could have kept track by their fights in the kitchen, dining room, and bedroom. At the beginning, when The Door first appeared, he'd suggested they try to leave. He could remember her crying, arguing; and before long he had stopped. Her fears had become his: They were safe in their rooms. Sounds came to the hallways outside their door. There were poundings on the walls, on the door, each day, and voices; but nothing seemed able to get in. And when the canned goods, Eversafe water bottles, and first-aid supplies began to replenish themselves—like miraculous fish, miraculous bread—without anyone's help, without the storeroom door even being opened, their decision was made for them. Something—someone—wanted them to stay. *It is not your business, what is happening outside,* it was saying. *Stay and you will be fed; you will be safe,* it was saying.

One day the television came on by itself. A picture appeared for a few seconds—a still frame, image grainy and unclear—and then was gone. He began to watch TV after that, the set hooked up to the generators, his eyes on the screen's blank static, pedaling until his legs ached. While he did this she stood behind him with one of her looks, feeling afraid and alone, saying instead that it was a waste of time and energy—only that. He remembered it clearly.

Twice, more pictures appeared—of the city as it had once been, of the park as it was now, of things that looked real but could not have been: a coiling black shape boiling from a strange sea, a sky with too many stars, a winged man glowing with a light that was more like a voice. They came quickly, these pictures—like accidents, like random thoughts. The phone did not ring. Human voices did not reach them from other parts of the building, and they never saw people walking on the land bridge below them. But he kept pedaling, hoping, while she stood behind him, judging.

One day the baby screamed, and they rushed in to find a ball of ragged yellow light hovering over the crib, moving slowly away, disappearing finally through the bedroom wall. The baby's eyes had rolled back to the whites. Her arm was twitching, two fingers burned, but she made no sound. And then, just as suddenly, the brown irises were back, the baby was breathing again, and so were they.

The next day, in the storeroom—which smelled oddly like ozone—he found a tube of salve that had not been there before, and he put it on the baby's fingers, and the fingers quickly healed.

A few days later he found three cans of vegetables on a storeroom shelf that had been empty the day before.

He grew aware that she was leaning against him. He started to say, "I've still got two hours left," knowing how she would answer, but she was asleep.

He thought of what he'd found in the old encyclopedia set and the embarrassingly few books they had in the apartment and wondered again what a public library would tell him. Even in the

books in these rooms, he had found the story everywhere.
Cherubim and seraphim.
The seven archangels.
Nabu, Karubu, Azazel, and Satan.
The Angel Rulers of the Seven Heavens. The angels of
Babylon and the *Zend Avesta*. Theophanic messengers, fallen
sons. The Armenian hreshtak—angels at the beginning of the
world. The Japanese winged "Bloom Lady," fairies, and
tennin—Japanese host of angels. The Persian *firishtah*, Hebrew
mal'ak, Slavic "angel of death," and the guardian angel of
Njals-saga. Dwarfs—fallen angels of the Danes. Allah's angels
sent to worship man. Africa's child of the angels who brought
rain. And the dark Panis, Hindu demons of the night.

*And the second angel poured out his vial upon the sea; and
it became as the blood of a dead man: . . . And the third angel
poured out his vial upon the rivers and fountains of waters; and
they became blood. . . . And the fourth angel poured out his vial
upon the sun. . . .*

But best of all, the poem he had taught only once in fifteen
years: Castor and Pollux, winged children of Leda . . . and her
godlike swan.

He thought of the creatures outside, of The Shadow that
shook the universes in its passage, and wondered how many
times this had happened—this Door—and what it must have been
like for other men and women—on the sands of Judaea, on
African veldts, in Asian jungles and European fjords long ago.
Abraham and Daniel. Guadalupe, Joan of Arc. Coming out of
nowhere, the white wings spread, a ragged ball of light that
could move anywhere, and the darker thing that would always
follow.

He thought of the darker things. He wondered which world
they had come from and was afraid he knew.

Ten days ago one of the things had appeared only a few
feet from their window as they sat looking out. Its form wasn't

clear. It wasn't real, and so they didn't move from the couch. It was the size of a man, dark, wingless, and perfectly still, floating there before them, changing before their eyes—jaws giving way to other jaws, eyes to other eyes, legs to other legs.

When the jaws struck—the glass bending with the blow, the teeth slipping along it with a dark smear that bubbled away into the twilight—he ran for the gun.

The thing was gone when he returned, and he stood looking at the cracked window, at the place where its saliva had etched deeply into the glass.

They waited, afraid, for it to return. For three days they did not fight.

He stared at the woman in the darkness and got up. He spoke gently to her, helped her to her feet, and guided her to the bedroom. There he undressed her and finally pulled the soiled covers up over her shoulders. She was tired. The baby, the worries, their fights—all of it tired her. She deserved her sleep.

He stepped quietly to the corner of the room, plugged the fan into the extension cord, and placed it on her bed stand. He turned it on, aiming it away from her head, and stood listening. The fan was old and loud, and he could not believe they had never laughed at its sound.

He waited. When she did not stir, he went to the kitchen. He removed the screwdriver and the loaded Walther .38 from the Tupperware bucket under the sink and went to the front door.

It took him ten minutes to remove the screws from the three bolt sheaths. It was slow work, but quieter than the bolts would have been.

When the last sheath was free, hanging against the doorframe, he laid the screwdriver and the screws on the floor where she would be sure to see them, picked up the Walther, and reached for the doorknob.

He would, he told himself, pound loudly on the door when he was on the other side. She would rush over; she would be able to get the screws back in easily. She would cry and plead with him, but she would get the screws back in.

His hand was shaking. He knew it wasn't fear. Anything was better than this—the fighting, a woman he didn't know anymore, the waiting, the not understanding. If he touched the doorknob, he knew his hand would stop shaking.

The storeroom would take care of the two of them, he told himself again. He was the one with first-aid training, the one who knew CPR, but whatever was making things appear on the storeroom shelves would take care of them. The woman and the child would be okay. He would come back as soon as he found other human beings, as soon as he understood the world outside better, or as soon as he could stand the thought of being in these rooms again.

When he turned, certain that she would be standing behind him at the bedroom door, contemptuous, silent—just as she'd been the other times—she wasn't there.

He stared at the empty doorway, remembering another woman, and began to replace the screws.

When he returned to the bedroom, she was asleep in the bed, the soiled covers over her shoulders where he had laid them.

In the morning he could not look at her. They said little, but she seemed rested, less afraid. Even when the scratching began at their door in the afternoon, they said nothing to each other, and he was grateful. The scratching stopped.

That evening he cranked on the generators as long as his legs could bear it. The pedaling made him want to scream. He could feel the walls, the slow suffocation, the looks of the woman. As his calves cramped, he saw himself reaching for the doorknob, saw himself walking in the perpetual twilight outside, across the land bridge toward dark cliffs. The pale wings were high above him, playing and teasing, then suddenly plummeting, bleeding. He looked up. The great Shadow was passing overhead, and he could see. . . .

They awoke that night to the sound of scratching—louder now.

"What is it?" she asked, stupid with sleep.

"Nothing," he said. What would his old textbooks say? How do feelings die? How does a man lose what defines his life—memories, affection, his very being?

Blunted affect, pathological bonding system, retrograde amnesia. But wasn't it more than this?

He barely remembered last summer. It was as hazy as someone else's memory or like a television set coming on by itself, the image grainy and random. Westport. The great long lake with its history, islands, and shore. They had made love just once, hating it, on a narrow, musty bed that could have been anywhere—Manhattan, Brooklyn, or Albany. She had cried, he remembered. They had tried one scenic drive to Middlebury—through the roadblocks, refugees, and National Guard—and had left two days later. It was not the soldiers that made them leave. They simply did not want to be together.

The baby had been a mistake. A slip of spermicidal foam. You don't bring a kid into a world like this if you can help it, do you?

An older memory washed over him then, dimmer and wrong. In it a boy met a girl. She, the nursing student. He, the wise psych major. They went to a party; he made silly jokes about "playing doctor" and was afraid to kiss her. Even after beers, he was afraid to kiss her. . . .

In that dream or in another, she laughed at his shyness, put her arms around his neck, and made love to him in the dark while the party went on forever below them.

She had never been a nursing student. She had never been

so full of laughter. He had always led. Wondering even as he did it, he touched her cheek, pushed hair away from her forehead, and—when the noise stopped—watched her face soften once again into sleep.

When it came again, it was a pounding on walls and doors that entered their bodies like adrenaline, snapping them upright like dolls. The walls shook.

Sounds that throats might make ululated with the pounding, which was louder than any he could remember.

"My God," she said, struggling up, heading toward the baby's room.

He was running to the kitchen on the balls of his feet. He grabbed the Walther from the bucket, ran back down the hallway, and crouched—naked—ten feet from the front door, hands shaking violently.

The pounding stopped.

A voice spoke. The words—if they were words—were not human.

A weight moved against the door. The scratching began again.

"Go away!" he found himself shouting. He made it louder. "*Go away!*"

Please, it seemed to say. A hoarse whisper. A word impossibly human.

He held the gun with both hands and listened. The baby made a sound. He heard her try to quiet it. On the other side of the door something moved again, whimpered once, and did not move again.

"Is it gone?" she asked. She was at the end of the hallway, afraid to come any closer to him or the door.

"I don't know," he said. The gun was heavy. His arms hurt. He continued to wait.

When after an hour nothing happened, he got up, walked

past her without a word, and got dressed.

As he sat at the generators, he laid the gun on the rug by his feet.

They had forgotten about it and were about to eat dinner. She had gone to their bedroom for something, the baby in her arms, and was passing the front door when it began again and she screamed and the baby began crying and he could barely hear them over the thunder of the pounding. When he reached her, she was two or three feet from the door. She had stumbled and was trying to get up with the baby. He grabbed her, yanked her back and away and behind him so that nothing stood between him and the door.

The whimpering was there again, barely audible under the pounding, and he opened his mouth to shout. And then, as always, he heard the other voices.

And as he heard them, he felt them in the marrow of his bones.

In the bowels of the building, high and nightmarish and so far from being human that at first he had imagined something else—straining wood, screaming hinges, blood thundering through his own skull—the other voices were moving up the stairwell like the wind, coming fast.

The thing on the other side of the door heard them and grew frenzied. Through its frantic scrabbling, its frantic rubbing against the door, he could hear it whisper. *Please.* He opened his mouth to shout, and stopped. There was something about it.

The voices were almost there.

It was, he realized then, like a child's whimpering. Like a child's fear.

Please.

He should have shouted, should have pounded back on the door, made it go away; but he did not. He looked back at her. Her eyes were wide. One of her hands was over the baby's face, as if to hide its eyes. He could hear the thing's frantic scratching everywhere now. The voices were nearly there. He knew what they were, had always known, he realized then: the black, leathery skin that burned to the touch; saliva that was like no other saliva; jaws colder than the vacuum between stars—all of it familiar now, the ancient enemy, its faces rising from the eons in his bones, from the sheaths of his nerves and the membranes in his skull, the waves of nausea washing over him now as darkness. He fought it, managed to keep from falling, to hold on to the gun.

Outside the thing whimpered, gibbered.

He took a step toward the door.

"No!" his wife shouted.

The voices were there now. The thing outside slid to the floor and began to scream. The door buckled, struck. Then it was hit again, the body tossed like a rag against it, the scream cut short.

And then the terrible grunting began, obscene and rhythmic, as something worked at flesh and its screams became rhythmic, too.

He was at the door, fumbling at the bolts with his free hand, before he heard her shout again. As he pulled it open, wanting to close his eyes but knowing he could not, he fired the Walther into the darkness only inches from his face, fired again and again until the clip was empty; and as the oily darkness spun away from him, twisting and writhing, his skull filled with unimaginable pain—with a scream of rage so old it knew no words—and he reached down, grabbed at the body that lay at his feet, pulled hard, and somehow closed the door. Nothing pushed against the door. Nothing fought him now. But the howling in his skull would not stop. It wanted him. It had wanted him for eternity. Without looking down, he slid the bolts in, refitted the chain, and closed his eyes against the sound.

When he turned, he saw that the thing had curled on the floor, making no sound. His wife was staring at it, afraid, and his daughter was crying.

Even where there wasn't blood, the body was dirty. The hair was twisted and snarled. Its arms and thighs were streaked with dirt, and there were scabs on the feet and knees. The shoulders were covered with deep wounds. The blood had pooled in the torn flesh, the white tendons of one arm showing where the meat had been ripped away. Where the long, graceful, articulated wings should have been, just behind the shoulder blades—anchored on the thick, broad spine—two bloody stumps glistened instead.

The thing smelled. It was the salt smell of blood but also the smell of a wet animal, so familiar from childhood; and he could only wonder at it. He crouched down. The thing saw him, eyes clearing suddenly in its pain, and jerked away from him.

He wanted to touch it. Never had he wanted to touch something so much.

The eyes were yellow, like those of certain dogs, and the chin was smooth, hairless. The skin was olive, darker than he had imagined. And the lips were full and cracked with sores.

Between its legs, where the thighs—astonishingly thin from the atrophy of flight—were streaked with dirt and shivering, lay the shadow of its organ, hairless and pale.

He wondered what it felt like to make love in the sky. To walk with legs not meant for walking. To die under such jaws.

He looked up at her, and as he did, he felt a dizziness; and something like ragged light filled the room. She looked back at him. The look on her face was not pure terror, no, not any more than his was. He had been wrong somehow. Had she always held the baby that way? Had she always stood so straight? And how, how could he have forgotten for all these months that *she* was the one who would be able to help keep this creature, and the others that would certainly follow it, alive and safe, Shadow willing.

"I'll get pressure bandages," she said. "There were some

in the storeroom yesterday." The baby had stopped crying. She would grow up knowing angels, he thought to himself.

He could remember last summer at last, so clearly now that it took his breath away. Westport, yes. The great long lake with its history, islands, and shore—beautiful even with the guardsmen everywhere. The two of them had swum to Picket Island more than once, naked in the night, and on the same warm ledge of limestone had made love again and again until their bodies hurt, their laughter skimming out across the lake like moonlight. They had stayed until the swamp maples turned flame-red and the ranks of soldiers began to thin. They had stayed until the air grew cold.

Joanna had not been an accident, he recalled. *I know it's an ugly world, Jerry. But we can do it. We can make something different for a child. I know we can.*

She had never been the woman he had thought she was. He understood that now. She had only been the woman he had been tempted to see. It wasn't over, but it would be different. They would be able to make the building—perhaps eventually the city—theirs, and it would be different: They had let the creature in.

He got up: and as he did, he saw what looked like teeth marks on the hands and feet of the creature beside him.

The marks were bleeding slowly. He remembered a painting from long ago.

And then the creature crossed its arms in pain.

Mother's Milt

by Pat Cadigan

Pat Cadigan lives in Overland Park, Kansas. She has been writing from the time she was a child in Massachusetts and has been publishing powerful, genre-crossing fiction since 1979 when she sold her first story to Marta Randall's *New Dimensions* anthology series. She is working on a horror novel.

Cadigan is equally at ease with science fiction, fantasy, and horror and has been nominated for every major award in the science fiction and fantasy field. Her first story in *Omni* was a nasty little chiller called "Vengeance is Yours." Since then *Omni* has published eleven more of her stories, including a couple starring Deadpan Allie (the protagonist of her first novel, *Mindplayers*), a vampire story (nominated for the Nebula), and, most recently, the science fiction story "Johnny Come Home" (June 1991). Cadigan's most recent novel, *Fools,* expanded from her award-nominated novella, "Fool to Believe," was recently published by Bantam. All of her fiction has an edge to it, and "Mother's Milt," appearing here for the first time, is no exception. There is nothing futuristic about this story—it could happen today. . . .

MOTHER'S MILT

Pat Cadigan

Milt appeared at breakfast, about as unsavory a sight as you could ever see at 7:30 on a summer morning: long stringy hair threatening to dip into the bowl of cereal, old faded sweatshirt with the sleeves hacked off showing wiry arms with a river of tattoos flowing up and down them, even older jeans faded to baby blue overlaid with a sheen of brown.

"Say hi to Milt, Lynn," my mother told me, planting a quart of milk on the table next to his technicolor elbow. "I bailed him out of jail last night instead of your father."

"Hi, Milt," I said.

His head moved slightly; I saw one watery hazel eye peering at me between the strands of hair, and I could tell he was amused by the wary tone in my voice. I might have been amused, too, if I'd been in his position, but I wasn't. I looked at my mother. As usual, the creases in her crisp, white coverall seemed sharp enough to cut flesh. My mother never failed to do mornings extremely well, even if she'd been up very late the night before.

"Drunk driving," she said, sitting down at Milt's left with her own bowl of cereal. "We can't go on like that."

"Drunk driving isn't funny, Ma," I said. Milt sat up straight. He looked like a knife-murderer.

"I meant your father," she said, "not Milt. Milt was in on a shoplifting charge."

"I know who you meant."

Milt glanced at my mother. She patted his arm. *"Don't worry.* I said you could stay, so you can stay. If you want to."

"And if I don't," he said, turning that psycho face to me, "ain't you afraid of forfeiting the bail?"

"My mother isn't afraid of anything," I said. "Haven't you figured that out yet?"

Before my mother left for work at Busy Hands, she presented Milt with a complete list of his chores for the day, reading it aloud to him just in case he was, in her words, literate-embarrassed. "Do the dishes, tidy the living room, vacuum all the rugs, dust all the downstairs furniture, change the linens on the beds upstairs—there are three bedrooms, including the one you're staying in—and clean both bathrooms. Do a good job, and I'll give you a treat when I get home from Busy Hands."

He took the list from her in what I thought of as Standard Dumb Amazement, blinking when she stood on tiptoe to pat him on the head, and then stared after her as she bustled out the door leading to the garage. Bustled was the only word for the way my mother moved; once you'd seen her do it, you understood exactly what it looked like. Milt went to the window over the sink and watched her drive away.

Finally, he turned back to me, holding the list the way I'd seen people hold bills from auto repair shops. "Is she kidding?" he asked me.

I spread a thin layer of cream cheese on the other half of my pumpernickel bagel. "Are you in jail?"

He laughed, crumpled the list, and tossed it over his shoulder into the sink. "What I am is outta here."

I got up, went to the junk drawer, and pulled out the gun. "I don't think so."

Those watery hazel eyes got very large. "Holy shit, girl! What are you doing?"

"Come on, *Milt,* what do *you* think?"

His gaze went from the gun to me, back to the gun and back to me.

"Give up?" I said. He started to raise his hands, just the way people did on TV. "The dishes. I'm helping you do the dishes."

He took a step toward me, and I aimed at his crotch. Most people make the mistake of aiming a gun at a man's head or chest, but, believe me, setting your sights lower will get their attention much better.

"Do I have to persuade you that I can and will use this on you? Do you think this is the first time I've had breakfast with a convicted felon on my mother's sufferance?"

He squinted at me. "Who *are* you people? *What* are you?"

"Conscientious citizens," I said. "Listen, I don't want you here any more than you want to be here. But here we are." I jerked my head at the table. "Stack 'em and rack 'em. I'll plead self-defense."

"Are you gonna keep that gun on me all day? That's what you'll have to do."

"We all gotta do what we gotta do, Milt," I said. "And you gotta get busy."

"How old are you?" he said suspiciously.

"Sixteen."

"My God." He didn't believe me, of course; I'm built like a linebacker, hostage to genetics.

"The house is a mess, Milt," I said. "Okay?"

He folded those skinny arms. "What if I just refuse to move?"

"Then it's going to be a boring day for both of us," I said. "And you'll go back to jail at the end of it."

That finally reached him. "I can't do that. And I can't stay here," he said. "Please, honey—Lynn—give a guy a break, will ya?"

"You got a break. You're out of jail."

He was staring at the gun again.

"Well, sort of," I added. "Look, my mother's eccentric even by your standards—"

"I heard *that*."

"—but don't get the idea she isn't serious. My mother doesn't kid around. She doesn't know how." I gestured at the dishes waiting on the table. "Come on, Milt. Is it going to kill you to do a dish?"

He got the point, but I could tell even he was surprised to find himself gathering up bowls and silverware and plates and taking them to the sink. The whole time he was rinsing things off and putting them in the dishwasher, I could practically hear the wheels turning in his head: when could he get a good opening to try to overpower this big, crazy bruiser of a girl, how far could he run and how fast, and what the hell was he doing, why had he accepted his release to a total stranger in the first place? My mother always chose well, though. Old Milt had obviously spent more than a few nights sleeping rough, and the prospect of spending at least one night indoors before he made off with anything that wasn't nailed down with a value of over five dollars had been too tempting to resist. Going along with the crazy little grey-haired lady who had chosen to foot bail for him over her husband had been a pretty good idea in the middle of the night.

The phone rang just after he'd gotten the vacuum cleaner out of the hall closet. My mother, of course; she was pleased to hear that Milt was on schedule, but dismayed that I still had to hold the gun on him. As if that were unusual. Anyone would think she'd have learned by now—they spend at least one whole day working under the gun. My mother, the eternal optimist, always hoping she'd get a quick study.

Just before lunch, he made a break for the front door. I let him yank on it and try to break the windows. Then I made him finish vacuuming the runner in the hall before I gave him his lunch. He kept muttering *I don't believe this* over and over while he spooned up tomato soup.

Dusting is when they usually try for the phone. I left the room briefly, just so he could get it over with. He was dabbing it with the feather duster when I came back. I wouldn't have brought it up, but he felt compelled to.

"How come you can get calls when the phone's dead?" he asked accusingly.

"The phone's not dead," I told him. "You just don't know how to use it."

"Jesus *Christ*." He threw down the feather duster. "I want to know what's going on here. Your mother said I could stay *if I wanted to*. Well, what if I don't want to?"

I hefted the gun slightly. "I think you want to."

He picked up the feather duster and finished doing the end tables and the bookcases.

There was another fuss about changing the beds. He didn't think he had to change his, since he'd just spent one night in it, and then he tried to tell me his back was too weak for him to turn the mattresses, a charade he insisted on playing out with all three of them, so it was a slow, clumsy process. But it got done. I let him have a snack break in front of the TV before I told him to set the kitchen table for dinner.

"That wasn't on the list," he said, unable to tear his eyes away from that skinny little game show hostess who waves her arms in front of washer-dryers as if they were miracles.

"My mother would want you to fill out the day with something useful," I told him.

"But really," he said, punching the couch cushion behind him, "I think I hurt my back with those damned mattresses. No fooling. I ought to get in a hot tub." He looked up at me and smiled for the first time. "God, a hot bath would be heaven right now. You could even stay there and keep the gun on me I wouldn't mind."

I just bet he wouldn't. But he wasn't the only one who'd seen *The Beguiled.* Still, if you don't let them try everything, they don't believe. Seduction occurred to some of them sooner, and some of them later, and the second group usually try it on my mother rather than me.

"What did you have in mind?" I said. "A bubble bath?"

His smile got bigger and more enthusiastic. "You got something sweet-smelling? I bet you have. Something you like for your boyfriends to smell on you."

"I wear Obsession," I told him. "Only Obsession. It wouldn't smell right on *you.* There's Obsession *pour l'homme,* but we don't have any."

"Obsession, eh?" His smile shrank a bit. He was looking at the barrel of the gun again and didn't realize I knew what he was staring at. "You obsessed with guns?"

"No. Cleanliness, actually."

He threw back his head and laughed. The studio audience coincidentally laughed right along with him, and he used the remote control to turn down the volume. "I can see that. All the more reason for me to take a bath before your mother gets home. So I can be as clean as the house when she comes in."

"This house isn't clean," I said. "The windows are filthy. You do those tomorrow."

He laughed again. "How's the old saying go? I don't do windows?"

"Yeah, sure, Milt. But it's just a saying. You change the drapes, too, and you vacuum upstairs and you clean the cellar and I don't know what all. My mother'll leave you a list, of course."

He slumped against the back of the couch. "Oh, come on,

141

little lady. Lynn. Are you gonna spend another whole day holding that gun on me?"

"If I have to."

"What about tonight? You and your mom gonna take turns guarding me?"

"We lock you in your room. You were locked in last night, but I guess you didn't know it."

He combed his fingers through that stringy hair. "Look. . . all this has been, you know, kinda weird and kinky and interesting, but it's gotten old. I gotta tell you, I was really wondering about your mom last night when she bypassed your old man and took me out instead. It seemed like one of those great opportunities, too good to be true. See, I know sooner or later my prints are gonna turn up with my real name and then I'm in the soup for sure. So I thought, well. I'll go with this Good Samaritan—Good Samaritan-ess?" He gave a little nervous laugh. "Well, whatever. I'll go with her, and I'll have a little something to eat and a good night's sleep, and then I'm off to Mexico, Canada, parts unknown—" He shrugged. "Then I get dishpan hands at gunpoint."

"You don't have dishpan hands," I said. "Dishwashers have made dishpan hands obsolete. You've got busy hands."

"Yeah, right. What is that, 'Busy Hands' where your mother works—a maid service?"

"You're exactly right. It's a maid service. My mother cleans houses for a living. But it's that old story—who shaves the barber? In this case, you do."

He stared at me, baffled. I guess they don't get much parlor philosophy in jail.

"Never mind," I said. "Break time's over. Set the table."

He hesitated, ready to argue further, and then thought better of it. "You'll have to talk me through this," he said, leading the way into the kitchen. "I can never remember which fork goes on the right."

"That's easy," I said, "you never put forks on the right. You don't want to risk accidentally piercing a dinner companion."

He looked over his shoulder at me. "Really?"

I just shook my head. "Oh, dammit. We forgot to run the dishwasher. Well, you'll have to wash a few dishes by hand. There isn't time for a complete cycle before my mother comes home."

I had to poke him in the ribs with the gun a few times to get him in the right frame of mind. "See, now I am gonna get dishpan hands," he said grumpily as he stood at the sink.

"Not with Softi-Bubbles," I said, sitting at the table. "It's specially formulated to leave your skin sweetly soft while it cuts the grease. You can also wash your fine linens in it and even use it for bubble bath."

He snorted. "Yeah. The bubble bath I'm never gonna get."

I was really getting tired of his whining. "You can take a bath after dinner if you really want to."

He stacked the dishes in the rack to let them drain. "You can make me clean, but I gotta tell you, I can't cook, even with that gun to my head. You can blow my brains out if you want, but there's nothing I can do."

"That's okay. My mother will be bringing dinner home with her. She's got a friend in the catering business."

"Great. Rubber chicken."

"You could always go on a diet." As I'd figured, that shut him up fast. After experiencing bail my mother's way, he didn't want to know what her idea of a diet would be. He was stubborn, but he was learning.

When he finished setting the table, I decided to let him go back to watching TV in the living room until my mother came home, rest his weary back. I was pretty sure my mother would be pleased with the job he'd done on the house, so she wouldn't mind my giving him a little extra relaxing time.

And I was right. My mother walked through the house beaming with pleasure, while Milt and I trailed along behind her in a little parade. I still had the gun on him, of course—there was no telling if he'd be stupid enough to try attacking my mother. But her effusive praise caught him off guard. After a day with me, he'd been expecting almost anything but that.

"I especially like the way you made the beds," she told him as we trooped back downstairs to the kitchen. "Is that how they do it in prison?"

"How'd you know I'd been in prison?" he asked.

"Get real, Milt," I said.

"Well, jail, yeah, but just about everybody's been in jail—"

My mother laughed. "Good heavens, where did you come by that idea? Young man, there are people who go their whole lives and never see the inside of a *jail*. Let alone the big house. Lynn's father was in the big house. We've learned to tell ex-cons by body language. And tattoos, of course." She ran a finger up his left arm as she ushered him into the kitchen. "Some of those are jailhouse tattoos. You really ought to have them worked on, covered over with better designs if you don't want to have them removed altogether."

All he could do was stare at her as she sat him at the table and took her place to his left.

"Lynn, you may serve now," she said, waving a hand at the white bags she had set on the counter. "And then afterwards, it'll be time for your treat," she added to Milt, wiggling her index finger in his stupefied face.

Tonight's offering was a stroganoff. I'd rather not eat so much red meat—in fact, I'd often thought of going vegetarian—but my mother wanted to keep me big. I worried about what the insides of my arteries looked like, even though my mother insisted that was no worry at all at my age.

"Jesus!" Milt said as the aroma hit him in the face. "I'm

starved! Your daughter didn't give me much for lunch."

"Eating heavily in the middle of the day would have made you sleepy," my mother told him. "Now, chow down. You've earned it."

He'd finished half his plate before it occurred to him that I wasn't holding the gun on him anymore. But I did have it in my lap, and it was pointing at him before he could make so much as a twitch in my mother's direction. She frowned at me and then gave Milt a look.

"Let's not fight at the table, you two." She turned back to me. "Okay?"

I shrugged. "He started it."

Milt's fork plopped in his food as he buried his face in his hands. "My God, my God," he moaned "How did I get here? What's happening? What kinda crazy deal is this?"

My mother gave his forearm a small push. "Elbows off the table, Milt."

He peeked at her from between his fingers. "Lady, I don't know what's going on here with your locked doors and your unbreakable windows and your dead phones and your gun-toting daughter, but I think I wanna go back to jail."

"Oh, no, you wouldn't like that," my mother said. "Jail's so risky. My friend Carol the caterer might bail you out then, and you'd like that a lot less than this, believe-you-me. She bailed out Lynn's father around lunchtime." My mother shook her head, going *tch-tch-tch*. "She'll forfeit the bail, of course, but it was a last-minute thing, this dinner she had to do, and they *insisted* on stroganoff. The Royal Lodge of Moose said they'd pay one-and-a-half times the normal fee for it, so even minus the lost bail money, Carol still makes out like a bandit."

"Carol *always* makes out like a bandit," I said. "She's the Robin Hood of the testimonial set."

"Yes, but catering is *so messy,*" said my mother. "I much prefer to clean up a mess than make one." She paused, contemplating a noodle on the end of her fork. "You know, I also think I prefer weather that's too cold to too hot. What about you, Milt?"

Milt's expression was completely despairing. "Huh?"

"Do you prefer your weather too cold or too hot? Or, let's put it this way—if you could, would you go to Canada or Mexico?"

"Why?" he asked tonelessly,

"This is just *dinner conversation,*" she said, a little exasperation creeping into her voice. "Everyone should know how to make small talk. Small talk's got a bad rap. If you could see the way some of the more bashful guests suffer sitting next to each other at one of the banquets my friend Carol caters, you'd understand the virtues of being capable of superficial conversation." She put down her fork and wiped her fingers on her napkin before laying a hand on Milt's arm. "Milt, this is *your* civilization, the one *you* have to live in, and you have *got* to get civilized."

"Okay," he said, "okay, okay, anything you say, whatever you like, lady. Just take me back to jail so I can plead guilty, pay my debt to society, and when I get out, I'll go get civilized."

"Well, *that's* the *good* news," my mother said brightly. "I was going to save it for after dinner, but I'm really impressed with those beds. The shoplifting charges have been dropped."

His mouth fell open. A very unoriginal reaction, but at least it was harmless. "How?"

My mother spread her arms. "How do you think?" She leaned toward him, beaming like mad. "You have a job! With Busy Hands!" She grabbed both his hands in hers and gave them a little shake. "You passed the audition! You aced the try-out! You made the team! But you know, I really thought you would." She turned to me without letting go of him. "Lynn? Dissenting opinion? Comments?"

I was still holding the gun on him while I ate. "You know

me, Ma. I bow to your superior judgment. Do you have a uniform that will fit him?"

"No," he said, snatching his hands away. "I won't do it. Blow my brains all over this kitchen if you want, but I won't do it. I won't be no crazy lady's slave. You can chain me up in the cellar, you can lock me in your attic, you can kill me. But I know my rights, and you're violating them. Ain't no way you can kidnap somebody from jail and make them be a slave for you."

"How do you kidnap somebody from jail?" I said. "Ma, do you know?"

"No, I don't." She chuckled. "Kidnapping's illegal. I've got all the official papers and everything—they signed him over to me, and he went of his own free will. What's the matter, Milt, housework got you down? I know you won't believe this, but it's actually easier to clean somebody else's house than your own. That's why this place looked the way it did, before you went to work on it. Tomorrow, you can do the windows and take care of the draperies, there's the laundry—"

"No! Didn't you hear me, lady? I said, no! That's capital N, capital O, N-O, no!" He gave me a frightened look, as if he expected me to shoot him for that.

"You're just tired," my mother said, picking up her fork again. "You'll feel better after a good night's sleep. Always works for me—I used to feel this way after slaving all day for Lynn's father, and then he'd come home drunk, mess everything up—" She tucked some stroganoff into her mouth and chewed thoughtfully. "I just had to get a system, you know. Work with a system, and you can conquer the world. And I really thought Lynn's father had finally gotten his mind right at last. You know, we did have to chain him in the cellar for a while. That was awful, even with the soundproofing. But he was doing so well and then—" She shrugged. "Well, we salvaged what we could, and there's no use crying over spilled stroganoff. Such as he is. I must say he's not half as gamy as I thought he'd

147

be for the age he was." My mother twiddled her fork in the noodles. "You're much younger. You've got a chance now. Go with it, hon. I really would cry over spilled Milt."

He looked down at the stroganoff and turned almost as white as my mother's uniform.

"May I be excused?" I said, wiping my mouth. "I've got some stuff I'd like to do and obviously I haven't been able to get to it today."

"Go ahead. Milt will clean up. A week's training here," she added to him, "and then you can wear the uniform. Have a good six-month probationary period, and I'll let you ride up front with me in the van, where Lynn's father used to sit. *Lynn!*"

I paused in the doorway. "What?"

She held out her hand and snapped her fingers. "The *gun,* silly."

I'd carried it off without thinking. And, of course, that was when Milt finally made his move. But he wasn't thinking either; he just lunged at my mother, and she smacked him right in the mouth with the heel of her other hand, knocking him off the chair onto the floor. When I left, she was dabbing at his split lip with a napkin, holding the barrel of the gun under his chin. I resisted a joke about crying over split Milt.

Upstairs in my room, I fired up the computer, turned on the modem, and got into the police computer. That was one of the few things I had learned that my mother hadn't taught me—in fact, I think it was the only thing she herself couldn't actually do. I tried to show her how once, but she just couldn't get it. Couldn't *hack* it was the way she put it, and she didn't even understand why I laughed when she said it.

Fortunately, the police still hadn't run Milt's prints, so I fingered some stuff around to fix it so that they never would. In a town of this size, there's very little urgency to run someone's prints—nobody expects someone on the Ten Most Wanted list to turn up on a shoplifting charge. My mother would say they were just lazy, good thing for us. Perhaps she was right, but I preferred to think that it was more like maybe the police were closing one eye and working with the Busy Hands system. There are lots of police families on my mother's client list, and you can practically eat off their floors.

I suppose it was cold, but I couldn't bring myself to feel particularly bad about my father. He'd never been a very good father; if he had, my mother would have given him a little more latitude. I took care of his records while I was in the police computer—Carol would appreciate the favor—and then downloaded the arrest reports for the day. My mother wouldn't be going out to the jail again for a while, but it's always good to keep current. And who knew but that Carol might have another rush job to fulfill? She would appreciate that favor, too.

And she'd remember all these little favors I did her, so when I turned eighteen, she'd back me up when I finally went to my mother and told her how I felt. I mean, Busy Hands is a wonderful service, and I'm very proud of the way my mother started it with nothing and built it into the fine operation it is today. But the fact is, I really, *really* hate housework, even when someone else is doing it. It's just so *boring*.

But I think I've developed a real taste for the catering business.

Black Velvet

by Maggie Flinn

One of the great pleasures of being an editor is to be able to encourage and publish new writers. Maggie Flinn's first published story, "50 More Ways to Improve Your Orgasm," was published in *Isaac Asimov's Science Fiction Magazine* early in 1992. "Black Velvet" is her second story. In addition to embarking on a promising writing career, Flinn is a rheumatologist and is on the faculty of Boston University School of Medicine—which probably explains why her description of medical conventions is so convincing. She grew up in Box Car Town, Pennsylvania, and now lives in Newton, Massachusetts.

"Black Velvet" is a subtle science fiction story of love and loss and guilt.

BLACK VELVET

Maggie Flinn

I wore black velvet that day. I think I look best in black. A sheath of a dress, just kissing the top of my knees, with buttons straight down the back. With a black velvet coat, a trapeze coat the sales lady called it. It flared out from the shoulders, draping a wide circle just above the hem of the dress. I couldn't wait to dance in it, his arms underneath the coat, finding the buttons, holding me. He said there'd be music at the wedding, to wear my dancing shoes. But I'm getting ahead of myself.

It started about two years ago. I'd met him a few times before, though. I remember the first time, working a convention. I'd been hired by one of the drug companies to do booth illustrations at various medical and surgical conventions. I'd been freelancing for a couple of years already, and this was one of my best contracts. I'd show up at eight at the advertising booth and draw life-size anatomically correct bits of bodies. An arthritic spine or an ulcerated stomach, sometimes a nice nude muscled torso or even a whole body. Drawing time would be one to two hours, three to five days for an adorable sum of money. The conventions were scheduled several years in advance. It was money and travel I could count on.

I was used to being asked for the drawings. That was when I first found out how cheap doctors really are. Each morning there would always be a couple of them. They say something nice at first, flattering. How beautiful my work is. And then, "So, if I come by at the end of the day, do you suppose I could have one? I mean, if you're going to throw them away that is." Or some variation of the same theme. I used to be nice and refer them to the people running the booth. Sometimes I say, "Sure, if you'll give me and my entire extended family free medical care for the rest of our natural born days." That usually works. Plus, I like the facial expressions that follow. This convention I'd tried something new. I pretended to be deaf. It wasn't quite as satisfying but it was definitely less aggravating on the whole. But this guy, he started to sign and I lost it. At first I giggled a bit, but he seemed so serious I broke down laughing.

"I can hear you just fine, but I'm afraid I don't understand sign language," I admitted, turning away from the half-finished sketch of a bony pelvis.

"I'm sorry," he said, "but the drug rep said you were deaf, and I wanted to ask you about your work. I had a roommate years ago who taught me a little sign language. I thought it was worth a try," he explained.

"Sorry, it was just pretense," I explained. "Fewer interruptions that way. The sooner I finish, the sooner I'm out of here."

He looked like he was about to apologize but didn't. He just stood there looking down at me, then at the drawings, then back at me. I noticed his eyes the most, so blue they were almost violet. And his moustache, streaked with a touch of grey. He didn't look old enough to have grey on his face.

"So, what were you trying to ask, anyway?" I asked, not knowing what else to do with the silence as he kept looking.

"How much?"

"Excuse me?"

"How much do you charge for one of these? I'd love to have one, but I figure I probably can't afford one."

I laughed.

"That much, huh?"

"No, not at all. It's just you're the first one who's ever asked to buy one—at a conference that is. It seems everyone else wants me to give them away."

"You're kidding," he said. To his credit, he seemed genuinely surprised.

"So, how much for the pelvis you're doing?" he continued.

We settled on a figure; I don't remember how much but it was more than I expected and probably less than I could have gotten, or so he later insisted. And we made the arrangements. He said it'd be better if I got it framed for him. I was to call him when it was done, and he handed me his business card. Then he started.

"Where have you been all my life?" he asked, widening his grin.

"Philadelphia," I said, reaching for more charcoal. I tried to concentrate on the sketch.

"Tell me this doesn't mean what I think it means," he said, taking my left hand in his.

"When you work with charcoal, you get dirty hands," I explained, deliberately misunderstanding him.

"The ring. Tell me you're not married."

"Sorry. I guess it means what you think. Eight years ago this July."

"Well, at least you have the decency to apologize for it. I finally meet the woman of my dreams. Talented, gorgeous, dirty hands and she's married. Why, god, why?" he moaned to the ceiling, two stories above us.

I was getting a bit nervous at this point. I'd received my fair share of compliments in my lifetime, but nothing like this. It seemed to me that people were staring, sideways of course, but staring. The drawings were supposed to be the attraction at the booth, not me. This was too sweet a job to risk. I smiled graciously, thanked him for the compliments, and told him I'd call when his picture was framed and ready for delivery. I explained how I really did have to get back to work, and surely he had to go to his meetings or the poster sessions or something. I knew I was mumbling, but he just bowed, smiled, and then blew me a kiss. I watched him walk away. The way his hips moved, I guess you'd say I watched him saunter away. From behind, they looked almost as good as his eyes. He was almost around the corner and out of view before I noticed the bulge at the base of his skull, just above his shirt collar.

I finished the picture carefully but quickly and went for coffee. I remember looking at his card while I drank the coffee. Robert Chamberlin, Ph.D., Paranormal Psychology. Well, that explained the bulge at the back of his head, the unmistakable sign of a Megson Implant. What the hell was someone with biomechanically enhanced paranormal abilities doing at an arthritis conference? I actually had a heart palpitation when I read the Philadelphia address. I blamed it on too much caffeine. The coffee at the hospitality suite was wonderful at that conference. I'd had a cup of cappuccino earlier before I'd started to work. This one was half coffee, half steamed milk, the whole thing flavored with hazelnut syrup. I didn't know anyplace in Philadelphia that made coffee like they did at that conference in Seattle. It had to be the caffeine that made my happily married heart dance like that.

I didn't see him again at that conference. Two weeks later, back home I didn't call him as I'd said I would but messengered over the completed sketch. I'd had it mounted in a sleek charcoal-colored steel frame, a few shades darker than the mat. Mean and modern. He sent the check by return mail, no note, just a check.

The next time was almost a year later in San Francisco. I was drawing a hip prosthesis. I didn't really like working the orthopedic conventions. Mostly I guess because I didn't like drawing devices as much as I did real parts, homegrown parts I called them to myself. The annual orthopedic meetings were also too big, running close to ten thousand doctors. How could anybody stand being around so many of them all at once? I almost felt sorry for them myself. And then, there he was.

"How's your sign language coming these days?" he asked from behind me as I was finishing the femoral shaft component to complete the last of the morning's work.

If I'd turned around any faster, I wouldn't have been able to stop before I'd made a complete circle and a complete fool of myself. I remember saying something real brilliant like "Oh, hi." I recognized him of course, even without the moustache. His grin was as big and beautiful in San Francisco as it had been in Seattle. He was also just as tall. I came up somewhere halfway between his navel and his armpits.

He didn't say anything else at first but took both my grimy hands in his, turned them palms down, and looked them over.

"Still married?" he asked, his eyes meeting mine.

"Still married," I affirmed, smiling more than was proper. I had given up coffee six months ago; but I was having palpitations again.

"Is your husband with you this trip?"

"No. Someone has to stay home with the kids," I explained, trying for some kind of barricade to hide behind.

"Good, then you're free to come have coffee with me."

"I don't drink coffee," I said, feeling stupider by the second.

"But I do," he insisted. "Besides, I want to hear about your kids and your work and what you've been doing this last year, and then you can explain to me how the sexiest woman I've ever met could possibly be already married."

So, sue me. I went with him. He had coffee, three cups of coffee. It was nearly eleven and I'd skipped breakfast, so I ordered herbal tea and two muffins. That was when I was still trying to acquire a taste for things that were supposed to be good for me. I told him about the twins and my husband the accountant. He told me I had bedroom eyes and a figure that would inspire an arsonist. I still haven't figured that last one out, but maybe it was how he said it. I told him about my years in and out of art school, and he asked me to fly to Barbados with him. We could catch a flight and be making love on the sand by midnight. I told him about my contract with the drug company that got me out of Philadelphia at least once a month, sometimes more. And how I had two more days at this convention to draw. He looked wistful and said he had to go. He was an invited speaker, something about his theory on why some people develop chronic pain. I remember asking him then why he attended conferences so far outside his field. He didn't really give me any more details then, but he did ask if he could walk me back to my hotel room before his talk, and we said goodbye at the elevators. He said he'd look for me later. I went to my room and changed my underwear.

I remember staring at myself in the bathroom mirror. It was one of those fancy hotels with a bathroom bigger than my living room at home, with lights all around. I ran the basin full of warm water as I tried to read which of the half dozen little identically shaped plastic bottles, perched so prettily in the calico lined basket, contained liquid soap as opposed to hair conditioner or bath oil. I finally settled on the boxed soap to clean my drenched panties. The face that stared back at me was my own, all right. It was what I was thinking, not what I was feeling, that was so out of the ordinary for me that I must have been expecting some visible difference. Fear and lust ought to look different, but there wasn't any change, not that I could see. I gathered up a few more bits of lingerie and dropped them in to soak. They didn't sink completely, so I stirred them under with my hands. I spent a few useless minutes trying to gouge the charcoal from under my nails before I lost all composure.

Grabbing my jacket, I headed out of the room, out of the hotel, away from the convention center. The jacket wasn't really warm enough for a November afternoon in San Francisco, but I walked all the way to Ghirardelli Square. I took an inside seat at the café and ordered solace in the form of hot chocolate with extra whipped cream. I didn't need the calories or the cholesterol, and for all I knew, I'd feel so guilty indulging myself I'd bring on a migraine. But what the hell, this situation was going to give me one hell of a headache anyway. I was married, I loved my husband and my kids, and I hadn't felt like this since I was fourteen and watched *Gone With the Wind* for the first time. And the guy had an Implant for god's sake; I knew better.

I left the square and hailed a cab after trying unsuccessfully to browse pleasantly through the stores. I spent the rest of the day watching the buffalo in Golden Gate Park. I stayed until it was too cold and dark to keep from being scared, so I found another cab and went back to the hotel.

The message light was on in the room, and there were flowers there that hadn't been there when I'd left. Yellow roses, it looked like more than a dozen, but I didn't stop to count before I read the card. It was an invitation. Dinner at eight, I'll pick you up, no blue jeans. It was signed Robert. I actually kissed the card before I replaced it in its envelope. I called the desk for messages; there was only one. The clerk apologized and said he hoped I would understand it, but the note he'd been handed just said "please" and was unsigned. But it was a tall guy with blue eyes who'd left it, if that was of any help.

I hung up the phone and began to work on my nails with a vengeance. Twenty minutes later, give or take a few, I was showered and almost ready. Ivory silk blouse with the french cuffs and gold cuff links, open one button too many to be professional. Black wool crepe skirt almost too short, sheer black hose and black suede heels. I left the matching jacket in the closet. It was the same outfit, with variations and replacements, that I'd been traveling with for several years. I reasoned it could take me from the few mandatory meetings with the drug company's people to dinner with an old friend who happened to live in a city I was drawing in. Like a good scout, I remember thinking, always prepared, as I looked at myself in the mirror. The unavoidable decision once again, to leave my hair down over my shoulders or to pin it up. I opted for what I hoped was sophisticated and gathered it up, twisted and clipped it in place. I loosened a few strands around my face, inserted my great grandmother's crystal and jet earrings, applied my lipstick, and was ready. For what, I wondered.

Better not to wonder about it, I thought as I checked my watch. A few minutes past seven. I called my husband, to save me, maybe; I don't know. He wanted to know why I hadn't called earlier; didn't I remember the time change? It was past ten o'clock, past his bedtime, I thought. The boys were fine, but I should have called when they were still up, he complained. When he started asking me about some charges on the MasterCard statement that had come in my absence, I said I had to go. He asked where? To dinner. With whom? Some of the people from the drug company, I told him. Oh. I asked him to kiss the boys for me and told him that I loved him and hung up.

According to my watch, it was still only a few minutes past seven. I left the room anyway and a message at the desk that I could be found in the hotel bar. I ordered a drink, Southern Comfort, no ice. I was still old-fashioned enough to believe that alcohol could steady my nerves. If this wasn't a date, I didn't know what was. I'd never liked dates anyway. I think that was one of the biggest reasons I got married. I wouldn't have to go through what I was now going through. The waiter slid up just as Robert entered the room.

He paused for a minute in the doorway. He was quite a sight standing there silhouetted in the lobby lights. But even his eyes needed time to adjust to the relative darkness of the bar. He smiled when he saw me; I remember that. He motioned to the waiter to stay as he crossed the room and then sent him on his way with an order for tonic and lime.

He paused for a moment before sitting and looked at me. He started at my head and slowly looked down and around the small table separating us until he reached my feet, and then his eyes moved more slowly back up, retracing the path they'd just taken.

"You look absolutely stunning," he said, his eyes meeting mine.

I stammered some kind of thank you and insisted that he sit down as I stared at my nails. It was either then, or maybe a few seconds later, that I knew for sure that I was in serious trouble. He could have taken my hand and led me right upstairs then and there, but he didn't. Instead he took my hand and talked to me.

"You're blushing," he said. "Don't tell me you're not used to compliments. Just what kind of a brute of a husband do you have?"

"I'm not blushing, and even if I were, it's too dark to see in here," I insisted. Brilliant repartee I thought, mentally kicking myself.

"The candle here is enough to see you by. Besides, why else would you avert your head in just that fashion, casting your eyes decorously downward?"

I looked up at him. "Now you're making fun of me?"

"I had to say something to get you to look at me, didn't I? But make fun of you, never."

He suddenly looked very serious. And then he changed the subject, sort of.

"It's my occupation, you know. I'm supposed to pick up on responses and not just rely on the subtleties of body language and nervous system discharges. What kind of parapsychologist would I be if I couldn't judge someone's response to a compliment in a darkened room?"

At a loss for an acceptable answer, I shrugged my shoulders and raised my eyebrows. I think I made some sort of vague gesture with one of my hands as well.

"Now you see that means you agree I'd be a lousy parashrink if I hadn't known you were blushing, but you don't want to agree with me that you were blushing, so you keep your mouth shut because you want to believe that I am good at what I do."

I had to laugh; the guy was good, and at more than one thing, or so it was beginning to look. And then I began to blush again, and then we both laughed.

"I like to get the business of my work out of the way right up front," he said as we both calmed down a bit as the waiter brought over his tonic and lime.

"I don't understand what you mean?"

"My being a parashrink, a paranormal psychotherapist."

"So, you read minds, I paint pictures," I said as lightly and gaily as possible.

"That's just it; I don't read minds. I think you know that."

"I do know that. It was a joke. Don't ask me to explain it, but it was a joke."

He smiled thinly.

"That much I figured out. For the record," he added, "I don't read minds. My implant allows me access to emotions and feelings not accessible by standard processing or input."

"Don't worry," I interrupted. "Even in art school we had to be screened. They told us all about you. That you are really just equipped with extra senses, other than ours. Instead of only hearing and seeing and tasting and all that, the Megson Implant accesses other brain areas. And Megson won the Nobel Prize for proving what Gypsies and fortune tellers have known for centuries. That psychic or paranormal abilities do exist, at least in some people, and can be exploited." I probably sounded snide, but I was feeling a bit on the defensive.

"And then she and her daughter developed the Megson Implant that enhances pre-existing paranormal abilities, and you found yourself a job," I added for good measure, when I realized he was staring.

"They screened you in art school?"

"Why should that surprise you? Doesn't the government want to know about anyone with any paranormal potential? Where else would they get more of you guys from?"

"I don't work for the government anymore," he said. "Besides, some things ought to be sacred, don't you think? Like beautiful women, beautiful women with artistic talents, for example."

I think I blushed again at that point but stayed with the subject.

"Anyone with latent paranormal abilities got plucked for the minimum two years government service; at least those who applied for assistance got screened. I didn't have the money up front, so I got screened like everyone else applying for government grants. I got lucky; I got just the money."

"You got a complete green light? No latency in any areas?"

"No, none," I replied. That was the truth. They hadn't found any. They'd tried hard enough all right, but I'd tried harder. That was when I'd learned that practice really did make perfect. "Why so surprised? What are the statistics now? Only one in a thousand or something have any real potential, right?"

"Something like that. But your headaches, with your headaches I'd have suspected something."

"How did you know—"

"It hurts now doesn't it?" he interrupted.

It had been throbbing on the right side steadily since the second sip of Southern Comfort.

I nodded in agreement.

"Part of my job, sensing these things, remember?" he said kindly. "Let me help," he said, extending his hands towards my temples.

"No, thanks," I said a little too quickly as I searched through my bag for the tiny inhaler. Finding it, I gave myself two quick puffs. A few seconds later the pulsing pain began receding.

"You still use medication? You haven't had release therapy?" he asked.

"Refractory case," I tried to explain. "They tried, even after I tested non-latent. They told me then that release therapy wasn't very effective in non-latents. Besides, the old-fashioned vasoconstrictors work pretty well," I said, indicating the inhaler I was replacing in my bag.

"I don't believe it," he said stubbornly.

"Don't believe what?"

"That you've no latent paranormal abilities. It goes against my whole theory."

"Your whole theory? Your whole theory of what?"

"Chronic pain. That patients with chronic pain without any apparent physical reason are actually experiencing the pain felt by others with actual physical abnormalities. For example, take low back pain. It's my belief that patients with chronic low back pain but normal physical exams and normal imaging studies are actually experiencing the pain via a psychic transference from individuals with actual anatomical disease such as tumors or herniated disks or the like."

"But I don't have chronic pain. I just get headaches. That's all. It's no big deal, really."

"I disagree," he said emphatically. "Headaches are one form of chronic pain. If you can identify and learn to control your paranormal abilities, your brain can begin to function more properly, and you shouldn't get the headaches anymore."

"I told you, I haven't any paranormal abilities. I just get headaches, you know, too much stress or something, that's all," I insisted.

"No, I don't think so. Somewhere someone's got a brain tumor or their head's just been split open, and you're on the psychic receiving end, so to speak."

"Doesn't make sense to me," I argued.

"Sure it does. Besides, it would explain why release therapy is so successful, particularly in latents. Bring latent paranormal abilities to the surface, bring them under conscious control, and the patient's somatic symptoms would resolve. Release the abilities, and the patient is released from their troubles. It it weren't for the proven value of release therapy, I don't think anyone would take my ideas about chronic pain seriously. And it was the effectiveness of the use of Megson Implants in release therapy that led to their widespread use in psychotherapy and other areas."

"If the patient didn't die during treatment," I added, interrupting his lecture. It was an interesting theory all right, but we were not dealing with one of my favorite topics. I remember trying to think of some way out of the conversation.

"Now, that almost never happens anymore," he went on. "Not since the Implant output modulation problem was fixed."

"After how many thousands of brains were pureed into squash?"

"You're right; I shouldn't have been so cavalier about it. I guess I just get tired of defending what I do all the time."

He looked so sincere, I stopped my attack.

"So, why don't we change the subject then?" I suggested. "Shall we adjourn for dinner and argue about something else?"

He agreed with the first suggestion but declined the second. We ate at some little bistro off the waterfront. It had red and white checked tablecloths and candles stuck in real glass wine bottles and wonderful sourdough bread. They served real butter with no extra charge. We didn't argue again that evening. We talked all about the cities we'd been in and which hotels we'd liked the best. Seems he attended several conferences a year in various medical specialties, anywhere they invited him to speak on his theory of the paranormal transfer of pain, he called it. But mostly we flirted. I mean we really flirted. I think I was downright seductive; I know for sure he was.

In the cab home he put his arms around me and kissed me, long and deep and sweet. I kissed back until I almost lost control and somehow began to pull away. I protested that if he didn't stop, I couldn't be responsible for myself, or something equally juvenile. I claimed I was married and wanted to stay that way. And he stopped. He did walk me to the hotel elevator and kissed me lightly on the cheek and thanked me for a wonderful evening. He didn't say a word about any next time.

I was back in my room before I even realized I didn't even know where he was staying. I called the front desk; he wasn't staying there. Do you know how many hotels there are in San Francisco? I didn't find one that had a Robert Chamberlin registered, but then I gave up after about the first dozen calls. I felt too stupid. I mean what if I'd found him. Then I'd have to decide something. I took his card out of my credit packet and stared at it till my head started to throb again.

Three days later I was home again. He hadn't called; there were no more flowers or messages. My husband was home when I got in; the twins were asleep. Maybe I got my coat off before I had his pants unzipped; I'm not sure.

The very next day I stopped by Robert's office. That's what he liked to be called, not Bob or Rob or anything. I didn't even have an excuse to explain my presence to his receptionist. I asked him if the doctor was available. What a question. He told me he'd be out of town until the following Monday. I declined to leave my name and number. I didn't even know if he was married or not. I just knew I had to see him again, Implant or no

Implant. Hell, I'd managed to keep my secrets from the experts; surely I could handle him.

It was a long few days. I waited outside his office Monday afternoon, and when he was leaving for the evening, I strolled over ever so casually and said, "Hi."

"Hi, yourself," he said with a wonderful smile.

"Can we go somewhere and talk?" I asked.

"How about my place?" he answered. So, he probably wasn't married.

His apartment was awful. He had a dog, and the dog had hair that was everywhere. But I don't think I noticed any of that then. We weren't even fully in the door before I melted into his arms. We were still both fully clothed when he asked me if I was sure.

"Of what?"

"That you really want to have an affair?"

I didn't have an answer for that. Instead, I asked him if he was married. Somehow it mattered to me. He said no, he wasn't even involved with anyone right then, but there was this relatively recent breakup he was still having some trouble with. Whatever that meant. Then I asked him if he wanted to have an affair. All this curled up together on a couch, panting heavily.

"Absolutely," he said. "But you're the one taking the risks, not me. Take your time; think it over. Call me in a week." And then he got up from the couch. He was actually smiling as he wrote down his home number and gave it to me.

I muttered something about an aerobics class and left. I didn't finish the class. Near the end I left and phoned.

"Do I have to wait a week, or can I come back over now?"

"Come back over now," he answered and hung up. I called my husband and told him I'd be working late at the studio and would he kiss the boys goodnight for me. I promised not to be too late.

And that was how it started. Did I feel guilty? Not then.

Later, that night. I didn't expect my viscera to feel quite so much like Chernobyl when I saw my husband. But I got over it; aside from a few minor meltdowns, I think I kept the guilt under control. And not having a phone in the studio worked out very well. I'd say I was working late, which I very often really did do, and then I never had to worry about getting called. Or checked on. We even had one weekend together at a conference where I drew and he spoke. It was in Chicago. It's the only time I've ever liked Chicago.

It was about three months along before he asked me if I loved my husband. I told the truth and said yes. And we talked about marriage and kids and families. He said he thought if I wasn't married, we'd have a wonderful future together *but*. It was a big "but" as I remember. That was when I learned he'd started seeing someone else. It seems he was feeling the urge to settle down. Since our relationship didn't fit smoothly into his view of the future he'd been designing, he'd been looking elsewhere. He claimed that it was something that happened to men his age. If he was ever going to have a family, he wanted to get started. He called it exploring other options. I took it in stride, at first at least. He was real hard to argue with. He still told me he loved me, that I was the sexiest person on the face of the earth. And when I was with him, he made me believe it.

And I tried to believe that she didn't matter. I kept telling myself that she didn't matter. But she did. Looking back, I'm not sure which happened first. He fell more in love with her, or I slipped up and he started to suspect. I think both happened at just about the same time, about another three months after he'd told me about her for the first time. We were in his apartment, and he'd told me that we wouldn't be able to meet freely there anymore because she was moving in. He'd warned me that it was probably going to happen. Oh, we could still see each other all right, just not there.

I didn't even cry. I figured we still had the studio, and I

could get a couch or something. We were getting ready to go out and he couldn't find his keys and that's when I made my mistake. I told him where they were. In his jacket pocket, outside left. Just like that. I hadn't made such a slip in so long, I couldn't remember. He looked at me kind of funny, but didn't say anything. I almost tried to explain it away, like I'd seen him put them there or something, but I thought it'd only raise more suspicion.

He did begin to suspect after that; at least he acted suspicious. He started bugging me about the headaches. And suggesting therapists for me. He even said he'd take me as a patient himself, even though it could be construed as unethical. I declined and became more careful. Let him think I'm hiding a little ability. So maybe I could find things that were lost, big deal. Let him think that somehow I managed to get through the screening procedures, without anyone catching on. After all, I really had been certified as nonlatent. It hadn't been easy, but I'd done it.

I'd heard what happened to people who had real abilities. I knew what had happened to my father. Daddy was picked by the government early. Before they fixed the Implant output modulation problem. He was tucked away in a VA hospital for seven years before his body caught up with his brain and managed to die.

He'd first explained it to me when I was about six, before any of Megson's work was being taken seriously. We were at the railway station; I think it was Grand Central Station in New York, but that part I'm not really sure about. I asked him why only one of the destination signs had such a pretty golden glow to it. He said people who got migraine headaches often saw such things but it was better not to tell anyone. I remember telling him I didn't have a headache. He said I would when I got older.

The next morning he showed me the newspaper. I couldn't read very well yet but there was a big picture of two crumpled trains, a head-on collision. Then he tried to explain about seeing the halo. And how important it was to never let anyone know about the halos or do anything at all about them. No matter what. He called it our secret. At first I was proud of it and was angry that he wouldn't let me tell anyone, not even Mother. He tried to explain that people don't want to know that other people might be able to know when or how they might die. I remember asking him if I could see when I was going to die, and he told me he didn't think it worked that way. Things only glowed about other people, not ourselves. At six, I didn't understand, but I kept the secret. By the time I was twelve, I think I had a glimmer of how sound my father's advice was. By then I knew enough not to let on about how I could find things that were lost or what the final game score was going to be. To this day, I don't understand why he failed to take his own advice. He actually volunteered for some of the original clinical trials exploring the applications of Megson's work. Maybe that was how the government found him so quickly. I never did know for sure how much they found out about his abilities.

But I kept my promise to him and kept our secret and kept on having an affair. But it wasn't the same, at least not after she'd actually moved in. I couldn't call him anymore, couldn't send him anything, not even a card. He said even the office really wasn't safe because she'd drop in unexpectedly. But we still had my studio, and I'd gotten a lovely futon with an imported silk Japanese mattress cover. We still saw a lot of each other. He called more often, still said he loved me, constantly and repeatedly. He even asked me to leave my husband, twice. Once I even thought he was serious. I said no, of course. And he kept bugging me about the headaches; he hadn't stopped wondering.

Then after one rare and particularly nasty argument over something I can't even remember now, he told me that she suspected. Suspected what, I asked. That he was seeing someone else. I think he picked a bar on purpose. He could have told me privately, but, no, he picked a public bar. Hell, I could throw a scene better in front of a public audience than anything I could manage in private. But I didn't. I stayed in control.

Leaning across the wide booth table as best I could, I asked him what exactly she'd said.

"Well, she didn't really say anything in so many words," he admitted, not meeting my eyes.

"Just what did she say?" I demanded.

"That she sensed a distance between us, that something was wrong."

"That's all?"

"Isn't that enough?"

I wanted to say no, not for me; it wasn't anywhere near enough. But I didn't. To this day I don't know why. Maybe I was sensing rejection, that he was loving her more and more and therefore me less and less. Or maybe I just came to my senses.

"So we'll stop. Sleeping with each other, I mean." The bastard agreed much too fast. Oh, we talked it out more all right. We must have spent at least three more hours in the bar. I even cried a little. It was like hammering out a treaty. We'd still see each other; after all he insisted he still loved me as much as ever, but we'd behave ourselves. No sex. Hugs and greeting kisses, but no sex.

I took that in stride as well. And still, we saw a lot of each other. We stayed lovers, without making love. I know that makes no sense, but that's what we did. We were trying to become just friends, but I still wanted him so badly I'm not sure that it was ever possible.

We were still working at it about a month later when he told me they were getting married. Soon. I told myself lots of things then. That it was much safer if he got married. That he deserved what I already had, a loving spouse, wonderful children, too many bills and fights over finances. The list went on and on. I even told him I was glad. We only saw each other a couple of times after that, and I remained civil and reasonable and promised to go to the wedding.

My husband went with me. I'd introduced Robert as someone I'd met at one of the conferences months before, and it seemed to work. I had other close male friends. My husband was not an unreasonable man. We had a good time. Not great, but good. The weather was lousy, and she looked too pretty. He laughed when I told him I'd bought the black velvet outfit. I insisted that it was only partially symbolic, that really I looked best in black. I promised not to wear a big red *A* over my chest. He'd laughed at that, too. I hardly cried at all during the ceremony. And the trapeze coat really did swing beautifully when we danced.

I never thought about it when he asked if we could drive them to the airport. They were off to Jamaica for their honeymoon. We'd gotten a sitter for the twins anyway, so we saw them off. We should have just left them at the curb, but my husband insisted on parking the car and escorting them in. The Philadelphia airport had just finished renovating all the information monitors. Lovely linear displays, green on black. Except for Flight 109 to Kingston which glowed. It glowed so brightly I couldn't read the information above and below it.

Robert looked at me as I said goodbye.

"Headache?" he asked.

"Just a bit."

"You've got to let me help you with those when we get back," he said smiling but concerned.

"When you get back," I repeated.

We all shook hands and kissed goodbye, and I walked away with my husband.

I kept telling myself that I had no way of knowing he wasn't a government agent. That's what I'd told myself the whole way home. That he was really a government agent and it was a trap to catch me. I knew it couldn't be true. It was a stupid, ridiculous idea, but I kept saying it over and over again in my head. When that didn't work, I told myself I'd promised never to try and change what had to happen. I'd promised my dad; hell, I'd promised myself I'd never act on halos.

By the time we got home, news of the explosion had already made TV. The boys had the screen on when we returned. You could see lots of smoke and parts of the plane and fire trucks. There must have been ambulances, but we didn't see them.

I wore the same black velvet to the funeral. I went alone. My husband said something about it being difficult to get away from the office, and I didn't argue. I was a bit overdressed for the occasion, but then so was she. I wouldn't have thought there were enough pieces of her left for an open casket, but they had her wedding veil down over her face so you couldn't see much anyway. And a bouquet of white lilies where her hands would have been.

Later that day I stopped at the hospital. I lied and told Robert that she'd looked beautiful and at peace. I assured him everyone knew that he'd wanted to be there but couldn't. He told me the doctors said he'd be transferring over to a rehabilitation unit by the end of the week, that he could expect a full recovery. Those were the words the doctors used, he said. He'll even be able to access his Implant within a few weeks.

He told me he felt guilty lying there in the hospital when so many had died. He'd been in the bathroom when the bomb exploded. She'd been strapped in her seat way up front. The reports were calling it a miracle that the plane stayed sufficiently intact to land. The flight crew was probably going to get some kind of medal for meritorious service under extreme duress or something. No one was even claiming credit for the bomb. There was speculation that someone had made a mistake and put it on the wrong flight. I didn't think any of that was going to make Robert feel better.

I told him it was probably normal to feel guilty even though it wasn't his fault. I told him how I'd read that survivors, and that's what he was, a survivor, often felt guilty. He just looked sad when he told me that he knew all that. Knowing it didn't help, he said. I kept telling him that there wasn't anyway he could have known. No one could have known exactly what was going to happen. I must have told him that a dozen times that afternoon, maybe more. Since no one knew, no one should feel guilty. I guess I'll probably be saying it again. And again and again. Maybe even enough to find out the truth to the old adage. Tell a lie often enough, and you might even get to believe it yourself. Now that would be real nice.

One Small Step for Max

by Dan Simmons

Born in Peoria, Illinois, Dan Simmons now lives in Colorado. His first published story appeared in *Twilight Zone Magazine,* as co-winner of the first *Twilight Zone Magazine* short story contest in 1982. His second published story, "Eyes I Dare Not Meet in Dreams" (*Omni,* Sept. 1982), was one of the first stories I bought for *Omni* as fiction editor. The story has since been transformed into the novel *The Hollow Man,* recently published by Bantam. Simmons' first novel, *Song of Kali,* won the World Fantasy Award in 1986; his second novel, *Carrion Comfort,* won the Bram Stoker Award in 1991; and his science fiction novel *Hyperion* won the Hugo Award for 1991. In addition to *The Hollow Man,* Simmons has another novel currently out, *Children of the Night,* about post-Ceausescu Romania and the plight of the orphans there. *Omni* has published several of his stories, including the novelette that eventually became *Carrion Comfort,* his epic novel on vampirism; "E Ticket to Namland;" and, most recently, the chilling "Two Minutes Forty-Five Seconds" (April 1988). These, and most of Simmons' other short stories, are collected in *Prayers to Broken Stones* (Bantam).

In "One Small Step for Max," published here for the first time, Simmons reveals his nasty sense of humor.

ONE SMALL STEP FOR MAX

Dan Simmons

On the day that Max Kine first set foot on the moon, he had larceny on his mind, Interpol on his tail, and six gel-wrapped diamonds in his lower intestinal tract.

The landing at Matsushita City in Crater Moltke was uneventful, and Customs was cursory. The lunie behind the counter asked Max whether he had anything to declare, slashed chalk across Max's suitcase, and waved him on. Max stood in line waiting for the maglev train into the city. "*Merde*," he muttered, "swallowed the goddamn rocks for nothing."

"What was that?" asked a startled Eurodame in line behind him. She wore a designer VR suit, but the blinking green diode on her peeper implants showed that she was tuned to realtime. She had a Berlin accent and that waxy, about-to-explode-from-tension skin that came from too many cosmetic bone moldings.

Max turned his brightest, most sincere smile on her. "I was just saying, Madam, that the word is that one can find some striking moonrocks in that gift shop for next to nothing."

The Eurodame scowled at him until a limo door irised open for her. The magtrain floated in a moment later. Max stowed his luggage under his seat and watched the rocky plain of Mare Tranquillitatis slide by as he levitated his way toward Matsushita

City past billboards announcing that there were only one hundred days left until the Gala 75th Anniversary of the First Lunar Landing.

The Tranquillity Oberoi Sheraton accepted the imprint of his counterfeit universal card and Max checked into an above-ground suite, ordered up dinner and a bottle of FasLax, and waited to retrieve his stolen diamonds. The stones were his last resort—a currency for bribes that had saved his life and liberty more than once. Max had met few officials who could not be bought off with diamonds in a time of hyperinflation.

The way Max figured it, he had four days in which to score here on the moon. After that, the wife of the missing South African merchant whom Max'd left in a flashback parlor in Riyadh—the merchant whom he'd left grinning and drooling his way through Strange Loop recyclings of his first sexual encounter—would get Max's postcard, retrieve her spouse, and call the cops. Max thought of what five days of constant flashback Strange Looping would do to the human brain and sincerely hoped that Mrs. South African Merchant had a vegetable garden big enough to stow her hubby with his intellectual peers.

Four days to make a big score. Max pondered his options. With most crooks who had grown up in the New Age Global Co-Prosperity Sphere, crime was a subtle, almost cerebral thing; white collar embezzlement by breeding new tapeworms to chew their way down the sphere credit streams, or complicated Virtual Reality scams, or the occasional counterfeit universal card. Not so with Max. He had grown up in the Detroit Badlands, a hive slum which had known neither the New Age nor Co-Prosperity. During the Nipponese Reconstruction of the U.S.A., the new masters had decided that Detroit in general and the Badlands in specific were not worth reconstructing.

Various judges and personality-reconfiguration therapists had said the same thing about young Max Kine.

Max had always preferred direct action in an age of pissant nuance. Despite the fact that Max was a small man, almost gaunt in a whipcord way, his specialties had been in armed robbery, extortion, and kidnapping. Most North Hem hive cops, with their doctorates in VR sleuthing and Gibsonian matrix detection, did not know how to cope with Max's type of one-man Neanderthal crime wave. Neither did his victims. By the time his kidnap victim's spouse and/or significant other had shelled out the ransom—always in negotiable merchandise, never credit—Max was long gone. Now approaching forty years of age, Max could still boast that he had served no time since he was sixteen.

But things and people were catching up to him. His modus operandi was too well known, his haunts too well established now that he had used up most of the great cities of the North Hem. And Max hated traveling the Second World with its insane, nonprofitable violence and its cyberprick VR crazies.

So Max Kine needed one more large score before retiring, and the only place left with rich pickings was the moon. Most professional criminals were afraid of operating on the moon, afraid of the pioneer justice reputed to be the lunies' swift response to even the most modest criminal act. Most professional criminals avoided the moon. But not Max Kine. Now, waiting for his diamonds, he sat in his luxury suite's WC, stared out through the crack in the door at the huge crystal chandelier in his main suite, and read his Oberoi Sheraton Traveler's Information booklet in hopes of finding some detail that would lead to his Big Score.

Americans had been the first to land on the moon almost seventy-five years earlier—this was one of the few facts that Max knew about the place—but almost a half century of eager American, EuroFed, and Russ Republic attempts at returning and colonizing had amounted to didley squat. A few rundown Quonset-hut research bases still lay scattered across the Mare like pimples on the moon's big, pale behind. The old Russ observatory complex sat empty in Karpinsky Crater on the far side. Not much to show for fifty years and several hundred billion old bucks.

Then the Nipponese had grown interested in the moon. Not for science—the rate of return on pure science was pitiful—but in the tourist and recreational aspects of lunar colonization. In a world jaded by VR and flashback drugs and total access to almost anywhere, the moon seemed a logical place to extend the luxury resort philosophy of the Nipponese underwater Pacific resorts and the Mt. Erebus condos. Within five years of that decision, the moon's population had gone from eighteen hundred forgotten researchers to more than a hundred and ninety thousand workers. Five years after that, the population was at twenty-five million and climbing. Tourists liked the place. VR could simulate the one-sixth gravity, and the flash of sunlight off the escarpments of Hyginus Rill during the three-day sunrise, and even the shouts and echoes at the Clarke Center Icarus Caves where tourists flew on feathered wings, but any hive dolehead could access VR . . . only the relatively well-to-do could go mooning and bring back the homemade holodisks to prove it.

At least it was true that the moon used to be a resort for the rich. Max scanned the tourist attractions. Lunaland Disney north in Mare Nectaris. The Honeymoon Grotto in The Sea of Fertility. Tranquillity Base Museum. The Bay of Rainbows Designer Outlet Discount Center. The Icarus Caves. The Sony-Tycho Pleasure Dome.

Merde, thought Max. Well, he'd just have to stick to the high-rent districts and find his Big Score there.

Four days.

Max retrieved his diamonds, polished them, dragged a table to the center of the main room, and set the diamonds in with the crystal prisms of the chandelier. Pushing the table back in place, Max frowned up at his hiding place. Usually he preferred having his diamonds within immediate reach; sometimes the authorities got surly if the bribe wasn't immediately visible and tangible.

Max considered hiding the diamonds behind a painting or within the hem of the curtains covering the fake window, but then he remembered the light gravity that had him moving in clumsy lopes, as if he were underwater. Crouching, Max coiled and jumped. He almost smashed his skull against the ceiling four meters above him. Pushing off from the ceiling, Max twisted, managed to avoid smashing into the chandelier, tinkled the crystal as he dropped in slow motion, and landed gently on his feet.

No problem retrieving the stupid things, thought Max. He stood looking at the chandelier and thinking that he might need the diamonds to bribe his way off this stupid chunk of airless rock if he didn't score in the next four days.

Four days.

On his second day on the moon, Max took the most expensive Sea of Tranquillity tour offered. He hated tours. They were for suckers and deeb feebs. *Rich* suckers and deeb feebs. Targets.

Besides, Max knew that he had to get the lay of the land. Robbery and kidnapping, his two central sources of income, required a careful knowledge of access and egress. Max was not a stickler for details—details tended to bore him—but when it came to his work, he usually paid attention.

The tour gave a fast overview of luxury recreation spots in half a dozen crater cities in Tranquillity basin: the Central Peak tidal pools in Torricelli, the Zen Gnostic meditation caves above Lamont, the botanic gardens in Maskelyne, the Sosigenas Spa, the Sabine-Ritter Links with eight kilometers of Jack Nicklaus low-g golf course, and the Arago Heights Extinct Species Safari. It was all bullshit to Max, but before the morning was half over he had chosen his victim.

It was the nosy Eurodame from Customs. She had exchanged her chic Tosada-Venturi VR suit for silk travel khakis, but her peeper diodes were blinking and Max was sure that she was enjoying the tour on every level VR could offer. She was old and traveling alone, and every time she flashed her platinum universal card, Max had images of the payoff from worried nephews and nieces back in Berlin.

It looked as if the snatch and disposal of the old lady would be easy enough—security appeared to be a joke with the lunies, and spacesuits and rovers were rentable if one wanted to get outside the city domes—but what about delivery of the ransom? Max had no intention of being stuck on the moon forever.

The tour was over and Max was swimming in the hotel pool when he saw a familiar face. Usually recognition was something that he would avoid at all costs, but in this case the face belonged to a woman he had known and lived with years before. She had even helped him with a Toronto credit heist before running away with an old accomplice of his.

She had not seen him as she walked through the pool area with her head down. Max pulled on a robe and followed. He noticed that she was wearing the green and blue outfit of an Oberoi employee.

Max followed her down a service dropshaft deep into the residential hive tunnels. The only illumination here was filtered sunlight through the occasional fiberoptic sun bundle. She did not look back before palming a door and entering her cubby. Max knocked and stared into the cheap watchdog lens, refusing to answer its queries, waiting for her to check the monitor. When she opened the door to let him in, she was also in a bathrobe, obviously ready to take a shower. Her eyes looked tired.

"Max. My God." She stepped back to let him into the four-by-six-meter efficiency.

"Swoozie." He jammed his hands in his pockets and

paced the length of the room. "How you doing, Babe?"

She shrugged and tugged her robe tighter. She looked twenty years older than when he had last seen her four years ago. "What do you want, Max?"

It was his turn to shrug. "Flashback maybe? We could tune into Toronto, sixty-five. Share a trip."

"I don't do F any more," she said. There was a bitter edge to her voice.

"How about some full-tactile VR, Swooz? Compatible alphas. For old times' sake?"

"I can't afford it, Max." She twitched her smile again and popped a standard inhaler. "The hardware, I mean," she added.

"I could never afford you."

Max plopped onto a padded bench. "Scotch then?"

She shook her head again. "What do you *want*, Max?"

"Why don't you start by telling me why you dumped me for Wild Bill."

She squeezed the lapels of her robe together. "He was decent to me and you weren't. Next question."

"What are you doing here, kid?"

"I work in the recycling vats in the Sheraton bio galleys." Her eyes were almost blank as they turned in his direction. "One more question, Max, and then I'm telling the watchdog to call the cops if you don't leave."

Max smiled at her. "Don't you want to know what I'm doing here, Swooz? What the past few years have been like for me?"

"No."

His smile faded. "All right, last question. Where's that miserable fuck Bill? He took half of my share from the Toronto job."

Her mouth twitched again. "Bill's in the Matsushita lunies' loony bin. A padded cave about three hundred meters beneath here. He's been there drooling and wetting himself for almost three years now."

Max frowned. "Why? What happened?"

"Your questions are all used up, Max." She reached for the door panel, but he grabbed her wrist and waited.

"Bill tried a simple Gibsonian matrix scam," said Swoozie. "Just moving a few credit blocks around. Harmless white collar stuff. No victims."

"And?" said Max, still gripping her wrist.

"And it worked for a few months. Then they caught him and put him in a Dante Suit."

"Dante Suit?" said Max. "Like those VR suits the Shining Path Vindicators used before joining the Sphere? The pain-giving thing?"

"Exactly," whispered Swoozie. "Let go of my arm before I scream."

Max released her. "Why would that drive Wild Bill nuts? He could take pain. I remember the time that street punk used a welding laser on Bill's arm in Detroit when   we...."

"This isn't just pain," whispered the woman, "it's pure pain. And they have all sorts of settings...crushed kneecap, dental extractions, pins in the eyeballs...and they gave Bill three days' worth of it."

"Still...," said Max, more to himself than to Swoozie.

"*Goodbye,* Max," she said and palmed open the door.

He reached for her, but she set her finger on the watchdog panel. He stepped into the corridor.

"Whatever you're planning," she said, "it's probably stupid and brutal and short-sighted. Just like you."

Max opened his mouth to answer, but the door had slid shut in his face. He walked back to the dropshaft whistling softly, his hands in the pockets of his robe. She was still crazy about him. He could tell. After his big score, he'd have her up to his suite for some flashback and introduce her to old times.

* * *

The next day he followed the Eurodame, Ms. Erma Schell of the clone dynasty Schells, as she visited Tranquillity Base Museum and the Lunar Landing Monument. There, half an hour into the tour, he forgot about her completely and found his Big Score.

The museum was way the hell out in the boonies, accessible only by tour shuttle. Besides the concession stand and the museum proper—a dark space filled with old spacesuits, photographs of some grinning 20th Century rocket yahoos, a yacking holo of some old astronaut yutz with thinning gray hair and a quirky smile—there was the Lunar Landing Monument itself.

Max's interest in all this ancient history stuff was zero–zero. But as he followed Ms. Schell into the circular perspex torus of the monument, things began falling into place.

A recorded voice was droning, "Here, on July twentieth, nineteen sixty-nine, men from the planet Earth first set foot on the moon. They came in peace for all mankind. First down the ladder of the landing module was Astronaut Neil Armstrong. . . ."

Max quit tailing his old Eurodame and walked over to the clear wall. Ten meters out on the bare lunar soil, protected only by a forcefield canopy overhead to keep micrometeorites from further degrading the ship and landing site, squatted the descent stage of the ancient and ungainly lunar lander. An old-style U.S. flag still leaned stiff and cockeyed away from where the ascent stage exhaust had almost knocked it over almost seventy-five years earlier. There was junk strewn around the open area—gold foil, bits of plastic, a camera knocked from an open bay on the lander, a lanyard, scraps of unrecognizable debris—but a spotlight illuminated the single item that caught and held Max Kine's gaze.

"This footprint," the voice was droning, "represents humanity's first step from the cradle of planet Earth. Its value to the lunar community . . . and to all mankind . . . is beyond estimation. Protected and preserved here by the harsh vacuum of the moon, Neil Armstrong's first giant step for mankind may last another billion years . . . ."

The bullshit spiel went on, but Max was no longer listening. He was staring, and the intensity of his stare, if observed, might have reminded the observer of a raptor's hungry gaze. And Max was smiling. Broadly.

It took Max less than a day to case the place. Information was free on the comnets. In two days he had visited the museum and monument three more times, twice wandering into restricted areas. Security guards intercepted him, but they bought his story of searching for the restrooms.

"Security guards" was too strong a term in Max's estimation. During the hours the museum was open—eighteen hours of the arbitrary twenty-four hour "day" the lunies kept in operation for the tourists' comfort—there were six rent-a-cop farts on duty. During the off-hours, just four guards and a handful of maintenance people. There was a central guard station, but it consisted of nothing more than video monitors that showed the interior halls of the museum and monument torus. The guards were armed with old-fashioned Malaysian-style stun wands.

Max turned his attention to access and egress. The former was a cinch; every resort rented rocket cars, moon buggies, and hoppers. The last was Max's choice: a sort of bicycle rocket thingee with thrusters and struts and—as far as he could tell— almost absolute exemption from any traffic control. The lunies were civil libertarians to the point of callousness. If guests wanted to kill themselves, fine. The hopper couldn't get enough altitude to get into the main transport lanes and the simple computer on board was just smart enough to avoid collisions with mountain peaks or other hoppers and to get the dumb tourist back to where he started from. Which took care of the egress.

Perfect, thought Max.

Max could rent a hopper in Matsushita City after dinner, be down at the Tranquillity Museum in less than an hour, do what had to be done while the museum was closed to tourists, and be back in his suite before the maid came in to turn down the sheets. *Perfect.*

Max studied maps and decided on the best place to stow what he would steal. There was an arroyo with a set of small caves about thirty klicks northeast of Tranquillity Base, far off any beaten tourist track.

The hoppers were not pressurized, so Max spent part of his third day renting a spacesuit and receiving instruction. The suit was idiot-proof: 36 hours of rebreathable air, self-sealing, computerized with its own simple navigation system, food slots in the helmet, and a Dr. Denton flap behind for a simple waste extractor.

Forty minutes into the lesson, Max grew restless. The instructor was droning on about getting lost. "If separated or the navigation computer were to fail—a near impossibility—don't worry about being found. The rescuers will find you. Each suit . . . ." Max keyed off his comm. He had no intention of getting lost.

The morning of his fourth day, Max took his rented suit and rented hopper out onto the Mare and practiced. First he found a gully far from prying eyes and stomped around a bit, leaving footprints in the soil. They seemed about the same depth and consistency as the one at Tranquillity Base. Then Max experimented.

He had brought a variety of tools and spray cans: trowels, shovels, plaster of Paris, fixative, flowfoam aerosols, boxes. It took almost two hours to find the right combination, but finally he was adept at digging around the footprint, spraying the cast into rigidity, loading it carefully in a flowfoam box, and tucking it into the saddlebag on the hopper. The whole process took less than eight minutes.

Max went back to the hotel and had a fine meal. Then he went up to his room, disassembled his Nikon imager, reassembled four of the flash components into a Colt deathwand, and velcroed it onto his black jumpsuit. The bottom of his camera bag came apart, and he removed a micro-thin layer of C-4-2 polymer explosive. Six microchips in the Nikon's focus system clicked out to serve as detonators.

Max sat on the edge of the bed for a minute. It was his opinion that two billion dollars would be about right for this ransom. Not in credit, but in black market new bucks. He would wait a while before even announcing his demands from the safety of Earth—from one of the Fiji archipelago states perhaps. He thought he would let the panic build for a week or two after he headed Earthside, then get in touch via his usual traceproof one-pad back channels. The money could be shipped to an offshore bank, transported by mule cutouts, and would have to be in Max's hands before he commed up directions for their little search teams. No harm done. Set for life.

Max stretched and looked at himself in the mirror. Then he went down to his rented hopper and flew south.

There were only four of the lunie-style personal rocket cars in the Tranquillity Museum parking lot. Max had come in from the north, skimming along only two meters above the rocks and craters, the shadow of his hopper and spacesuit bobbing over dusty boulders and looking like a clumsy doll stuck in a flying bedstead.

He jinked the hopper's controls and set down on the roof of the museum. Hopping off his bicycle seat, Max pulled the deathwand from his spacesuit pocket, set it on widest dispersal, and walked the length of the building, spraying down through the roof. He did the same for the observation torus around the Apollo landing site. There was no defense against a deathwand; anything inside the structure which had a synaptic system more complicated than a grasshopper's was dead.

The spraying had taken less than a minute.

Max pulled C-4-2 from his spacesuit pocket, tore off a piece, molded it into a lump, coded the detonator for 20 seconds, and moved back to the hopper while the explosive blew off a ventilator access cover and three layers of pressure seal. He stayed back while the atmosphere geysered out of the museum, littering the rooftop and surrounding area in a cloud of detritus: papers, loose office crud, a spacesuit glove from an open exhibit, cups . . . even a set of dentures.

Max checked his suit chronometer. Less than three minutes had elapsed since he had landed on the roof. He grabbed his bag of equipment from the saddlebag and dropped easily down the ventilator shaft, kicking open the remaining grills. Max landed in a corridor where loose garbage still stirred in the last wisps of escaping atmosphere, oriented himself quickly, and went to the guard station. The three security guards were in no condition to challenge him. Max was only slightly interested in the bubbling and boiling going on—he had never seen the effects of explosive decompression on a corpse before—but he wasted no more than a glance at the phenomenon before stepping across them and checking the security panels. Max Kine was an expert at security panels.

The museum computer had closed airtight doors throughout the complex. Max opened them with a manual override. He also turned off the polarizing forcefield above the landing site monument. Alarm diodes and holos were flashing, and Max assumed that he would hear bells and voices if there were atmosphere in the room, but a quick scan showed him that there had been no automatic radio calls for help. The computer was desperately trying to alert security people or others in the complex, but it had no program to call anyone else in the first five minutes of a disaster. Max checked his suit chronometer. Four minutes and eight seconds had elapsed.

Max lobotmized the security computer and bounced down the hallways toward the observation torus. He found the fourth guard in the central corridor and noticed several bodies through open office doors along the way—at least five men and three women—but it wasn't this fault if these stupid administrators and maintenance people had come in to work at the wrong time. Truth be told, Max Kine had never considered *anything* to be his fault.

There were no bodies in the torus. Max took only a second to stare out at the Apollo historical site; then he set his second wad of C-4-2 shaped charge against the perspex window and blew an almost perfectly round hole in it. Max stepped through and bounced lightly across the lunar surface. Dust rose in slow, one-sixth-g arcs as he trod across the historical footprints.

For a second Max considered taking the flag as well, but then decided not to vary from the script. On a whim, he tugged the cockeyed flagstaff out of the gray soil and launched it like a javelin. The wire-stiffened plastic flag messed up the trajectory and the whole thing tumbled clumsily out of sight over the torus roof.

No more goofing around, Max warned himself.

It was not hard finding Armstrong's first footprint; the laser spot still illuminated it in a golden glow. Max opened his bag and bent to his task. Trowels, spade, fixative, flowfoam. The whole thing took less than five minutes.

Max transferred the flowfoam container to his bag, tossed his tools in, bounced back across the regolith, and leaped easily to the roof of the torus and then to the top of the museum. He stowed everything in his saddlebag, tweaked the handlebar controls, and went skimming off a meter above Mare Tranquillitatis. The emergency and police channels were as silent as the tomb he had just left.

In the arroyo thirty klicks northeast along a low rill that ran out from a crater rim, Max parked his hopper on solid rock in an ink-black shadow and began the transfer of the bag. He had already slid everything back into a crevice when curiosity got the better of him and he removed the flowfoam container, cracked the seal, and peered in for one last glance at Neil Armstrong's immortal footstep, the legacy of the human race that was to outlast humanity itself.

His gloves slipped on the edge of the flowfoam and he made too quick a motion to catch the container before it fell. The flowfoam stopped, but the rigid cast and footstep inside slid out with almost frictionless grace, did three slow revolutions just beyond Max's flailing gloves, and smashed into a thousand globs of dust and shattered plaster against a sharp-edged boulder.

"Oops," said Max.

For a moment he could only lean against the boulder and concentrate on not throwing up in his space helmet. Then a thought struck him and he brightened up considerably.

He didn't need the footstep! The ransom was the thing; once he had that, let the lunies go diddle themselves.

Max slumped back against the boulder in a new wave of discouragement. The lunies were famous for their frontier justice but even more famous for their pragmatism. If they got their footprint back, they probably wouldn't bear the expense and effort of sending their hit teams to Earth. But if they paid the ransom and got nothing . . . .

Merde, thought Max. *All this over a stupid footprint just like a million other footprints in the dust up here. . . .*

Max grinned behind his polarized visor, bounced down the rocky slope to a dusty bit of Mare, stomped around a bit, chose the cleanest footstep, and then did his magic with fixative and flowfoam. He took the newly preserved footstep, sealed it away, and slid the bag back in the same crevice he had chosen earlier. Then he fired up the hopper and brought it down to the dust below to let its exhaust scatter any other footsteps he had left there.

He turned in his hopper and suit to a bored attendant behind the rental counter and was back in his suite before the maid had come in to turn down his sheets and set a chocolate mint on his pillow.

One thing, he thought before dropping off to sleep. *I'll have to deal with little Swoozie before I leave on the Earthbound shuttle in the morning. She doesn't know anything, but she knows me.* No problem. He had returned the components for the deathwand to the Nikon. He'd use it once more and then dump the pieces before boarding the shuttle.

They burst in less than half an hour later—at least a dozen goons—clubbed Max senseless even before he had time to sit up and dragged him out in his silk pajamas. His toenails made slight scraping noises on the tiled floors. They dragged a chair to the center of the suite, slapped him into it, and continued to pummel him even while other men were setting up equipment around him.

He came to just as they were fitting the black and red Dante Suit over his naked body.

"Trial?" managed Max between pulped and swollen lips.

"Fuck the trial," said the big lunie with a wild red beard and forearms bigger than Max's thighs. "We know you done it." The man grinned through his beard. "Besides, I'm the judge."

"Proof?" rasped Max through the stubs of his teeth.

"Should've listened to your spacesuit instructor," said the huge bald man who was wrestling the suit's headpiece over Max's face.

"Instructor?" Max's attention was suddenly diverted by a glimpse of the settings on the control box that was the nexus for filaments running from the greasy-feeling Dante Suit. The words on the rheostat started at CRUSHED TESTICLES, worked their way up through SCREWDRIVER IN EYEBALL, and quickly escalated to phrases and images that Max's mind did not want to accept. "Spacesuit instructor?" he said a second before they drove the VR peeper filaments directly and painfully into his right optic nerve.

During the brief interlude before he began screaming for the rest of his natural life, Max heard the bald man say, "Spacesuit instructor. Yeah. If you'd listened you would've heard him tell you that every spacesuit boot has a barcode engraved on the sole so's we can identify and track you if you get lost. The ones back at Tranquillity Base weren't perfect, but they led us to the suit and hopper rental. We just backtracked the hopper's navigation memory. The footprint you left us in the bag back at the arroyo was perfect."

Max started to say something else—something clever and legally irrefutable and salvation-winning—but the Dante Suit had stitched his lips shut. He screamed anyway. The cry echoed in his skull.

Dimly, through the nausea of panic, Max heard the red-bearded judge say, ". . . and sentence you to the rest of your natural life in this suit. May God have mercy on your putrid soul. Go ahead, Charlie, crank 'er up."

The diamonds! thought Max with a surge of relief that made him giddy. They had thrown him into a chair directly beneath the chandelier. The Dante Suit was wrapped around his entire body now, like some clinging parasite, but his arms and hands were still free. A simple vertical leap in the one-sixth gravity would take him to the ceiling, and before they could grab him, he would have the diamonds in his hands, the bribe offered.

Coiling with the superhuman strength of absolute desperation, Max leaped for his life.

But Max was tightly wrapped in the Dante Suit, the Dante Suit was connected to the console of instruments by a dozen short cables, and two of the stocky lunies grabbed the console as Max jumped.

The Dante Suit cables were made of high-tensile carbon-carbon conducting filament. They would not have snapped if a thousand Maxes had pulled at them in a full one-gee field. They did not break now. The heavy console did not budge a centimeter. Max rose a little more than a meter and a half to the end of the cables' reach, bounced back to his chair like a wayward balloon being tugged down by an irate child, and screamed silently as the lunies tethered him in place, threw the switch, and spun the rheostat up.

All in all, it was one puny leap for Max Kine.

The Cave Painting

by Garry Kilworth

Garry Kilworth was born in England. He has lived and worked in Africa, Asia, and the Middle East. He and his wife have recently returned to Sussex, England, after spending three years in Hong Kong. He is the author of several adult and young adult novels including *Theatre of Timesmiths, Witchwater Country, The Abandonatti, The Foxes of Firstdark,* and *The Drowners* and of the short story collection, *The Songbirds of Pain.* He has been a regular contributor to *Omni* since 1985 when we published "The Songbirds of Pain." His most recent *Omni* story was "In the Country of Tattooed Men" (Sept. 1990), and it will be the title of an upcoming collection to be published by Edgewood Press. Kilworth is another writer whose fiction roams seemingly without effort between the boundaries of science fiction, fantasy, and mainstream. Yet even his mainstream fiction has a peculiar edge to it, which is probably what consistently attracts me to his work, whether I publish it in *Omni* or elsewhere. "The Cave Painting," a new story by Kilworth, draws the reader into his world by constructing extraordinarily realistic characters, only to "go strange" once he's hooked you. This is a technique at which Kilworth is expert.

THE CAVE PAINTING

Garry Kilworth

We had hoped to reach the cave by noon.

The long drive across the Gibson Desert had made us testy and irritable. Somewhere along the gravel road, chips of stone had shattered the windscreen of the Honda, turning it into glass hail which the wind blew into the car. Janet was cut a little around the cheeks, and Mace, who had been driving, had specks of blood like a rash of measles over his whole face. I was in the back seat and consequently escaped unhurt.

Once the screen was gone the car filled with choking red dust and the air conditioner ceased to function with any degree of efficiency. We soon got the full force of the Australian desert sun, somewhere in the region of 50 Celsius, and began to bake inside our cake tin on wheels. The lung-grabbing blast of air coming through the hole was hot and full of grit. By the time we saw the rock, Mace had gone into the sulks, and Janet stated she was ready to strangle anyone who tried to treat our situation with flippancy. This remark had followed an attempt by me to treat the episode lightly.

"I *hate* people trying to cheer me up," she grumbled.

"I'm British," I said, my tone almost apologetic; "we always make jokes when the chips are down."

She gave me another blood-and-dust glare, I suppose

wondering whether my mention of the word "chips" was alluding to the gravel that had been the cause of our present condition. Her left arm was draped along the back of Mace's seat, her fingers lightly touching his shoulder. Long black hair tumbled down to her (now dirty) white blouse and obscured most of her face as she turned to face front again and presumably stare into the billowing red dust, rolling ahead of us like the bow wave from a marine landing craft.

I studied Mace in the rearview mirror. There was no indication from his expression that he was aware of the touch of those slim fingers. I wished they were on my shoulder, not his. When Janet and I had begun our ten-month tour of Australia, we had been lovers as well as good friends. Things happen on the road, though, and now we were, as they say, just good friends.

It would be more accurate to say I was "just good friend." For my part, I still had much stronger feelings. I still wanted her, emotionally and physically, as a lover again. God, my guts ached for the touch of those fingers. She had become supremely beautiful, wondrously fascinating since we had parted. What was once taken for granted was now unattainable, and the fact that I had once had it all—love, intimate companionship, sex—made the craving that much worse. I wanted it back. I still loved her, but I didn't dare let her know it. She would have sent me away. So I maintained this minor war with her, taking ground, giving ground, remaining interested and, hopefully, still interesting.

Mace was a second generation Japanese-Australian we met on our travels. We stopped for him because he had a backpack and was obviously travelling on the cheap. Leaning in through Janet's window, he told us he'd just passed his medical exams and was celebrating by going on *walkabout*. I didn't like the way he was looking into Janet's eyes or the way she was returning that look, so I replied that if he was on *walkabout* he wouldn't need a lift in our car.

"It's just an expression," he told me, with a pained look. "It just means I've got no set destination, not that I've got to do the whole thing on foot."

"Don't mind him," Janet said, dismissing me with a flick of her head, "he's a pom."

Janet is English too, but since we'd stopped sleeping together, she was about as approachable as a Martian. We were still going through what she called our "period of adjustment," which to her meant getting rid of all those uncomfortable pieces of emotion that still surfaced during unguarded moments. As soon as she recognized one of these flimsy remnants of past love, she dealt with it ruthlessly in some way unknown to me. Her expression hardened, and she suddenly became very brisk and businesslike in whatever she had been doing when the unwelcome feeling struck. How did she do it? If she had let me in on the secret I would have gladly employed the same technique. Instead, I found myself anticipating such moments, looking for them, and (I suppose) enjoying the hurt they brought with them. Such pain is better than nothing at all.

This tall doctor with his Melbourne drawl very soon slipped into my place inside her sleeping bag. I couldn't believe how quickly it happened, and the pain was then no longer pleasurable. Janet had once told me she had to be in love with a man to sleep with him. Yet here was the first unattached guy she had met since falling out with me, and he took over as smoothly as if he had been ordained my replacement. He had come to my tent late one evening, about a month ago.

"I want you to know I intend going to bed with Janet. She's in agreement with this. Do you have any objections?"

Mace was a gentleman. He wanted what he saw, and intended to have it, but felt the need to declare war before he bombed Pearl Harbour so that there could be no accusations of sneak treachery later.

"If you've already got her permission," I tried to keep the

emotion out of my voice, "what do you need mine for? I'm not in any position to object anyway."

"You were lovers—"

"Right. Past tense."

The worst of it was, I had actually grown to like Mace. From that point on I hated his guts. I was sure I hated both of them, and I only stayed because . . . because . . . hell, I don't know why I stayed. Maybe I thought it wouldn't last, that Janet and I would drop back in together again, the way it had been before. There were these fantasies in my head, of her coming to my tent one night, weeping and saying it was no good, she couldn't do without me. Or looking into my face suddenly, in the campfire light, and no words being necessary, just putting our arms around each other, and Mace getting the message, walking away into the night with his pack without even saying goodbye.

Once, when Mace was off somewhere collecting wood, she turned to me and said, "Why didn't you object?"

"Object?"

"When Mace came to you that night."

I became very angry then.

"I don't know how to play these games," I said. "I'm a practical man. I like to know the rules first."

She smiled, not unfriendly.

"Practical man? You're a dyed in the wool romantic, Jimmy, and you know it."

And thereafter I was plagued by the thought that she had been testing the waters that night, to see if I still loved her, and I'd failed to recognize it. Should I have leapt on Mace and beaten him senseless? (Since Mace was a head taller that me, there would probably have been a very different result.) Or perhaps I should have said in a very dignified tone that I objected very much, because I was still in love with her? I don't know. The skills necessary, the nuances of a three-cornered *affaire,* were beyond me. When it came to playing the game, I was hopeless; my head spun with possibilities, none of which seemed right for me. I ended up being flat and pathetic.

Janet was right about one thing, I am a terrible romantic. There were even times when I convinced myself that although they slept in the same tent, they weren't doing anything, that Mace was still waiting for her to say yes.

So I had had a month of being the outsider, the observer. I thanked the lord that Janet was not one of those women who like canoodling in public, so I didn't have to watch them kissing and cuddling and whispering into each other's ears. The light touch on the shoulder was bad enough. Just that small show of affection was enough to turn on the flow of acid in my stomach. I suppose I still couldn't understand how she could do this thing to me: fall for the first man she saw on the road. I could go a lifetime and not find someone to replace *her.*

The rocky outcrop appeared to rush toward us, yet remain unreachable. It seemed we had been driving toward it forever. Overhead the sky was a hard brittle blue, without a cloud. I could see no signs of life, either in the air or out on the desert.

There's a lot of space on the Australian continent, and we'd been using it well. We'd been keeping away from towns, and the radio in the car had died on us, so we had little news of the outside world. The trading posts we stopped at for goods and petrol were run by thin men with faces like burned lizards: taciturn men who could spit twenty feet, but apart from that hardly opened their mouths. I had asked the last one if the civilized world was all right.

"Who the hell cares?" he snapped.

He had been one of those crusty frontiersmen who feel the place is getting crowded when someone moves into a neighboring valley. There were several like him, and they never looked unhappy to see us go, even though we were probably the only people they saw all week. Month?

I stared out of the dustcovered side window at the passing desert. I found the apparent stillness, the facelessness of the wilderness, disconcerting. Nothing appeared to have moved since it was all part of the great Gondwanaland. In Europe we expressed fears about the way the human race was reshaping the world, but out here the landscape mocked us for being ineffectual and fleeting. It had a spiritual presence that was undeniable.

To me, the desert felt like a deity, all knowing, all powerful. I wondered if anyone had ever prayed to the desert, revered it in the way that animists worship single trees and rocks. The Aborigines? As I stared out over the wasteland, I indulged in one of those banal daydreams where Janet and I were all that remained of the human race. A desert island, an Adam and Eve, a begin-again dream. Everyone has one of these mellifluous fantasies at one time or another. They're hackneyed, it's true, but then love itself is a cliché, the emotional patterns eternally repetitive.

The desire behind this well-used vision was strong enough. I suppose I prayed, to the desert, in those few moments.

Let it happen. Let it happen.

Janet's voice brought me sharply out of my reverie.

"What's the name of the place again?" I heard her yell, trying to make herself heard over the tire and engine noise.

"Wallabenga Cave," Mace shouted.

The hill which housed the cave had been suggested by Mace as an alternative to visiting Ayers Rock . . . "Everybody goes to Ayers Rock. Let's try for something different—whaddya say? There's some wall paintings in Wallabenga—a special one, I heard, not like the rest of them. . . ."

So we had driven out into the head-flattening heat of the Gibson, to brave the kraits and spiders, under a sun whose rays could probably light paper, into dust that found every crease, every fissure of our bodies. On top of that, Mace had only three

201

tapes for the car's cassette, all of them by Midnight Oil. I had to listen to *Dust and Diesel* six times a day. I used to like it.

We finally reached the rock, a sandstone crag like a natural giant cathedral, standing proud of the desert. Bas-relief formations bulged from an otherwise smooth face. There was something faintly familiar about these projections, as if they had been carved at one time into forms representing human features or perhaps the heads of animals. The whole crag looked as if it had been chiseled from a mountain somewhere else, then tossed out into the Gibson, where its contours had been worked by itinerant craftsmen. I had to admit that its red colour and projections made it look magnificent under the afternoon sun, like the burning palace of some desert king. It had the same feel about it as Petra, except that there was no city carved out of this conglomerate, only the merest suggestion of architecture running like wet paint down the walls of the cliff.

Mace switched off the car engine and then untied the handkerchief he had used as a dust filter. It left a whitish mark around his mouth in contrast to the rest of his engrimed face. He pulled a pack onto his right shoulder by one strap.

I said, "Are you taking that in the cave with you?"

"Thought it would be a good idea," he replied. "We might want to sleep in there, just for tonight. Then we can set out in the cool tomorrow, early."

"Good thinking," said Janet, grabbing her own pack.

No one ever consulted me, asked me what I thought of an idea. Once the other two had accepted something from each other, I was expected to go along, like a family pet. I wanted to argue, but I didn't. Mace was right anyway; the cave would be better than a tent or the car. I was waiting, longing for him to say something stupid, so I could tear into him and let out a little pressure, but he never did.

I took my time getting my own pack, until Janet yelled, "Jimmy, are you coming, or what?"

She had her hands on her hips, as if she were scolding a three-year-old. I stared back, noticing that she was getting a little chubby around the middle.

"You can't lay down the law with a tummy like that," I said. "You ought to lay off the boiled sweets."

She glanced down at herself, but instead of the distressed expression I was expecting, she looked up again with soft eyes. That one look startled me for a moment. Then she disappeared into the cave entrance.

I ran after the pair of them. They were waiting for me just inside. Mace had a flashlight, and he switched it on.

"The guide book says we have to keep going until we come to a cavern. We can't get lost because there's only one tunnel."

He set off, and Janet and I followed behind, in single file. After a long while I realized that while the book might have been right about there being no run-offs, it hadn't mentioned the length of the cave. We seemed to be walking for decades—or *stumbling* might be a better description—until finally I could detect a strong odor of something burning.

"What's that smell?" I said, using the opportunity to touch Janet's shoulder.

"Oil," replied Mace. "There's an old Abo who lives in here. He burns oil lamps for light. They call him the 'guardian of the painting' or something."

"Aboriginal tribesman," I stressed.

Janet said, "Don't be so prim. You think he's worried what we call him? Anyway, Mace has spent three summers with Aborigines. He's got friends amongst them, so I guess he can call them what he thinks is right."

My own reply was cut short as we entered a world glowing with yellow light. We had reached the central cavern. The three of us stepped into a great natural hall, with fluted columns on either side, and magnificent scalloped rock curtains hanging from the ceiling. There were lamps in many of the recesses, some balanced on rounded stalagmites. Our footsteps echoed as we crossed a floor worn smooth by running water. It was strange how all around this hill was a desert, while within it there was water in plenty. In the far right-hand corner of the cavern was a pool some twenty meters in diameter. We went to this and washed ourselves, getting rid of the dust and stale sweat, before exploring further.

Mace had spoken of a side chamber, which we found after a short search, inside which sat the old man who had been given the task of caretaker by his tribe. The walls and ceiling of this offshoot cavern were amazing. Not several normal-sized paintings as I had expected, but a single work covering all the available space within the large chamber, even the floor. It was dazzling—not with colour, for the usual ochres and stains had been used, but with intricate detail. A desert scene, with rocks, mountains, waterholes, and strange elongated figures, who seemed to be on a slow laborious trek across the hot sand-and-stone world of the picture. The scope of the work took my breath away. Such a painting must have taken decades to complete, and by people with such an eye for perspective that when you stared into the chamber you could have been looking down on a vast landscape from a cloud. Yet each individual stone, soak or patch of sand was evident with all its tiny markings, as if you were holding it in your hand and studying it closely. One moment I got the giddy feeling of being suspended, even flying, above a ruddled countryside worked over in places with orpiment; yet the next second I was peering at a small desert bloom from just inches away, its petals seeming to close against the fierceness of the sun.

"Wow, this is really something!" I said. "This was worth the drive."

"You're not kidding," cried Janet. "Does the old man speak English, Mace?"

"Try him," said the Australian.

The wizened round face of the dark-skinned man beamed at us. He was squatting on his haunches. There were no shoes on his feet, the skin of which looked tougher than any leather. He was wearing a red-chequered shirt, stuffed into an ancient pair of slacks.

"Speak a small bit, boss," he said, showing us a tiny space between his thumb and forefinger, and he grinned.

Janet squatted down to his level but stayed in the entrance, careful not to tread on the painting.

"What is this?" she indicated the picture with a wave of both arms.

"Him one world, boss," he replied. "This what happen outside, see? Him hare-wallabies come and put 'em here, tell us what's what."

Mace said, "The hare-wallaby people. They're a mythological race from the *Dreamtime*. He's saying they did the painting."

I interrupted.

"I've heard that some educated Aborigines object to the word *Dreamtime*. They say it's not accurate. It's supposed to be their *Genesis,* isn't it?"

"Yeah, when the world was formed by their forefathers, tribes like the carpet-snake men and hare-wallaby people— strange hybrid creatures—and the songs were made which they use as maps to find water. The animal-people were instrumental in shaping the earth, giving it form. Abos will point out striations of rocks where they say ancient battles were fought and lumps of stone that are dead ancestors."

Then Mace spoke to the old man quietly, and the old man replied in similar hushed tones.

"What's he saying?" asked Janet.

Mace said, "Just what he said before, that this painting represents the world, but I was curious. The book says that the meaning of the picture changes. It's dynamic, not static. The content remains the same of course, no one alters the painting in any way, but the interpretation varies according to what's happening in the outside world."

I asked the inevitable question.

"How does *he* know what's going on outside? I mean, we're in the middle of nowhere. . . ."

"Middle is right," replied Mace. "This chamber is supposed to be the center of the earth. Outside the cavern everything is mutable, subject to time and tide, decay, growth. In *here* things are always the same."

"I still don't understand," said Janet. "How can it reflect the outside world if it doesn't change itself?"

Mace was patient with us.

"It has to be interpreted. The changes aren't evident to us, but they are to the painting's guardian. This is a sacred trust, handed down from a tribal elder to his successor. At this time only this one man can read the picture and tell us what it means."

"But how does he *know?*" I insisted.

"He sees it in the picture," remarked Mace, losing patience at last. "What do you want me to say? I don't understand the mystique of this thing. If I did, I would be him. I only know what the book tells us."

He spoke again to the old man, who replied with a smile.

"What?" cried Janet, obviously unhappy that she couldn't be directly privy to the conversation. "Tell me!"

"I just asked him how it is with the world," laughed Mace.

"And what did he say?" said Janet.

"Fine, I suppose."

"What do you mean, you *suppose?*"

Mace shrugged. "The picture's full of calmness. Yes, I think that's the closest meaning of the words he used, 'there is a calmness over the earth.'"

Although I didn't mention it at the time, the old man might have meant "stillness": a stillness over the world. The state that is said to exist immediately before a holocaust or the fulfillment of an apocalypse. Expectation.

We decided we would sleep in the cave that night, so we went out and got the rest of the gear from the car. I took a look at the night sky while I was out there. It was all right. It seemed fine. Not that I knew much about the bottom of the globe. There were unrecognizable constellations embedded in the darkness: my familiarity with the heavens ended at the equator. This wasn't my sky, it belonged to the south lands. I could find the Southern Cross, but there my knowledge ended. The Polynesians used this sky like a dynamic chart, to navigate by, following star paths as they moved up individually from below the horizon and crossed the heavens. They could interpret the oceans too, the swells, the currents, even water temperatures, gaining navigational insights from them. I knew this for a fact. Western seamen, with their finely drawn paper charts and shiny sextants, had challenged Polynesians to navigational runs from one island to another, and had lost.

So who was I to challenge this old man, who said he could read the world in a painting? We opened a can of beans, and I took him some. He ate them with relish.

We slept uneasily that night, not for any reason but that it was an unusual bedroom. I could hear beetles, or lizards, or something, scuttling in amongst the stones, going down to the water to drink. The old man kept the lamps going too, so there was no sense of night or day. It induced insomnia in all of us. I played a game with Mace.

"What if you were to go to a planet," I said, "where everything was the opposite. Where night was actually day and day was night. *Exactly* the opposite from what we have now. A place where black men were white, and white men were black. A *negative* world. Would you know it?"

"If it was the exact opposite to this world, then it would be the same. Left-handed people using their right hands to do things, and vice versa. It would be the *same*."

"No, but things would *feel* different, because they would *be* different. You'd have a kind of *déjà vu* sensation, only not that, just a sense that something's wrong. Like when you look *out* of a mirror at yourself from the glass, and you think, 'I can't tell us apart; we look exactly the same, yet he's the real one, not me . . . I'm just two-dimensional quicksilver.'"

"When you look *out* from a mirror? Boy you are one wacky . . . ."

"Go to sleep you two," interrupted Janet, "before mamma deals a few heavy hands."

And we did manage it then, sleeping well into the day, if it was day.

We trooped over to the old man after we'd had breakfast and asked him to interpret the picture for us. He started in by showing us where the sun was, and the mountains and seas, until Mace said, yes all that was very interesting, but what was happening out there, anything special? The old man smiled and said, nothing was happening, and Mace took this to mean nothing had changed, but there's a difference. Nothing's changed means that things are going on the way they normally do, whereas nothing's happening *might* mean that, but it could also be interpreted as meaning *absolutely nothing is happening out there.*

We knew it was midday outside, so we didn't bother leaving the cavern. It would be hot, dusty, and no place for delicate skin. So we opened a pack of cards and played poker for matchsticks, then read our books, then when all was tranquil and I was deeply engrossed in my novel, Janet rolled over on her sleeping bag and said in a quiet voice that she wasn't getting fat on boiled sweets, she was having a baby.

"WHAT?" cried Mace.

I studied his expression as it went through various emotions, from horror to delight and back again, finally to settle on something between these two extremes. I couldn't see Janet's face. I just wanted to kill them both. I felt like I had a rock jammed in my windpipe.

"I'm going to be a father," Mace cried at last.

And Janet said in the same quiet voice, "No, I don't think so."

Everyone was silent after that, and I listened to the dust settling on the floor of the cavern and the microbes battling it out in my body, before I said, "Me?"

She looked up and nodded.

"I missed one before we met Mace."

"And you didn't say anything?"

"I wasn't sure; I've missed before, and anyway we weren't talking at the time. Are you angry?"

I didn't even think about it.

"No. No, not really, as long as I get to have something to do with him...her—whatever. What are you going to do now? I mean, about us?"

She rolled onto her back.

"I don't know. I'll have to think about it."

Mace said acidly, "Well *do* let us know when you've made up your mind, sweetheart."

But she had already started crying by then, and we both rushed to comfort her at once, and it got all confused, arms and arms, and bodies, and legs, until the three of us lay there in a knot, no one willing to let go, least of all me. All I knew was that I was being hugged, and it felt good. I was going to be a father! The whole world had changed its face in a split second. One moment I'd been at the bottom of a deep pit, with no hope of ever getting out. I'd been solitary, bitter, sent out into the wilderness and close to despair. Suddenly, I was back in the garden, with people touching me, *hugging* me. And I was going to have a child by the woman I loved. Just like that, without me doing anything but waiting patiently. I could've waited a million years, without anything happening, but I didn't have to. One second the world was a dark lonely place, the next a place full of light and laughter. Just like that. Just like that.

We stayed wrapped around each other for quite a while, until we heard voices coming from the cave, and then we untangled ourselves only just in time. A middle-aged couple came into the cavern, blinking, and staring around with their mouths open. Mace started giggling, and Janet and I followed, until we were all snorting and snuffling, trying to stifle our laugher in case the couple thought we were making fun of them, which we weren't.

The woman, tall and slim in a floppy hat, went in to see the old man. The male half of the pair, also hatted, came over to us.

"Sky's looking kinda red out there," he said.

"Red?" Mace repeated.

"Yeah. Sort of. Think we're in for a storm?"

Mace said, "I don't know. The book doesn't say anything about inclement weather at this time of the year. We're tourists too. That is, I'm from Melbourne, but this is my first time out here in the desert."

"Well, the sky looks kinda funny," said the man, glancing toward the picture chamber. "We're pretty far out, here. I wouldn't want to get stuck in a flash flood or anything. I'm from the U.S.—Mississippi. Place called Platten. You wouldn't have heard of it, I s'pose?"

We shook our heads.

"No. Anyway, name's Carter, like Jimmy only I'm called John. My wife's Sarah." He smiled and nodded in her direction. "I'd better see what's doin'."

I said, "My name's Jimmy. Together we make an ex-president."

He smiled. "I don't think so," he said.

As we watched him making his way over the uneven floor a ripple went through the ground. It felt like the skin of the world had just shivered. The American tottered, almost lost his balance. I found myself gripping at the wavy stone floor with my fingernails. I had a sense of falling for a moment, as if the earth were slipping away from underneath me. When I turned to look at Janet, she had a frightened expression on her face.

"What was that?" she whispered.

"Felt like an earth movement," said Mace.

"An *earthquake? Here?*" I said.

We all waited for a follow-up. John Carter was standing, looking at his feet, as if he expected something more too.

After a while nothing had happened, and we all began to relax. Sarah Carter came out of the picture chamber. She had a short conversation with her husband, who immediately left the cavern by the tunnel exit. Then she came over to us.

"Mind if I sit with you?" she said, not waiting for an answer, but settling on the hard stone next to Janet. "I'm not quite ready to go outside. It's so *hot* out there. We're going to have a picnic in here, like you. John's gone to check on our car. That was a peculiar thing, now wasn't it? That *judder?*"

"Yes it was," replied Janet.

Mace asked, "What did the Abo tell you?"

"Ab . . . ? Oh, he said lots of things. I asked him what the little figures were doing, and he said, 'Him run for rock, boss.' Why does he use that word, *boss?*"

"Just an expression. He's not being servile."

"He looks a thousand years old, especially with that grin."

Mace said rather unnecessarily, "His race is one of the oldest on the earth."

Something was bothering me, and I voiced it.

"Listen, he told you that the creatures were *running* for the rocks?"

Sarah Carter blinked hard.

"I think so. Yes, that's what he said."

I got up and walked over to the side chamber. When I had studied those figures yesterday, they had been painted as if they were struggling against tired muscles, weary bones. As if they were just managing to pull themselves along, nearing the end of a great journey and were looking forward to a long rest. There had been no suggestion of *running* in their stances.

I stood in the entrance and stared around the chamber. There was no evident change in the painting. The people in the picture were in the same positions that I'd seen before. I heaved a sigh of relief, then immediately felt very silly. What had I been expecting? That the old man had modified the painting, altered it while we slept? Or that it really was a mirror image of the outside world?

I pointed to a little group of brown-skinned people.

"Walkabout?" I suggested.

The old man shook his head.

"Him *run,* boss. Him hide."

I stared hard at the primitive two-dimensional beings. When I stepped a little closer, looking down on the figures, concentrated on them, I admitted to myself there was the possibility of fast movement, of haste. It was a matter of viewpoint. One of those tricks of perception, like staring at an Escher print and accepting that water can flow uphill. Or better still, a line drawing of a square figure. One moment it looks solid, but if you concentrate on a different perspective, it becomes hollow.

"Hide? What do they want to hide from?" I said at last.

"Nothin', boss. Him hide from the nothin'."

"*The* nothing?" Was that just the way it came out in pidgin, or did it mean the "nothing" was a frightening nonthing? A thing that was not a thing. A no thing. A negative *something.* Hell, an athletically obsessive mind like mine can do somer-

212

saults with such thoughts.

I returned to the others but kept the old man's words to myself. I wasn't sure what they meant anyway, and Mace might've made a meal out of my unease. Sarah Carter was speaking to Janet, who now looked as if she'd forgotten the tremor and was listening and chatting with an animated expression on her face. Maybe we had just had too much of each other, the three of us, and had become too internalized? Fresh company was making all the difference, putting our feet back on the ground. We talked for a good hour after that, until every one of us was taking surreptitious glances at the tunnel, waiting for Carter to make an appearance.

John Carter never came back.

Finally, Sarah Carter said, "I'd better go out and see what's the matter. Will you look after my things?" She gave Janet a rather heavy-looking crocodile skin handbag and a Pentax camera. "I'll be back in a while. John's probably looking for the drink. I put it under the front seats to keep it out of the sun."

She left the cavern.

Sarah Carter never came back.

"What's happening?" asked Janet, after a couple of hours had gone by. "Even if he'd had a heart attack or something, she would've come back for us. And what about her things?"

I said, "The old man thinks there's something going on out there. He said everyone was running and hiding from something."

Janet said, "You're scaring me, Jimmy."

Mace got up and went to the side chamber. He stayed there quite a while, talking to the old man. When he came back he looked a little shaken.

"Well?" I said.

He glanced down at Janet, who said, "Don't mind me. I'm all right now. I *want* to know what he said."

Mace squatted beside us and his words were like a line from a fairy tale. They sent a chill down my back and had my skin tingling unpleasantly, the way it had done when I was told my father had died. The same faint buzzing in my brain, too.

"He told me that there's no world out there."

Janet said in a choked voice. "What do you mean, *no world?*"

Mace looked a little angry.

"I don't know, I'm just telling you what he said. The world's gone—at least, the world as we knew it. It's changed. It's not *our* world any more."

"Crap," I said, and laughed. "Come on, folks. Lighten up a little. This place is spooking us. Screw him and his picture. He probably wants us to stay here and feed him."

It was true we had been giving the old man scraps.

Janet said a little wildly, "I'm not going out there until I know it's safe. Those people didn't come back. This bag must be worth, I don't know, it's a Gucci for Christsakes. And the camera. I don't want to put my baby at risk. . . ."

So that was it. The baby. It was probably her hormones causing the hysteria. Mace and I exchanged significant male looks. The protector surfaced in both of us.

"One of us will check first," Mace said, soothingly. "I know what you're thinking. That maybe they tested a bomb or something, in the Gibson. We'll have a look. I mean, if the air's not clean, we'll know."

"The world," she snapped. "The whole world."

Mace laughed.

"Look, to the Aborigines the 'whole world' is Australia. That *is* their world. One of us will check. . . ."

"You go, Mace. I want Jimmy to stay here. I want the father of my child *here*."

Mace's face darkened. His eyes narrowed and he ran a hand through his long black hair. I took his arm and led him aside.

"Look, she's just a bit overwrought. We've been in here too long. Go out and have a quick look; then come back in and get us. I think we should drive to a town straightaway, find a few people and get our heads back to normal."

He sighed. "Yeah, you're right, Jimmy. We're cracking up in here. I won't be a minute."

He strode toward the tunnel.

Mace never came back.

We lay in each other's arms that night, if it was night. I kept telling her that Mace had gone off in a huff, driven away, and was cooling down somewhere, feeling guilty.

"I don't think he'll abandon us, not completely. He's just punishing us for something."

"He's punishing me," she said.

After that we fell asleep.

When I woke I went to the old man. He grinned at me. I said, "Those people in the picture...," but he interrupted with, "Not *people,* boss," and when I went right up to a group of them, got down to their level by kneeling on the floor, I realized only then that they might not be human. You see what you want to see, just like when you revise a document full of errors, but miss the obvious ones time and time again. Your eyes send the *expected* messages to your brain. In fact, when I got *right* down to it, studied their outlines very closely, they were really quite weird, though the flat style of the painting had made them little more than dark shadows against the white landscape.

"The world changed?" I asked.

He nodded. "All gone, boss."

"The *whole* world? Or just Australia?"

"All things change, boss. Him different place now. Me and you, we're not here, not properly, see?"

I shook my head.

"No, I *don't* see. How the hell did it change, just like that?" and I snapped my fingers.

"S'how things happen, boss. One time this, one time that."

"Was it a bomb? A war? What then?"

He shook his head and smiled, the texture of his skin looking like a dry river bed.

"No bombs. Nothin' like that. *Dreamtime* come again. New world, see."

"The world's re-formed? What the hell are you grinning at? Aren't you scared? What about the hare-wallabies, or the poisonous snake people? Are they here? Aren't you worried about it?"

"Old man, boss," he said apologetically. "Gonna die soon, see."

I left him there and went back to Janet.

"What did he tell you?" she asked.

I made a sudden decision.

"He said it was okay to go outside now."

"Are you sure?"

I forced a smile. I was thinking that there had to be a reason for all this, and the only one I could think of was that I had prayed to the landscape, to the ancient dust and rocks, to wipe out everyone but Janet and me. And when I got it into those terms, I didn't feel guilty, I just felt stupid. It was ridiculous. I would've needed an ego a mile high to believe that anything out of my mouth could make the slightest difference to the world as a whole. Who did I think I was? No, the world was the same place we had left it. There was just something funny going on out there, that was all. Something a bit weird but with an explanation behind it. Everything has a rationale, doesn't it? Sure it does. Absolutely. The world reduced to *nothing* and then the landscape gardeners being sent in, creatures whose purpose it was to shape it again? How could I bring all that about with a single prayer? There must have been millions of prayers like it, gone before, to no effect. It was stupid. It was ridiculous.

There was something at the back of my brain that nagged at me a little, a cliché that began, "The final straw . . . ," but I suppressed it under the heavy weight of logic I had accumulated in my short lifetime.

I said, "Of course I'm sure. It's all right, really. We'll just walk out of here. I don't believe in all that crap anyway. I don't know what happened to Mr. and Mrs. Carter, but Mace is probably on his way back to us right at this minute, with a new windscreen as his excuse. I don't want to stay in here, Janet. Let's go outside and wait for him there?"

With that speech I convinced both her and myself that this whole unhealthy scene was the product of overactive imaginations. The old man had had us dancing to some strange tune. He was playing with us for reasons of his own, using his damn painting to put the fear of God in us. Well, I wasn't having any more of that. We were getting out of the cavern and back to sanity. I had a family to take care of.

"Let's go," I said, but before I could pull Janet to her feet, we heard voices coming from the tunnel.

"*There!*" I said, triumphantly. "It's probably the Carters."

I walked over to the tunnel and peered down it, waiting for them to come into the light. Janet followed me, staying at my shoulder. I felt an enormous sense of relief washing through me, and it was then that I realized I *had* believed, subconsciously, in the old man's words. He had been quietly persuasive: a powerful personality in a passive way. Well, we had been delivered from the nightmare. A nightmare that never really was. A return to the *Dreamtime?* It seemed so silly now, now that those voices were on their way.

Listening hard, I glanced over at the old man.

He gave me a tight smile, the equivalent of a Western

shrug.

They didn't sound like American accents. They sounded foreign: a language I couldn't recognize.

When they turned the corner, coming into the light I could see it wasn't the Carters. It wasn't anybody. Although I had seen silhouettes like them, just a short while ago, I actually didn't know *what* they were.

All I know is that as soon as we saw each other we all froze, and the air was fouled by the stink of fear.

In the Month of Athyr

by Elizabeth Hand

Elizabeth Hand has published short fiction in *Twilight Zone Magazine, Pulphouse,* and the anthology *Full Spectrum* and book reviews and criticism in *The Washington Post Book World* and *Science Fiction Eye.* She lives on the coast of Maine. Her first novel, *Winterlong,* was dreamlike, provocative, gender-bending science fiction. It was nominated for the Philip K. Dick Award. *Aestival Tide,* set in the same universe as *Winterlong,* was recently published by Bantam Spectra. A third novel in the series will be out in 1993. Hand is currently working on *Waking the Moon,* a contemporary supernatural novel.

"In the Month of Athyr" is another gender-bending story, and according to the author it was inspired by Connie Willis's classic story on male/female relationships "All My Darling Daughters." This is the first publication of this provocative novelette.

IN THE MONTH OF ATHYR

Elizabeth Hand

In the month of Athyr   Leucis fell asleep.
                                    –C.P. Cavafy, "In the Month of Athyr"

The argala came to live with them on the last day of Mestris, when Paul was fifteen. High summer, it would have been by the old Solar calendar; but in the HORUS station it was dusk, as it always was. The older boys were poring over an illustrated manual of sexual positions by the sputtering light of a lumiere filched from Father Dorothy's cache behind the galley refrigerator. Since Paul was the youngest he had been appointed to act as guard. He crouched beside the refrigerator, shivering in his pajamas, and cursed under his breath. He had always been the youngest, always would be the youngest. There had been no children born on the station since Father Dorothy arrived to be the new tutor. In a few months, Father Dorothy had converted Teichman Station's few remaining women to the Mysteries of Lysis. Father Dorothy was a *galli*, a eunuch who had made the ultimate sacrifice to the Great Mother during one of the high holy days Below. The Mysteries of Lysis was a relatively new cult. Its adherents believed that only by reversing traditional gender roles could the sexes make peace after their long centuries of open hostility. These reversals were enacted literally, often to the consternation of non-believing children and parents.

On the stations, it was easier for such unusual sects and controversial ideas to gain a toehold, and the Mysteries had made quite an impact. This was not surprising. The current ruling Ascendancy embraced a particularly repellent form of religious fundamentalism, a cunning synthesis of the more extreme elements of several popular and ancient faiths. For instance, the Ascendants encouraged female infanticide among certain populations, including the easily-monitored network of facilities that comprised the Human Orbital Research Units in Space, or HORUS. Because of recent advances in bioengineering, the Ascendants believed that women, long known to be psychologically mutable and physically unstable, might also soon be unnecessary. Thus were the heavily reviled feminist visionaries of earlier centuries unhappily vindicated. Thus the absence of girl children on Teichman, as well as the rift between the few remaining women and their husbands.

To the five young boys who were his students, Father Dorothy's devotion to the Mysteries was inspiring, if not downright terrifying. Their parents were also impressed. Since his arrival, relations between men and women had grown even more strained. Paul's mother was now a man, and his father had taken to spending most of his days in the station's neural sauna, letting its wash of endorphins slowly erode his once-fine intellect to a soft soppy blur. The argala was to change all that.

"Pathori," hissed Claude Illo, tossing an empty salt-pod at Paul's head. "Pathori, come here!"

Paul rubbed his nose and squinted. A few feet away Claude and the others, the twins Reuben and Romulus and the beautiful Ira Claire, crouched over the box of exotic poses.

"Pathori, come *here!*"

Claude's voice cracked. Ira giggled; a moment later Paul winced as he heard Claude smack him.

"I *mean* it," Claude warned. Paul sighed, flicked the salt-pod in Ira's direction and scuttled after it.

"Look at this," Claude whispered. He grabbed Paul by the neck and forced his head down until his nose was a scant inch away from the hologravures. The top image was of a woman, strictly forbidden. She was naked, which made it doubly forbidden, and with a man, and smiling. It was that smile that made the picture particularly damning; according to Father Dorothy, a woman in such a position would never enjoy being there. The woman in the gravure turned her face, tossing back hair that was long and impossibly blonde. For an instant Paul glimpsed the man sitting next to her. He was smiling too. Like the woman he had the ruddy cheeks and even teeth Paul associated with antique photographs or tapes. The figures began to move suggestively. Paul's head really *should* explode, now. He started to look away, embarrassed and aroused, when behind him Claude swore—

"—move, damn it, it's Dorothy!—"

But it was too late.

"Boys . . . ."

Father Dorothy's voice rang out, a hoarse tenor. Paul looked up and saw him, clad as always in salt-and-pepper tweeds, his long grey hair pulled back through a copper loop. "It's late; you shouldn't be here."

They were safe: Their tutor was distracted. He looked behind him, past the long sweep of the galley's gleaming equipment to where a tall figure stood in the shadows. Claude swept the box of hologravures beneath a stove and stood, kicking Paul and Ira and gesturing for the twins to follow him.

"Sorry, Father," he grunted, gazing at his feet. Beside him

Paul tried not to stare at whoever it was that stood at the end of the narrow corridor.

"Go along, then," said Father Dorothy, waving his hands in the direction of the boys' dormitory. As they hurried past him, Paul could smell the sandalwood soap Father Dorothy had specially imported from his home Below, the only luxury he allowed himself. And Paul smelled something else, something strange. The scent made him stop. He looked back and saw the figure still standing at the end of the galley, as though afraid to enter while the boys were there. Now that they seemed to be gone the figure began to walk towards Father Dorothy, picking its feet up with exaggerated delicacy. Paul stared, entranced.

"Move it, Pathori," Claude called back to him, but Paul shook his head and stayed where he was. Father Dorothy had his back to them. One hand was outstretched to the figure. Despite its size—it was taller than Paul, taller than Father Dorothy—there was something fragile and childlike about it. Thin and slightly stooped, with wispy yellow hair like feathers falling onto curved thin shoulders, frail arms crossed across its chest and legs that were so long and frail that he could see why it walked in that awkward tippy-toe manner: If it fell its legs would snap like chopsticks. It smelled like nothing else on Teichman Station, sweet and powdery and warm. Once, Paul thought, his mother had smelled like that, before she went to stay in the women's quarters. But this thing looked nothing like his mother. As he stared, it slowly lifted its face, until he could see its enormous eyes fixed on him: caramel-colored eyes threaded with gold and black, staring at him with a gaze that was utterly adoring and absolutely witless.

"Paul, come *on!*"

Ira tugged at him until he turned away and stumbled after the others to the dormitory. For a long time afterwards he lay awake, trying to ignore the laughter and muffled sounds coming from the other beds, recalling the creature's golden eyes, its walk, its smell.

At tutorial the next day Father Dorothy said nothing of finding the boys in the galley, nor did he mention his strange companion. Paul yawned behind the time-softened covers of an ancient linguistics text, waiting for Romulus to finish with the monitor so he could begin his lesson. In the front of the room, beneath flickering lamps that cast grey shadows on the dusty floor, Father Dorothy patiently went over a hermeneutics lesson with Ira, who was too stupid to follow his father into the bioengineering corps, but whose beauty and placid nature guaranteed him a place in the Izakowa priesthood on Miyako Station. Paul stared over his textbook at Ira with his corkscrew curls and dusky skin. He thought of the creature in the galley— its awkwardness, its pallor, the way it had stared at him. But mostly he tried to remember how it smelled. Because on Teichman Station—where they had been breathing the same air for seventeen years and where even the most common herbs and spices, cinnamon, garlic, pepper, were no longer imported because of the expense to the the station's dwindling group of researchers—on Teichman Station everything smelled the same. Everything smelled of despair.

"Father Dorothy."

Paul looked up. A server, one of the few that remained in working order, lurched into the little room, its wheels scraping against the door. Claude snickered and glanced sideways at Paul: The server belonged to Paul's mother, although after her conversion she had declared it shared property amongst all the station women. "Father Dorothy, KlausMaria Dalven asks that her son be sent to her quarters. She wishes to speak with him."

Father Dorothy looked up from the monitor cradled in his hand. He smiled wryly at the ancient server and looked back at Paul.

"Go ahead," he said. Ira gazed enviously as Paul shut his book and slid it into his desk, then followed the server to the women's quarters.

His mother and the other women lived at the far end of the Solar Walk, the only part of Teichman where one could see outside into space and realize that they were, indeed, orbiting the moon and not stuck in some cramped Airbus outside of New Delhi or one of the other quarantined areas Below. The server rolled along a few feet ahead of him, murmuring to itself in an earnest monotone. Paul followed, staring at his feet as a woman passed him. When he heard her leave the Walk he lifted his head and looked outside. A pale glowing smear above one end of the Walk was possibly the moon, more likely one of the station's malfunctioning satellite beacons. The windows were so streaked with dirt that for all Paul knew he might be looking at Earth, or some dingy canister of waste deployed from the galley. He paused to step over to one of the windows. A year before Claude had drawn an obscene figure in the dust along the edge, facing the men's side of the Walk. Paul grinned to himself: It was still there.

"Paul, KlausMaria Dalven asks that you come to her quarters. She wishes to speak with you," the server repeated in its droning voice. Paul sighed and turned from the window. A minute later he crossed the invisible line that separated the rest of Teichman from the women's quarters.

The air was much fresher here—his mother said that came from thinking peaceful thoughts—and the walls were painted a very deep green, which seemed an odd choice of colors but had a soothing effect nonetheless. Someone had painted stars and a crescent moon upon the arched ceiling. Paul had never seen the moon look like that, or stars. His mother explained they were images of power and not meant to resemble the dull shapes one saw on the navgrids.

"Hello, Paul," a woman called softly. Marija Kerenyi, who had briefly consorted with his father after Paul's mother had left him. Then, she had been small and pretty, soft-spoken but laughing easily. Just the sort of pliant woman Fritz Pathori liked. But in the space of a few years she had had two children, both girls. This was during an earlier phase of his father's work on the parthogenetic breeders, when human reproductive tissue was too costly to import from Below. Marija never forgave Paul's father for what happened to her daughters. She was still small and pretty, but her expression had sharpened almost to the point of cunning; her hair had grown very long and was pulled back in the same manner as Father Dorothy's. "Your mother is in the Attis Arcade."

"Um, thanks," Paul mumbled. He had half turned to leave when his mother's throaty voice echoed down the hallway. "Marija, is that him? Send him back—"

"Go ahead, Paul," Marija urged. She laughed as he hurried past her. For an instant her hand touched the top of his thigh, and he nearly stumbled as she stroked him. Her fingers flicked at his trousers, and she turned away disdainfully.

His mother stood in a doorway. "Paul, darling. Are you thirsty? Would you like some tea?"

Her voice was deeper than it had been before, *when she was really my mother,* he thought; before the hormonal injections and implants, before Father Dorothy. He still could not help but think of her as *she,* despite her masculine appearance, her throaty voice. "Or—you don't like tea, how about betel?"

"No, thanks."

She looked down at him. Her face was sharper than it had been. Her chin seemed too strong, with its blue shadows fading into her unshaven jaw. She still looked like a woman, but a distinctly mannish one. Seeing her, Paul wanted to cry.

"Nothing?" she said, then shrugged and walked inside. He followed her into the arcade.

She didn't look out of place here, as she so often had back in the family chambers. The arcade was a circular room, with a very high ceiling; his mother was very tall. Below, her family had been descended from aristocratic North Africans whose women prided themselves on their exaggerated height and the purity of their yellow eyes and ebony skin. Paul took after his father, small and fair-skinned, but with his mother's long-fingered hands and a shyness that in KlausMaria was often mistaken for *hauteur*. In their family chambers she had had to stoop, so as not to seem taller than her husband. Here she flopped back comfortably on the sand-covered floor, motioning for Paul to join her.

"Well, *I'm* having some tea. Mawu—"

That was the name she'd given the server after they'd moved to the women's quarters. While he was growing up, Paul had called it Bunny. The robot rolled into the arcade, grinding against the wall and sending up a little puff of rust. "Tea for me and my boy. Sweetened, please."

Paul stood awkwardly, looking around in vain for a chair. Finally he sat down on the floor near his mother, stretching out his legs and brushing sand from his trousers.

"So," he said, clearing his throat. "Hi."

KlausMaria smiled. *"Hi."*

They said nothing else for several minutes. Paul squirmed, trying to keep sand from seeping into his clothes. His mother sat calmly, smiling, until the server returned with tea in small soggy cups already starting to disintegrate. It hadn't been properly mixed. Sipping his, bits of powder got stuck between Paul's teeth.

"Your father has brought an argala here," KlausMaria announced. Her voice was so loud that Paul started, choking on a mouthful of tea and coughing until his eyes watered. His mother only stared at him coolly. "Yesterday. There wasn't supposed to be a drop until Athyr; god knows how he arranged it. Father Dorothy told me. They had him escort it on board, afraid of what would happen if one of the men got hold of it. A sex slave. Absolutely disgusting."

227

She leaned forward, her long beautiful fingers drumming on the floor. Specks of sand flew in all directions, stinging Paul's cheeks. "Oh," he said, trying to give the sound a rounded adult tone, regretful or disapproving. *So that's what it was,* he thought, and his heart beat faster.

"I wish to god I'd never come here," KlausMaria whispered. "I wish—"

She stopped, her voice rasping into the breathy drone of the air filters. Paul nodded, staring at the floor, letting sand run between his fingers. They sat again in silence. Finally he mumbled, "I didn't know."

His mother let her breath out in a long wheeze; it smelled of betel and bergamot-scented tea powder. "I know." She leaned close to him, her hand on his knee. For a moment it was like when he was younger, before his father had begun working on the Breeders, before Father Dorothy came. "That's why I wanted to tell you, before you heard from—well, from anyone else. Because—well, shit."

She gave a sharp laugh—a real laugh—and Paul smiled, relieved. "It's pathetic, really," she said. Her hand dropped from his knee to the floor and scooped up fistfuls of fine powder. "Here he was, this brilliant beautiful man. It's destroyed him, the work he's done. I wish you could have known him before, Below—"

She sighed again and reached for her tea, sipped it silently. "But that was before the last Ascension. Those bastards. Too late now. For your father, at least. But Paul," and she leaned forward again and took his hand. "I've made arrangements for you to go to school Below. In Tangier. My mother will pay for it; it's all taken care of. In a few months. It'll be fall then, in Tangier; it will be exciting for you. . . ."

Her voice drifted off, as though she spoke to herself or a server. "An argala. I will go mad."

She sighed and seemed to lose interest in her son, instead

staring fixedly at the sand running between her fingers. Paul waited for several more minutes, to see if anything else was forthcoming, but his mother said nothing more. Finally the boy stood, inclined his head to kiss her cheek, and turned to go.

"Paul," his mother called as he hesitated in the doorway.

He turned back: She made the gesture of blessing that the followers of Lysis affected, drawing an exaggerated *S* in the air and blinking rapidly. "Promise me you won't go near it. If he wants you to. Promise."

Paul shrugged. "Sure."

She stared at him, tightlipped. Then, "Goodbye," she said, and returned to her meditations in the arcade.

That night in the dormitory he crept to Claude's bunk while the older boy was asleep and carefully felt beneath his mattress, until he found the stack of pamphlets hidden there. The second one he pulled out was the one he wanted. He shoved the others back and fled to his bunk.

He had a nearly-new lumiere hidden under his pillow. He withdrew it and shook it until watery yellow light spilled across the pages in front of him. Poor-quality color images, but definitely taken from life. They showed creatures much like the one he had seen the night before. Some were no bigger than children, with tiny pointed breasts and enormous eyes and brilliant red mouths. Others were tall and slender as the one he had glimpsed. In one of the pictures an argala actually coupled with a naked man, but the rest showed them posing provocatively. They all had the same feathery yellow hair, the same wide mindless eyes and air of utter passivity. In some of the pictures Paul could see their wings, bedraggled and straw-colored. There was nothing even remotely sexually exciting about them.

Paul could only assume this was something he might feel differently about, someday. After all, his father had been happy with his mother once, although that of course was before Paul

229

was born, before his father began his work on the Breeders Project. The first generations of geneslaves had been developed a century earlier on Earth. Originally they had been designed to toil in the lunar colonies and on Earth's vast hydrofarms. But the reactionary gender policies of the current Ascendant administration suggested that there were other uses to which the geneslaves might be put.

Fritz Pathori had been a brilliant geneticist, with impressive ties to the present administration. Below, he had developed the prototype for the argala, a gormless creature that the Ascendants hoped would make human prostitution obsolete—though it was not the act itself the Ascendants objected to, so much as the active involvement of women. And at first the women had welcomed the argala. But that was before the femicides, before the success of the argala led Fritz Pathori to develop the first Breeders.

He had been an ethical man, once. Even now, Paul knew that it was the pressures of conscience that drove his father to the neural sauna. Because now, of course, his father could not stop the course of his research. He had tried, years before. That was how they had ended up, exiled to Teichman Station, where Pathori and his staff had for many years lived in a state of house arrest, part of the dismal constellation of space stations drifting through the heavens and falling wearily and irretrievably into madness and decay.

A shaft of light flicked through the dormitory and settled upon Paul's head. The boy dove beneath the covers, shoving the pamphlet into the crack between bedstand and mattress.

"Paul." Father Dorothy's whispered voice was surprised, shaming without being angry. The boy let his breath out and peered up at his tutor, clad in an elegant grey kimono, his long iron-colored hair unbound and falling to his shoulders. "What are you doing? What do you have there—"

His hand went unerringly to where Paul had hidden the

pamphlet. The shaft of light danced across the yellowed pages, and the pamphlet disappeared into a kimono pocket.

"Mmm." His tutor sounded upset. "Tomorrow I want to see you before class. Don't forget."

His face burning, Paul listened as the man's footsteps padded away again. A minute later he gave a muffled cry as someone jumped on top of him.

"You idiot! Now he *knows*—"

And much of the rest of the night was given over to the plebeian torments of Claude.

He knew he looked terrible the next morning, when still rubbing his eyes he shuffled into Father Dorothy's chamber.

"Oh dear." The tutor shook his head and smiled ruefully. "Not much sleep, I would imagine. Claude?"

Paul nodded.

"Would you like some coffee?"

Paul started to refuse politely, then saw that Father Dorothy had what looked like real coffee, in a small metal tin stamped with Arabic letters in gold and brown. "Yes, please," he nodded, and watched entranced as the tutor scooped the coffee into a silver salver and poured boiling water over it.

"Now then," Father Dorothy said a few minutes later. He indicated a chair, its cushions ballooning over its metal arms, and Paul sank gratefully into it, cupping his bowl of coffee. "This is all about the argala, isn't it?"

Paul sighed. "Yes."

"I thought so." Father Dorothy sipped his coffee and glanced at the gravure of Father Sofia, founder of the Mysteries, staring myopically from the curved wall. "I imagine your mother is rather distressed—?"

"I guess so. I mean, she seems angry, but she always seems angry."

Father Dorothy sighed. "This exile is particularly difficult

for a person as brilliant as your mother. And this—" he pointed
delicately at the pamphlet, sitting like an uninvited guest on a
chair of its own. "This argala must be very hard for KlausMaria
to take. I find it disturbing and rather sad, but considering your
father's part in developing these—things—my guess would be
that your mother finds it, um, *repellent*—?"

Paul was still staring at the pamphlet; it lay open at one of
the pages he hadn't yet gotten to the night before. "Uh—um, oh
yes, yes, she's pretty mad," he mumbled hastily, when he saw
Father Dorothy staring at him.

The tutor swallowed the rest of his coffee. Then he stood
and paced to the chair where the pamphlet lay, picked it up and
thumbed through it dismissively, though not without a certain
curiosity.

"You know it's not a real woman, right? That's part of
what's *wrong* with it, Paul—not what's wrong with the thing
itself, but with the act, with—well, *everything.* It's a geneslave;
it can't enter into any sort of—relations—with anyone of its own
free will. It's a—well, it's like a machine, except of course it's
alive. But it has no thoughts of its own. They're like children,
you see, only incapable of thought, or language. Although of
course we have no idea what other things they *can* do—strangle
us in our sleep or drive us mad. They're incapable of ever
learning, or loving. They can't suffer or feel pain or, well,
anything—"

Father Dorothy's face had grown red, not from embarrassment, as Paul first thought, but from anger—real fury, the boy
saw, and he sank back into his chair, a little afraid himself now.

"—institutionalized rape, it's exactly what Sofia said would
happen, why she said we should start to protect ourselves—"

Paul shook his head. "But—wouldn't it, I mean wouldn't
it be easier? For women: If they used the geneslaves, then they'd
leave the women alone. . . ."

Father Dorothy held the pamphlet open, to a picture

showing an argala with its head thrown back. His face as he turned to Paul was still angry, but disappointed now as well. And Paul realized there was something he had missed, some lesson he had failed to learn during all these years of Father Dorothy's tutelage.

"That's right," his tutor said softly. He looked down at the pamphlet between his fingers, the slightly soiled image with its gasping mouth and huge, empty eyes. Suddenly he looked sad, and Paul's eyes flickered down from Father Dorothy's face to that of the argala in the picture. It looked very little like the one he had seen, really; but suddenly he was flooded with yearning, an overwhelming desire to see it again, to touch it and breathe again that warm scent, that smell of blue water and real sand and warm flesh pressed against cool cotton. The thought of seeing it excited him, and even though he knew Father Dorothy couldn't see anything (Paul was wearing one of his father's old robes, much too too big for him), Father Dorothy must have understood, because in the next instant the pamphlet was out of sight, squirreled into a cubbyhole of his ancient steel desk.

"That's enough, then," he said roughly. And gazing at his tormented face Paul thought of what the man had done to become an initiate into the Mysteries, and he knew then that he would never be able to understand anything his tutor wanted him to learn.

"It's in there now, with your father! I saw it go in—"

Ira's face was flushed, his hair tangled from running. Claude and Paul sat together on Claude's bunk poring over another pamphlet, a temporary truce having been effected by this new shared interest.

"My father?" Paul said stupidly. He felt flushed and cross at Ira for interrupting his reverie.

"The argala! It's in there with him now. If we go we can listen at the door—everyone else is still at dinner."

Claude closed the pamphlet and slipped it beneath his pillow. He nodded, slowly, then reached out and touched Ira's curls. "Let's go, then," he said.

Fritz Pathori's quarters were on the research deck. The boys reached them by climbing the spiral stairs leading up to the second level, speaking in whispers even though there was little chance of anyone seeing them there, or caring if they did. Midway up the steps Paul could see his father's chambers, across the open area that had once held several anaglyphic sculptures. The sculptures had long since been destroyed, in one of the nearly ritualized bouts of violence that periodically swept through the station. Now his father's balcony commanded a view of a narrow concrete space, swept clean of rubble but nonetheless hung about with a vague odor of neglect and disrepair.

When they reached the hallway leading to the chief geneticist's room, the boys grew quiet.

"You never come up here?" Claude asked. For once there was no mockery in his voice.

Paul shrugged. "Sometimes. Not in a while, though."

"I'd be here all the time," Ira whispered. He looked the most impressed, stooping to rub the worn but still lush carpeting and then tilting his head to flash a quick smile at himself in the polished metal walls.

"My father is always busy," said Paul. He stopped in front of the door to his father's chambers, smooth and polished as the walls, marked only by the small onyx inlay with his father's name engraved upon it. He tried to remember the last time he'd been here—early autime, or perhaps it had been as long ago as last Mestris.

"Can you hear anything?" Claude pushed Ira aside and pressed close to the door. Paul felt a dart of alarm.

"I do," whispered Ira excitedly. "I hear them—listen—"

They crouched at the door, Paul in the middle. He *could*

hear something, very faintly. Voices: his father's, and something like an echo of it, soft and soothing. His father was groaning—Paul's heart clenched in his chest but he felt no embarrassment, nothing but a kind of icy disdain—and the other voice was cooing, an almost perfect echo of the deeper tone, but two octaves higher. Paul pressed closer to the wall, feeling the cool metal against his cheek.

For several more minutes they listened, Paul silent and impassive, Claude snickering and making jerking motions with his hands, Ira with pale blue eyes growing wide. Then suddenly it was quiet behind the door. Paul looked up, startled: There had been no terminal cries, none of the effusive sounds he had heard were associated with this sort of thing. Only a silence that was oddly furtive and sad, falling as it did upon three pairs of disappointed ears.

"What happened?" Ira looked distressed. "Are they all right?"

"Of course they're all right," Claude hissed. He started to his feet, tugging Ira after him. "They're finished, is all—come on, let's get out of here—"

Claude ran down the hall with Ira behind him. Paul remained crouched beside the door, ignoring the other boys as they waved for him to follow.

And then before he could move, the door opened. He looked up and through it and saw his father at the far end of the room, standing with his back to the door. From the spiral stairs Claude's voice echoed furiously.

Paul staggered to his feet. He was just turning to flee when something moved from the room into the hall, cutting off his view of his father, something that stood teetering on absurdly long legs, a confused expression on its face. The door slid closed behind it, and he was alone with the argala.

"Oh," he whispered, and shrank against the wall.

"*O,*" the argala murmured.

Its voice was like its scent, warm yet somehow diffuse. If the hallway had been dark, it would be difficult to tell where the sound came from. But it was not dark, and Paul couldn't take his eyes from it.

"It's all right," he whispered. Tentatively he reached for it. The argala stepped toward him, its frail arms raised in an embrace. He started, then slowly let it enfold him. Its voice echoed his own, childlike and trusting.

It was irresistible, the smell and shape of it, the touch of its wispy hair upon his cheeks. He opened his eyes and for the first time got a good look at its face, so close to his that he drew back a little to see it better. A face that was somehow, indefinably, female. Like a child's drawing of a woman: enormous eyes surrounded by lashes that were spare but thick and straight. A round mouth, tangerine colored, like something one would want to eat. Hair that was more like feathers curled about its face. Paul took a tendril between his fingers, pulled it to his cheek and stroked his chin with agonizing slowness.

His mother had told him once that the argalae were engineered from human women and birds, storks or cranes he thought, or maybe some kind of white duck. Paul had thought this absurd, but now it seemed it could be true—the creature's hair looked and felt more like long downy filaments than human hair or fur. And there was something birdlike about the way it felt in his arms: fragile but at the same time tensile, and strong, as though its bones were lighter than human bones, filled with air or even some other element. Paul had never seen a real bird. He knew they were supposed to be lovely, avatars of physical beauty of a certain type and that their power of flight imbued them with a kind of miraculous appeal, at least to people Below. His mother said people thought that way about women once. Perhaps some of them still did.

He could not imagine any bird, anything at all, more beautiful or miraculous than this geneslave.

Even as he held it to his breast, its presence woke in him a terrible longing, a yearning for something he could scarcely fathom—open skies, the feel of running water beneath his bare feet. Images flooded his mind, things he had only ever seen in 'files of old movies. Small houses made of wood, clouds skidding across a sky the color of Ira Claire's eyes, cream-colored flowers climbing a trellis beside a green field. As the pictures fled across his mind's eye, his heart pounded: *Where did they come from?* Sensations spilled into him, as though they had been contained in too shallow a vessel and had nowhere else to pour but into whomever the thing touched. And then suddenly the first images slid away, the white porch and cracked concrete and saline taste—bitter yet comforting—of tears running into his mouth. Instead he felt dizzy. He reached out and his hands struck at the air feebly. Something seemed to move at his feet. He looked down and saw ripples like water and something tiny and bright moving there. A feeling stabbed at him, a hunger so sharp it was like love; and suddenly he saw clearly what the thing was—a tiny creature like a scarlet salamander, creeping across a mossy bank. But before he could stoop to savage it with his beak (*his beak?*), with a sickening rush the floor beneath him dropped, and there was only sky, white and grey, and wind raking at his face; and above all else that smell, filling his nostrils like pollen: the smell of water, of freedom.

Then it was gone. He fell back against the wall, gasping. When he opened his eyes he felt nauseous, but that passed almost immediately. He focused on the argala staring at him, its eyes wide and golden and with the same adoring gaze it had fixed on him before. Behind it his father stood in the open doorway to his room.

"Paul," he exclaimed brightly. He skinned a hand across his forehead and smiled, showing where he'd lost a tooth since the last time they'd met. "You found it—I wondered where it went. Come on, you!—"

He reached for the argala, and it went to him, easily.
"Turned around and it was gone!" His father shook his head,
still grinning, and hugged the argala to his side. He was naked,
not even a towel draped around him. Paul looked away hur-
riedly. From his father's even, somewhat muffled, tone he could
tell that he'd recently come from the neural sauna. "They told
me not to let it out of my sight, said it would go sniffing after
anyone, and they were right. . . ."

As suddenly as he'd appeared he was gone, the metal door
flowing shut behind him. For one last instant Paul could see the
argala, turning its glowing eyes from his father to himself and
back again, lovely and gormless as one of those simulacrums
that directed travellers in the HORUS by-ports. Then it was only
his own reflection that he stared at and Claude's voice that he
heard calling softly but insistently from the foot of the spiral
stairs.

He had planned to wait after class the following morning
to ask Father Dorothy what he knew about it, how a mindless
creature could project such a powerful and seemingly effortless
torrent of images and sensations; but he could tell from his
tutor's cool smile that somehow he had gotten word of their
spying. Ira, probably. He was well-meaning but tactless, and
Father Dorothy's favorite. Some whispered conference during
their private session and now Father Dorothy's usual expression, of perpetual disappointment tempered with ennui, was
shaded with a sharper anger.

So *that* was pointless. Paul could scarcely keep still during
class, fidgeting behind his desiccated textbooks, hardly glancing at the monitor's ruby scroll of words and numerals when his
turn came to use it. He did take a few minutes to sneak to the
back of the room. There a huge and indescribably ancient
wooden bookcase held a very few, mostly useless volumes—

Reader's Digest Complete Do-It-Yourself Manual, Robert's Rules of Order, The Ascent of Woman. He pulled out a natural history text so old that its contents had long since acquired the status of myth.

Argala, Paul read, after flipping past *Apteryx, Aquilegia, Archer, Areca,* each page releasing its whiff of Earth, mildew and silverfish and trees turned to dust. *Adjutant bird: Giant Indian Stork, living primarily in wetlands and feeding upon crustaceans and small amphibians. Status, endangered; perhaps extinct.* There was no illustration.

"Hey, Pathori." Claude bent over his shoulder, pretending to ask a question. Paul ignored him and turned the pages, skipping *Boreal Squid* and *(Bruijn's) Echidna,* pausing to glance at the garishly colored Nebalia Shrimp and the shining damp skin of the Newt, *Amphibian: A kind of eft (Juvenile salamander).* Finally he found the Stork, a simple illustration beside it.

Tall stately wading bird of family *Ciconiidae,* the best-known species pure white except for black wing-tips, long reddish bill, and red feet, and in the nursery the pretended bringer of babies and good fortune.

"... you *hear* me?" Claude whispered hoarsely, pinching his ear. Paul closed the book and pushed it away. Without a word he returned to his desk, Claude following him. Father Dorothy raised his head, then went back to explaining the subtleties of written poetry to Ira Claire. Paul settled into his seat. Behind him Claude stood and waited for their tutor to resume his recitation. In a moment Father Dorothy's boyish voice echoed back to them

". . . I make out a few words—   . . . 'SORROW,'
then again 'TEARS,'   and 'WE HIS FRIENDS MOURN'
It seems to me that Leucis   must have been dearly beloved . . . "

Paul started as Claude shook him, and the older boy

repeated, "I have an idea—I bet he just leaves it alone, when he's not in the room. We could get in there, maybe, and sneak it out. . . ."

Paul shrugged. He had been thinking the same thing himself, thinking how he would never have the nerve to do it alone. He glanced up at Father Dorothy.

If he looks at me now, he thought, *I won't do it; I'll talk to him later and figure out something else. . . .*

Behind him Claude hissed and elbowed him sharply. Paul waited, willing their tutor to look up; but the man's head pressed closer to his lovely student as he recited yet another elegiac fragment, wasted on the hopeless Ira—

"A poet said, 'That music is beloved
that cannot be sounded.'
And I think that the choicest life
is the life that cannot be lived."

"Paul!"

Paul turned and looked at Claude. "We could go when the rest are at dinner again," the older boy said. He too gazed at Ira and Father Dorothy, but with loathing. "All right?"

"All right," Paul agreed miserably, and lowered his head when Father Dorothy cast him a disapproving stare.

Trudging up the steps behind Claude, Paul looked back at the narrow plaza where the sculptures had been. They had passed three people on their way here, a man and two women, the women striding in that defiant way they had, almost swaggering, Paul thought. It was not until they turned the corner that he realized the man had been his mother, and she had not acknowledged him, had not seen him at all.

He sighed and looked down into the abandoned courtyard. Something glittered there, like a fleck of bright dust swimming across his vision. He paused, his hand sliding along the cool brass banister.

On the concrete floor he thought he saw something red, like a discarded blossom. But there were no flowers on Teichman. He felt again that rush of emotion that had come when he embraced the argala, a desire somehow tangled with the smell of brackish water and the sight of a tiny salamander squirming on a mossy bank. But when he leaned over the banister there was nothing there. It must have been a trick of the light or perhaps a scrap of paper or other debris blown by the air filters. He straightened and started back up the stairs.

That was when he saw the argala. Framed on the open balcony in his father's room, looking down upon the little courtyard. It looked strange from this distance and this angle: less like a woman and more like the sombre figure that had illustrated the Stork in the natural history book. Its foot rested on the edge of the balcony, so it seemed that it had only one leg, and the way its head was tilted he saw only the narrow raised crown, nearly bald because its wispy hair had been pulled back. From here it looked too bony, hardly female at all. A small flood of nausea raced through him. For the first time it struck him that this really *was* an alien creature. Another of the Ascendants' monstrous toys, like the mouthless hydrapithecenes that tended the Pacific hydrofarms or the pallid bloated forms floating in vats on the research deck of Teichman Station, countless fetuses tethered to them by transparent umbilical cords. And now he had seen and touched one of those monsters. He shuddered and turned away, hurrying after Claude.

But once he stood in the hallway his nausea and anger faded. There was that scent again, lulling him into seeing calm blue water and myriad shapes, garnet salamanders and frogs like candied fruit drifting across the floor. He stumbled into Claude, the older boy swearing and drawing a hand across his face.

"Shit! What's that smell?—" But the older boy's tone was

not unpleasant, only befuddled and slightly dreamy.

"The thing," said Paul. They stood before the door to his father's room. "The argala . . . ."

Claude nodded, swaying a little, his dark hair hiding his face. Paul had an awful flash of his father opening the door and Claude seeing him as Paul had, naked and doped, with that idiot smile and a tooth missing. But then surely the argala would not have been out on the balcony by itself? He reached for the door and very gently pushed it.

"Here we go," Claude announced as the door slid open. In a moment they stood safely inside.

"God, this is a mess." Claude looked around admiringly. He flicked at a stack of 'files teetering on the edge of a table, grimaced at the puff of dust that rose around his finger. "Ugh. Doesn't he have a server?"

"I guess not." Paul stepped gingerly around heaps of clothes, clean and filthy piled separately, and eyed with distaste a clutter of empty morpha tubes and wine jellies in a corner. A monitor flickered on a table, rows of numerals and gravid shapes tracing the progress of the Breeders Project.

"*Not*," a voice trilled. On the balcony the argala did not turn, but its bright tone, the way its vestigial wings shivered, seemed to indicate some kind of greeting.

"All right. Let's see it."

Claude shoved past him, grinning. Paul looked over, and for a second the argala's expression was not so much idiotic as tranquil, as though instead of a gritty balcony overlooking shattered concrete, it saw what he had imagined before, water and wriggling live things.

"*Unh.*"

Claude's tone abruptly changed. Paul couldn't help but look: The tenor of the other boy's lust was so intense it sounded like pain. He had his arms around the argala and was thrusting at it, his trousers askew. In his embrace the creature stood with its head thrown back, its cries so rhapsodic that Paul groaned himself and turned away.

In a minute it was over. Claude staggered back, pulling at his clothes and looking around almost frantically for Paul.

"God, that was incredible; that was the best—"

Like what could you compare it to, you idiot? Paul leaned against the table with the monitor and tapped a few keys angrily, hoping he'd screw up something; but the scroll continued uninterrupted. Claude walked, dazed, to a chair and slouched into it, scooped up a half-full wine jelly from the floor and sucked at it hungrily.

"Go on, Pathori, you don't want to miss *that!*" Claude laughed delightedly and looked at the argala. "God, it's amazing, isn't it? What a beauty." His eyes were dewy as he shook his head. "What a fucking thing."

Without answering Paul crossed the room to the balcony. The argala seemed to have forgotten all about them. It stood with one leg drawn up, staring down at the empty courtyard, its topaz eyes glittering. As he drew near to it, its smell overwhelmed him, a muskier scent now, almost fetid, like water that had stood too long in an open storage vessel. He felt infuriated by its utter passivity, but somehow excited, too. Before he knew what he was doing he had grabbed it, just as Claude had, and pulled it to him so that its bland child's face looked up at him rapturously.

Afterwards he wept, and beside him the argala crooned, mimicking his sobs. He could dimly hear Claude saying something about leaving and then his friend's voice rising and finally the *snick* of the door sliding open and shut. He gritted his teeth and willed his tears to stop. The argala nestled against him, silent now. His fingers drifted through its thin hair, ran down its back to feel its wings, the bones like metal struts beneath the breath of down. What could a bird possibly know about what he was feeling? he thought fiercely. Let alone a monster like this. A real woman would talk to you, afterwards.

To complain, he imagined his father saying.

... never enjoyed it, ever, his mother's voice echoed back, and Father Dorothy's intoned, *That's what's wrong with it; it's like a machine.*

He pulled the argala closer to him and shut his eyes, inhaling deeply. A wash of yellow that he knew must be sunlight: Then he saw that ghostly image of a house again, heard faint cries of laughter. Because it was a woman, too, of course; otherwise how could it recall a house, and children? But then the house broke up into motes of light without color, and he felt the touch of that other, alien mind, delicate and keen as a bird's long bill, probing at his own.

"Well! Good afternoon, good afternoon. . . ."

He jumped. His father swayed in the doorway, grinning. "Found my little friend again. Well, come in, come in."

Paul let go of the argala and took a few unsteady steps. "Dad—I'm sorry, I—"

"God, no. Stop." His father waved, knocking a bottle to the floor. "Stay, why don't you. A minute."

But Paul had a horrible flash, saw the argala taken again, the third time in what, half an hour? He shook his head and hurried to the door, face down.

"I can't, Dad. I'm sorry—I was just going by, that's all—"

"Sure, sure." His father beamed. Without looking he pulled a wine jelly from a shelf and squeezed it into his mouth. "Come by when you have more time, Paul. Glad to see you."

He started to cross to where the argala gazed at him, its huge eyes glowing. Paul ran from the room, the door closing behind him with a muted sigh.

At breakfast the next morning he was surprised to find his mother and Father Dorothy sitting in the twins' usual seats.

"We were talking about your going to school in Tangier,"

his mother announced, her deep voice a little too loud for the cramped dining hall as she turned back to Father Dorothy. "We could never meet the quotas, of course, but Mother pulled some strings, and—"

Paul sat next to her. Across the table, Claude and Ira and the twins were gulping down the rest of their breakfast. Claude mumbled a goodbye and stood to leave, Ira behind him.

"See you later, Father," Ira said, smiling. Father Dorothy waved.

"When?" said Paul.

"In a few weeks. It's nearly Athyr now—" that was what they called this cycle—". . . which means it's July down there. The next drop is on the Fortieth."

He didn't pay much attention to the rest of it. There was no point: His mother and Father Dorothy had already decided everything, as they always did. He wondered how his father had ever been able to get the argala here at all.

A hand clamped his shoulder, and Paul looked up.

"—must go now," Father Dorothy was saying as he motioned for a server to clean up. "Class starts in a few minutes. Walk with me, Paul?"

He shook his mother's hand and left her nodding politely as the next shift of diners filed into the little room.

"You've been with it," the tutor said after a few minutes. They took the long way to the classroom, past the cylinders where vats of nutriment were stored and wastewater recycled, past the spiral stairs that led to his father's chamber. Where the hallway forked Father Dorothy hesitated, then went to the left, toward the women's quarters. "I could tell, you know—it has a—"

He inhaled, then made a delicate grimace. "It has a smell."

They turned and entered the Solar Walk. Paul remained at his side, biting his lip and feeling an unexpected anger churning inside him.

"I like the way it smells," he said, and waited for Father Dorothy to look grim. Instead his tutor paused in front of the window. "I love it."

He thought Father Dorothy would retort sharply, but instead he only raised his hands and pressed them against the window. Outside two of the HORUS repair units floated past, on their interminable and futile rounds. When it seemed the silence would go on forever, his tutor said, "It can't love you. You know that. It's an abomination—an animal—"

"Not really," Paul replied, but weakly.

Father Dorothy flexed his hands dismissively. "It can't love you. It's a geneslave. How could it love anything?"

His tone was not angry but questioning, as though he really thought Paul might have an answer. And for a moment Paul thought of explaining to him: about how it felt, how it seemed like it was showing him things—the sky, the house, the little creatures crawling in the moss—things that perhaps it *did* feel something for. But before he could say anything, Father Dorothy turned and began striding back in the direction they'd come. Paul hurried after him in silence.

As they turned down the last hallway, Father Dorothy said, "It's an ethical matter, really. Like having intercourse with a child, or someone who's mentally deficient. It can't respond; it's incapable of anything—"

"But I love it," Paul repeated stubbornly.

"Aren't you listening to me?" Father Dorothy did sound angry, now. "*It* can't love *you*." His voice rose shrilly. "How could something like *that* tell you that it *loved* you!? And *you* can't love it—god, how could you love *anything,* you're only a boy!" He stopped in the doorway and looked down at him, then shook his head, in pity or disgust Paul couldn't tell. "Get in there," Father Dorothy said at last and gently pushed him through the door.

* * *

He waited until the others were asleep before slipping from his bunk and heading back to his father's quarters. The lights had dimmed to simulate night; other than that there was no difference in the way anything looked or smelled or sounded. He walked through the violet corridors with one hand on the cool metal wall, as though he was afraid of falling.

They were leaving just as he reached the top of the spiral stairs. He saw his father first, then two others, other researchers from the Breeders Project. They were laughing softly, and his father threw his arms around one man's shoulders and murmured something that made the other man shake his head and grin. They wore loose robes open in the front and headed in the opposite direction, towards the neural sauna. They didn't see the boy pressed against the wall, watching as they turned the corner and disappeared.

He waited for a long time. He wanted to cry, tried to make himself cry; but he couldn't. Beneath his anger and shame and sadness there was still too much of that other feeling, the anticipation and arousal and inchoate tenderness that he only knew one word for and Father Dorothy thought that was absurd. So he waited until he couldn't stand it anymore and went inside.

His father had made some feeble attempt to clean the place up. The clothing had been put away and table tops and chairs cleared of papers. Fine white ash sifted across the floor, and there was a musty smell of tobacco beneath the stronger odors of semen and wine jelly. The argala's scent ran through all of it like a fresh wind.

He left the door open behind him, no longer caring if someone found him there or not. He ran his hands across his eyes and looked around for the argala.

It was standing where it usually did, poised on the balcony with its back to him. He took a step, stopped. He thought he could hear something, a very faint sound like humming; but then it was gone. He craned his neck to see what it was the creature looked at but saw nothing, only that phantom flicker of red in the corner of his eye, like a mote of ruby dust. He began walking again, softly, when the argala turned to look at him.

Its eyes were wide and fervent as ever, its tangerine mouth spun into that same adoring smile; but even as he started for it, his arms reaching to embrace it, it turned from him and jumped.

For an instant it hung in the air, and he could imagine it flying, could almost imagine that perhaps it thought its wings would carry it across the courtyard or safely to the ground. But in that instant he caught sight of its eyes, and they were not a bird's eyes but a woman's, and she was not flying but falling.

He must have cried out, screamed for help. Then he just hung over the balcony, staring down at where it lay motionless. He kept hoping that maybe it would move again, but it did not, only lay there twisted and still.

But as he stared at it, it changed. It had been a pale creature to begin with. Now what little color it had was leached away, as though it were bleeding into the concrete; but really there was hardly any blood. Its feathers grew limp, like fronds plucked from the water, their gold fading to a grey that was all but colorless. Its head was turned sideways, its great wide eye open and staring up. As he watched, the golden orb slowly dulled to yellow and then a dirty white. When someone finally came to drag it away, its feathers trailed behind it in the dust. Then nothing remained of it at all except for the faintest breath of ancient summers hanging in the stale air.

For several days he wouldn't speak to anyone, not even responding to Claude's cruelties or his father's ineffectual attempts at kindness. His mother made a few calls to Tangier and, somehow, the drop was changed to an earlier date in Athyr. On the afternoon he was to leave they all gathered, awkwardly, in the dormitory. Father Dorothy seemed sad that he was going but also relieved. The twins tried to get him to promise to write, and Ira cried. But, still without speaking, Paul left the room and walked down to the courtyard.

No one had even bothered to clean it. A tiny curl of blood stained the concrete a rusty color, and he found a feather, more like a furry yellowish thread than anything else, stuck to the wall. He took the feather and stared at it, brought it to his face and inhaled. There was nothing.

He turned to leave, then halted. At the corner of his eye something moved. He looked back and saw a spot on the ground directly beneath his father's balcony. Shoving the feather into his pocket he walked slowly to investigate.

In the dust something tiny wriggled, a fluid arabesque as long as his finger. Crouching on his heels, he bent over and cupped it in his palm. A shape like an elongated tear of blood, only with two bright black dots that were its eyes and, beside each of those, two perfect flecks of gold.

An eft, he thought, recognizing it from the natural history book and from the argala's vision. A juvenile salamander.

Giant Indian stork, feeding upon crustaceans and small amphibians.

He raised it to his face, feeling it like a drop of water slithering through his fingers. When he sniffed it, it smelled, very faintly, of mud.

There was no way it could have gotten here. Animals never got through by-port customs, and besides, were there even things like this still alive, Below? He didn't know.

But then how did it get here?

A miracle, he thought, and heard Father's Dorothy's derisive voice—*How could something like that tell you that it loved you?* For the first time since the argala's death, the rage and despair that had clenched inside him uncoiled. He moved his hand, to see it better, and with one finger stroked its back. Beneath its skin, scarlet and translucent, its ribs moved rapidly in and out, in and out, so fine and frail they might have been drawn with a hair.

An eft.

He knew it would not live for very long—what could he feed it, how could he keep it?—but somehow the argala had survived, for a little while at least, and even then the manner of its dying had been a miracle of sorts. Paul stood, his hands folding over the tiny creature, and with his head bowed—though none of them would really see, or understand, what it was he carried—he walked up the stairs and through the hallway and back into the dormitory where his bags waited, past the other boys, past his mother and father and Father Dorothy, not saying anything, not even looking at them, holding close against his chest a secret, a miracle, a salamander.